The Contemporary British Historical Novel

The Contemporary British Historical Novel

Representation, Nation, Empire

Mariadele Boccardi

First published 2009 by
PALGRAVE MACMILLAN

Palgrave Macmillan in the UK is an imprint of Macmillan Publishers Limited, registered in England, company number 785998, of Houndmills, Basingstoke, Hampshire RG21 6XS.

Palgrave Macmillan in the US is a division of St Martin's Press LLC, 175 Fifth Avenue, New York, NY 10010.

Palgrave Macmillan is the global academic imprint of the above companies and has companies and representatives throughout the world.

Palgrave® and Macmillan® are registered trademarks in the United States, the United Kingdom, Europe and other countries.

ISBN-13: 978–0–230–20007–4 hardback
ISBN-10: 0–230–20007–9 hardback

This book is printed on paper suitable for recycling and made from fully managed and sustained forest sources. Logging, pulping and manufacturing processes are expected to conform to the environmental regulations of the country of origin.

A catalogue record for this book is available from the British Library.

Library of Congress Cataloging-in-Publication Data

Boccardi, Mariadele, 1972–
    The contemporary British historical novel : representation, nation, empire / Mariadele Boccardi.
        p. cm.
    Includes bibliographical references and index.
    ISBN-13: 978–0–230–20007–4 (alk. paper)
    ISBN-10: 0–230–20007–9 (alk. paper)
    1. Historical fiction, English – History and criticism. 2. English fiction – 20th century – History and criticism. 3. History in literature. 4. Great Britain – In literature. 5. Literature and history – Great Britain – History – 20th century. I. Title.

PR888.H5B63 2009
823'.081090914—dc22   2009013633

10 9 8 7 6 5 4 3 2 1
18 17 16 15 14 13 12 11 10 09

Printed and bound in Great Britain by
CPI Antony Rowe, Chippenham and Eastbourne

To Bob and Nicholas

Contents

Acknowledgements

I would like to thank the Faculty of Humanities, Languages and Social Sciences at the University of the West of England for granting me a semester of research leave, during which this project took its final shape, and my colleagues in the Department of English for their willingness to exchange ideas on the subject of historical fiction, even when it did not fall within their research interests. I am also indebted to Professor Berthold Schoene and Dr. Michael Greaney, who read the initial proposal for the project and gave valuable advice on its contents as well as on its publication. Finally, thank you to Bob.

Introduction: The Novel of History 1969–2005

In *On Histories and Stories* (2000), A.S. Byatt notes 'the sudden flowering of the historical novel in Britain' in the post-war period (9). She sees the newly reacquired seriousness of a genre that in the twentieth century had largely been confined to escapist literature as a sign that 'history' has become 'imaginable and important again' (9). It is a phenomenon that has not escaped the attention of other scholars writing at the turn of the millennium, from a position, that is, of retrospection analogous to that assumed by historical novelists. Thus, Tony E. Jackson (1999) confidently claims that 'the turn to history as a theme may be the definitive element in British fiction in the last three decades' (170), while Del Ivan Janik (1995) relates the 'acute consciousness of history and ... sharp focus on its meanings or potential for meaning' (161) in contemporary English novels to a reaction against post-structuralist and postmodern arguments for the end of history.

A visit to any bookshop will ascertain the truth of these claims for the popularity of the historical novel, as fiction concerned with the recuperation and representation of the past forms a significant proportion of the volumes on the shelves and display tables, evidence that the concern with history Byatt, Jackson and Janik identify has persisted even beyond the millennial conditions which initially invited a reflection on the past. Indeed, the genre's reach has expanded further than the experimental, self-referential works that are the subject of these critics' studies: the historical novels one encounters in bookstores can in turn be sub-divided into ever narrower categories among which crime, romance and adventure are

1

easily detectable. The fact that these reproduce the best-selling genres in fiction more generally is perhaps the most visible evidence of the popularity of the historical novel amongst both authors and readers and, in turn, this provides the clearest indication that there is a need for a scholarly approach to the genre such as this study proposes, and which aims to examine the late twentieth-century re-emergence of the historical novel both contextually and theoretically. My investigation of the contemporary British historical novel seeks to probe the conditions for the initial recuperation and subsequent success of the genre and to rely on the evidence provided by the texts to pursue recurrent elements, from formal strategies to thematic convergences, in novels published between 1969 and 2005. The year that marks the earlier limit of my discussion saw the publication of John Fowles's *The French Lieutenant's Woman*. This was the book that heralded the revival of an interest in the Victorian period both for its persisting influence on the present and for its psychological, social and cultural distance from it. The latest novels I discuss, Ronan Bennett's *Havoc in Its Third Year* and Gregory Norminton's *Ghost Portrait*, turn their attention from the social and cultural birth of modernity in the nineteenth century to the political birth of the modern nation with the English Civil War.

If the resulting analysis is to have any value in the light of the sheer number of novels concerned with the representation of past events, it is essential to establish some principles of selection and, with them, a working definition of the contemporary historical novel and a tentative theory of the genre. Selection, definition and theoretical framework have proved the prime concern and the ultimate downfall for scholars of the post-war historical novel. In *Shadows of the Past in Contemporary British Fiction* (1984), David Leon Higdon was among the first to remark on the attention to the past in post-war fiction. Working within a framework that combines contextual and literary-historical elements, he suggests that the difference between modernist and post-war fiction rests on their respective attitudes towards the past: where, for the former, history was 'a nightmare to be fled, ... an irrelevancy to be ignored' (3), the latter aims to engage with the 'three major manifestations' of the past, 'memory, tradition, and history' (6). Higdon observes that what accompanies and partly explains the contemporary British novel's interest in the past is a 'new sensibility', whose defining trait is an emphasis on continuity (in contrast with modernist exhortations to break with what preceded it) and a 'recognition that the future is vitally related to the past' (7). This reference to a new sensibility is perceptive and, while Higdon does not attempt to give it a name, later critics have had no qualms, rightly or wrongly, in identifying it with postmodernism. More problematic is his reliance on notions of continuity and discontinuity. While it may be true that modernist authors keenly felt their programmatic break with the Victorian past, what contemporary novelists long for is to re-establish the interrupted line with the narrative forms of the nineteenth century bypassing their immediate predecessors, the modernists. They therefore create another line interrupted at an alternative point and for aesthetically different reasons. Questions of continuity and discontinuity are ultimately contingent on the choice of which literary past it may be worth claiming allegiance to, and which pronouncing the rejection of. Higdon's difficulties are largely a consequence of his desire for comprehensiveness, whose corollary is the conflation of the literary past (implied in his mention of tradition) and the historical past, which, in turn, he considers the prerogative of memory and the historical record equally. As a result, his study comprises a large range of works broadly concerned with the retrieval of, and engagement with, the past, but it does not consistently explore the substantial differences in the process of retrieval and in the nature of the engagement inherent in whether the past is the site of direct or mediated experience, of memory or of history.

While these two forms of evocation of the past share the essential quality of the retrospective articulation of events, only the latter properly discloses the difficulties of gaining access to a reality that is available only in textual form and always in part. One of the defining characteristics of the historical novel as a recognisable genre is precisely its complex relationship to the existing textual records of the past, on the one hand, and to the competing representation of that past in the discipline of historiography, on the other. In more recent studies, David Cowart and Margaret Scanlan draw attention to the textual and imaginative dimension of the historical novel's narrative recreation of the past. In *History and the Contemporary Novel* (1989), Cowart relates the 'technical innovations in the novel'

in the late twentieth century (1) to the historical novelists' awareness that 'the past can only be known imaginatively' (28), because
its accessible remains are fragmented, incomplete and contradictory.
Similarly, Scanlan's *Traces of Another Time* (1990) is constructed on
the premise that '[t]he contemporary English novel often empha-
sizes the difficulties of knowing the truth about the past' because
the epistemological enterprise is limited in its scope and findings by
the inescapable 'reliance on narratives' (12). Her examination of the
persistence of the past into contemporary fiction concentrates on
what she calls 'the contemporary skeptical historical novel' (3). The
genre is defined by its awareness of the constructed and falsifying
nature of any comprehensive and coherent account of the past,
while its aim is precisely to reopen the gap that exists between the
event and its articulation in textual form. The result is a combination of estrangement from the actuality of the historical event and
narrative self-referentiality that is crucial to understanding the relationship between the contemporary historical novel and postmodernism, even if the latter is not mentioned explicitly in either
study.

As was the case with Higdon's 'new sensibility', Cowart and Scanlan
usefully point to a change in attitude towards the past since World
War II that sees a heightened interest in the events that shaped the
present and a concomitant resistance to accepting the version of that
past transmitted by official, already encoded history. However, again
like Higdon, the framework they establish for their discussion in fact
serves to widen rather than restrict the applicability of the term 'historical novel'. Thus, alongside his analysis of the nuances of the contemporary novel's engagement with the past, Cowart includes a
section concerned with the representation of the future. While this
may illustrate the inherently historicising operation of narrative, it
also diverts the focus of his study from what is recognisable as a historical novel, whether intuitively understood or rigorously theorised,
namely an imaginative representation of a period (and in some
instances a sequence of events) whose reality is confirmed by other
sources even if its experiential dimension is irretrievable and has to
be approximated by an act of the imagination. In other words, if it is
in the nature of the historical novel, like all fiction, to rely on invention, that process is always embarked on in relation to contiguous
textual engagements, academic as much as fictional, with the same

historical setting. As Ann Rigney points out,

> what defines the historical novel as a genre is precisely the inter-
> play between invented story elements and historical ones. As
> novels, they are written under the aegis of the fictionality con-
> vention whereby the individual writer enjoys the freedom to
> invent ... a world "uncommitted to reality." As *historical* novels,
> however, they also link up with the ongoing collective attempts
> to represent the past and invite comparison with what is already
> known about the historical world from other sources. [...] They
> are not "free-standing fictions" ..., they also call upon prior his-
> torical knowledge, echoing and/or disputing other discourses
> about the past. (2001: 19)

Scanlan is certainly aware of this productive interaction between
history and fiction, so that the novels she examines perform the role
of commentaries on historical situations at the same time as reimag-
ining them. However, her emphasis on the novel's function as a self-
conscious contribution to the historical record leads Scanlan to
extend the definition of historical novel to works whose setting is
the very recent past and which indeed depict events whose outcome
and consequences are still indecipherable (most notably, in her case,
the fate of Northern Ireland in relation to the Union and the
Republic). This approach deprives the historical novel of its key formal feature, retrospection, and with it of the dual temporal dimension in which the genre operates, the time of the writing (the present)
and the time of the setting (the past). It is precisely this double frame
of reference that permits the historical novel its claim to be 'both an
entry into the past ... and a coherent interpretation of that past from
a particular standpoint in the present' (Fleishman 24). This is an
aspect hinted at in the subtitle of what is, by general consensus, the
first example of the genre, Sir Walter Scott's *Waverley, or 'tis sixty years
since* (1813).

The gap of 60 years has particular relevance for the period of
Scottish history that forms the subject of Scott's novel. However, it
can also be taken to signify a temporal distance beyond the reach of
the personal memory of the writer, and therefore requiring an
engagement with the sources that mediate the reality of the past for
consumption in the present, and yet it refers to a time not so distant

as to have acquired romantic or legendary status. The retrospective view to a time beyond direct experience forces the historical novelist to confront the textual nature of the material at his or her disposal, with the corollary lack of a comprehensive and unified image of the past, and to acknowledge the imaginative leap from the fragmented evidence to the finished representation of the period or events that are the setting and subject of his or her work. At the same time, and somewhat contradictorily, the elapsed time between the past of the events and the present of their writing situates the author in a position of privileged knowledge, in that he or she is aware of the outcome of events and their effect on those events' future, which is the writer's present. As a result, purely by virtue of its being written retrospectively, a historical novel either contains in inchoate form or outlines explicitly the workings of the historical process. What these two aspects of retrospection reveal is the dual, or even paradoxical, nature of historical fiction, tending towards a self-referential limitation of its access to the object of representation, on the one hand, and benefiting from the formal trappings of omniscience, on the other. As I will argue in the following pages, this makes the historical novel inherently metafictional and as such not only ideally receptive to postmodernism's positions on narrative, representation and knowledge but also supremely equipped to probe their validity. Indeed, it is my contention that the historical novel is, at once, the genre where postmodernism manifests itself most clearly and that where it proves theoretically inadequate.

Cowart and Scanlan, then, dilute or obscure the salient features that distinguish the historical novel and consciously neglect to examine the genre's relationship, in its contemporary incarnation, with postmodernism. This is in spite of the fact that their work, introducing such concepts as the 'open, skeptical form' of historical representation (Scanlan 7) or 'the technical license or opportunities' afforded to it (Cowart 28), is clearly indebted to ideas on narrative, representation and knowledge articulated by Hayden White in the discipline of historiography, and Linda Hutcheon in literary theory and criticism. White's and Hutcheon's theories are closely related not only in their approach to their respective fields of enquiry but also in the effects of their conclusions. White's premise in *Metahistory* (1973) is that the historical work is 'most manifestly ... a verbal structure in the form of a narrative prose discourse that purports to be a model, or icon, of past structures and processes in the interest of *explaining what they were by representing* them' (2, emphasis in the original). By providing what is essentially a literary discussion of notable examples of historiography, White seeks to draw the attention of the historian from the content of his or her work to its form, challenging the purported objectivity and neutrality of narrative as merely a carrier of prior and external meaning and instead foregrounding its role as a defining contributor to the generation of historical meaning. This analysis, which relies on such literary-critical interpretive strategies as discourse, form, representational modes and figurative meaning, tends to narrow the substantive distance between historical and fictional representation, to the extent that it underlines the difference between events and their articulation in narrative, between the knowledge acquired through scholarly research and the presentation of that knowledge in persuasive, authoritative and seemingly objective form. Although White in no way denies the existence or even the accessibility of the past, his approach points to the doubly mediated relationship between the historian and his or her subject: not only are the events only available in textual form, they are in turn conveyed to readers by means of another text, the historian's own. The encoding thus taking place (what White calls emplotment) employs techniques analogous to those of fiction, in so far as

> [t]he historian arranges the events ... into a hierarchy of significance by assigning events different functions as story elements in such a way as to disclose the formal coherence of a whole set of events considered as a comprehensible process with a discernible beginning, middle, and end. (7)

By foregrounding the artificial and inescapably ideological nature of historical narrative, White deprives history of its self-constituted distinction with respect to fiction (and it is worth noting that the formulation of this distinction coincided with the emergence of the figure of the professional historian at a time, the early nineteenth century, that also marked the first recognisable examples of historical fiction), namely its claim to truthfulness. In this climate, contemporary historical fiction can ambitiously aspire to granting imaginative apprehension of the past just as effectively as historiography.

The questioning of the very notion of historical truth, the insistence that historical knowledge is always textually mediated, and the recognition of the ideological component of all narratives are precisely the elements that Hutcheon identifies in *A Poetics of Postmodernism* (1988) as characteristic of the postmodern attitude towards representation and narrative generally, and historical representation and narrative particularly. Indeed, her claim that postmodernism disrupts such 'cultural and social assumptions' as 'origins and ends, unity, totalization, logic and reason, consciousness and human nature, progress and fate, representation and truth, ... causality and temporal homogeneity, linearity, and continuity' (86) confronts the enduring legacy of the Enlightenment and of nineteenth century historicism. It is no coincidence that these are the very systems of thought that provided the philosophical underpinning for the historical novel at the time of its first emergence as an identifiable genre. It is therefore not surprising that Hutcheon should trace the literary manifestation of these postmodern concerns to what is, for her, a new kind of historical novel, for which she coins the term 'historiographic metafiction' (5). The label denotes 'novels which are both intensely self-reflexive and yet paradoxically also lay claim to historical events and personages' (5). Historiographic metafiction preserves its generic roots in the work of Scott and other nineteenth-century practitioners, but precisely because of this clear genealogical connection it can operate a more thorough disruption of the genre's representational assumptions. In other words, the genre that most directly owed the underlying principles of its practice to the Enlightenment and nineteenth-century historicism is used effectively to undermine their epistemological assumptions and ontological certainties in the late twentieth-century postmodern context. Hutcheon hails the new form as having restored history to its rightful place at the core of novelistic practice, but of a novel which, by the constant attention it pays to its own ontological and epistemological status, calls into question the very possibility of knowing the past in any reliable way and of representing it as a coherent narrative.

I welcome the challenge, implicit in Hutcheon's approach to her subject, to the widespread and reductive description of postmodernism as a phenomenon whose defining feature is an a-historical consumption of all representations, all placed equally on a plane that has only surfaces and no depths, only presents and no diachronic perceptions, only prices and no values. If, as even its critics recognise, postmodernism deals in narratives (whether we call them fabulation or metafiction), then it also deals with time, since any narrative encompasses a process of temporal unfolding purely by virtue of its congenital structure of beginning, middle and end. And time, in relation to the unfolding of events, is also the subject of historiography and historical fiction. However, in her eagerness to emphasise the novelty of historiographic metafiction Hutcheon ignores the fact that a self-referential dimension can be detected in the earliest examples of the historical novel and, in so far as she does not insist on the significance of the recuperation of the conventions of a Victorian genre for contemporary purposes, she misses an opportunity to further confirm the interest in the literary past of postmodern fiction. Similarly, by discussing side by side and with few concessions to their individuality novels that align themselves with very different national literary traditions, her work risks replicating the assumptions of the primacy of surface connections and presentness she seeks to refute, at the expense of a historically informed examination of contemporary historical fiction. These unexplored paths, if followed, lead to an examination of the specific literary and cultural conditions for the recuperation of the historical novel in Britain within a nationally inflected appropriation of postmodernism.

A degree of metafictionality is inherent in the historical novel *qua* historical novel. On a purely formal level, in fact, the historical novel makes literal the historicising dimension of narrative. The use of verbs in the past tense as the basic starting point for the temporal architecture of any narrative is, for the majority of novels and certainly for realist ones, a convention and artifice designed to imply the meaningful closure of retrospective (i.e. historical) knowledge by mimicking it formally. Thus, although the action and events the narrative relates may be in the present, their rendition by means of the past tense grants them a degree of fulfilment and inherent significance they would not otherwise possess: 'plotting presupposes and requires that an end will bestow upon the whole duration and meaning', so that 'that which was conceived of as simply successive becomes charged with past and future' (Kermode 46). In other words, the organisation of narrative into a beginning, middle and end constructs a textual temporality which imitates the temporality of events in the real world and also complements the actual temporality of the reading experience. As Peter Brooks (1984) puts it, while it is true that when reading a narrative 'we realize the action progressively, segment by segment, as a kind of present in terms of our experience of it', we do so 'precisely in anticipation of its larger hermeneutic structuring by conclusions' (23). By its very nature, on the other hand, in the historical novel the formal conventions of narrative representation (the grammatical past tense) and the actual position in time of the object of representation (events in the past) coincide. What was a constructed retrospective understanding confined to a narrative domain becomes in the historical novel actual hindsight guaranteed by the passing of real, not just narrative, time beyond the confines of the narrative. In other words, although the form the narrative of a historical novel takes may be identical to that of any novel, the awareness that that form corresponds more closely to the relationship between events and their appearance in the novel alters the perception of that relationship. The result is an attenuated consciousness of the formally codified traits of narrative representation and the greater impact of the impression of reality, even if this is a somewhat paradoxical outcome in view of the inevitably more substantial contribution of the imagination to the recreation of the past rather than to the reproduction of the present.

What emerges from this description is a close formal connection between the historical novel and the realist novel. The addition of a formal link between realism and historical fiction complements the socio-economic points of contact in their genesis, which were first outlined in Georg Lukács's *The Historical Novel* (1937). Lukács's analysis, among the earliest attempts to understand the historical novel as a genre within a theoretical framework, is particularly interesting for the approach this study takes to the contemporary British historical novel, because it allows for a national specificity in the experience of history and in the search for a form that can accurately convey that experience. He draws a connection between England's 'post-revolutionary' (21) condition in the early nineteenth century, which he contrasts with that of France and other European countries, and the attention of 'the great social novel[s]' to 'the concrete ... significance of time and place, to social conditions and so on' (21). These, in turn, led the novelists of the time to the moulding of 'the realistic, literary means of expression for portraying this spatio-temporal (i.e. historical) character of people and circumstances' (21).

Initially, however, realist novels envisage history in synchronic terms, that is to say they concentrate on what makes the period in which the action takes place, be it the present or the past, particular to itself. It is only when the novelist is confronted with the visible impact of history on an identifiable mass and tries to understand what is happening by narrating it that the historical novel in its proper sense comes into existence: its subject is the process that causes the transition from one historical period or coherent set of beliefs to another and marks the connection between them. Therefore historical novels are 'an attempt to prove that man and his society develop as part of a process which includes and envelops the present' (Sanders 11). In the case of Scott, whom Lukács heralds as the first author whose novels can properly be called historical, this moment of historicising insight occurred when he witnessed the gradual but inexorable disappearance of the Highlands way of life at the hands of the ever-expanding bourgeois modernity of commerce and money.

Lukács goes on to assert that the example of Scott's fiction gave voice and at the same contributed to the middle classes' understanding of themselves as historical subjects, a trait which is pursued in the realist novels of the mid-Victorian period to the extent that there is no real substantive difference between the two genres:

> The ultimate principles are in either case the same. And they flow from a similar aim: the portrayal of a total context of social life, be it present or past, in narrative form. [...] The classical historical novel arose out of the social novel and, having enriched and raised it to a higher level, passed back into it. (Lukács 242)

Shaw specifies what that enrichment consisted of, arguing that it is the example of the historical novel that 'made a sense of history part of the cultural mainstream and hence available to novels in general, not simply to historical novels' (22). Lukács's statement in particular suggests two important observations concerning the recovered academic and popular success of the historical novel in the late twentieth and early twenty-first centuries, one contextual and one literary.

The traditional form of realism as it had evolved from the experiment of historical fiction is no longer a satisfactory means of expression of identity for the middle classes at a historical moment such as the present one, which is marked by socio-economic conditions labelled 'late capitalist'. These consist of the disjunction of consumption from production, of the pre-eminence of the former over the latter as an identity-defining activity which, however, proves elusive when compared with the solidity and materiality of production, but which is nonetheless endlessly promoted by means of the glitzy surfaces of advertising. Indeed, the very notion of a middle class is in the process of being redefined in so far as it is no longer the ownership of the means of production but rather the conspicuous display of items appropriated for consumption that marks its visible existence. Following Lukács's model, one possible explanation for the return to the historical novel on the part of contemporary writers and readers is the need to articulate anew the experience and impact of the historical process on the recently ideologically deracinated bourgeoisie. The mid-Victorian period, which marked the summit of self-confidence for British middle class capitalism, holds particular fascination for its contemporary epigones, and provides a variously romanticised setting for the vast majority of historical novels published in the last three decades. It is therefore only after confronting the antecedents of the present socio-economic condition by means of historical fiction that the contemporary novel can rediscover the awareness of history essential even to settings and plots univocally preoccupied with the present, and shape a contemporary instance of realism which, while formally different from its nineteenth-century counterpart, is substantively comparable.

There is a clear national dimension to the engagement with the condition of postmodernity that I have just described: the canonical significance of the mid-Victorian period, as the name itself suggests with its reference to Victoria, Queen of England and Empress of India and all the colonies, is a specifically British phenomenon. The period's importance ranges from the economic and commercial (British industry and trade) to the political and military (imperial expansion and technological innovation), while the value of the certainties derived from the awareness of canonicity is translated into the pre-eminence granted in literary practice to the hegemonic literary form of the time, the realist novel. The revisiting of what appears as the epitome of successful representation from the perspective of a present largely devoid of standpoints to define itself and, consequently, of a unifying narrative form, equally acquires national overtones.

The contemporary historical novel's attention to the Victorian fictional model signals a formal and literary-historical equivalent to the search for origins and fault lines in historical continuity that characterises postmodernity in Britain more generally and which is the consequence of a loosening of the historical co-ordinates that favour an understanding of the present in relation to the past which is a feature of postmodernity. Formal success in the representational enterprise, which contemporary historical fiction denies for itself even as it projects it backwards onto Victorian novels, becomes symptomatic of a broader nostalgic aspect inherent in British postmodernism. Nostalgia exceeds the literary domain in which it is most clearly articulated to form a significant element of culture more generally, as well as of popular expressions of interest in the past. Thus, it is not simply the confidence of realist narrative practice, with its corollary aspiration to comprehensiveness, that is found missing in the present and is instead located in the past. The confidence of the Victorian nation, whose expansionary ambitions and comprehensive mastery of territory as much as diplomacy contemporary historical novels do not hesitate to outline, is also lacking at a time when Britain's importance on the world stage is steadily decreasing and when, arguably, the nation as a concept or political unit is ever less relevant in the context of dominantly global economic, social and cultural perspectives. There is therefore a political dimension to the seemingly innocuous, if ideologically conservative, hankering for the past glory of realist fiction in the present. It may well indicate a displaced and thinly disguised nostalgia for the national glory of the period when that representational form had its apogee, an attitude made acceptable by its being articulated on the traditionally escapist ground of historical fiction. This mutual exchange between formal concerns and political reflections is a persistent feature of contemporary historical fiction generally and of the novels examined in this study particularly. The use of the formal *as* the political is, in turn, a mark of postmodern fiction.

There is a further dimension to the historical novel that makes it particularly relevant to a literary moment sensitive to a redefinition of realism. Given its status as a genre defined by its participation in both artistic invention and historical accuracy, the historical novel calls attention to the porous border between reality and fiction, a porosity exploited and a border trespassed by Walter Scott's predilection for adding sometimes multiple prefaces and postscripts to his novels. The proliferation of narratorial personae, respondents, addressees and sources in the prefaces and postscripts constructs a complex paratextual apparatus to accompany the novels' representation of history which is inextricable from the novels themselves and serves a double purpose. On the one hand, the author's professed reliance, in his fictional practice, on oral and written accounts of the past as well as on its material traces aims to clarify and validate their contents by 'underscoring the presumably basic referentiality of the historical novel itself' (Gaston 31), which becomes a complement to historiography and equally authoritative about its subject. On the other hand, the conspicuous presence of historical reality (even if in the form of its textual remnants) on the margins of a fictional text calls attention to the fact that the genre of the historical novel cannot but conflate the past and its representation in the present because both belong to the same linear, continuous, homogenous historical reality. Thus, '[t]he connection between the discourse and the historical events it represents is not only that of historical connection, that is, of the fact that the discourse follows the events in time'; instead, 'there is also an *ontological* connection: both the discursive act and the event represented are posited as belonging to the same historical world' (Rigney 1990, 26).

In the 'Introductory' section and the 'Postscript' to *Waverley* Scott outlines the characteristics of his work, which will in turn come to define the genre of the historical novel more generally, namely, a limiting of the historical scope of the representation, an awareness of the historical process, a qualified retrospective view of events, and the use of imagination at the service of truth. Here Scott describes his subject as something other than 'a romance of chivalry' or 'a tale of modern manners' (Weinstein 9), appropriating a space for his story that, while past and therefore benefiting from hindsight, is still recognisable as continuous and homogeneous with the present in which he is writing. The conventional image of the river, which stands for the unidirectional flow of time – and of history – reinforces this point. By noting that 'like those who drift down the stream of a deep and smooth river, we are not aware of the progress we have made until we fix our eye on the now distant point from which we have been drifted' (4), Scott certainly implies that retrospective distance is necessary to apprehend the significance of past events.

Equally, though, he situates himself as still part of the same river, so that there is no ontological alterity between the two moments, only historically contingent differences. This premise allows for an awareness of the historical process, while at the same time justifying the reliance on 'imaginary scenes' and 'fictitious characters' (9) to provide a true representation of the past. If, in fact, past and present are not radically other but belong instead to the same metaphorical river, and if hindsight gives access to the workings of the historical process symbolised by the more or less noticeable flowing of its waters, then plausible behaviours, events, even speeches can be invested with truth value in so far as they clarify the circumstances for historical change and the latter's impact on those that participated in it or simply suffered its consequences.

Scott's belief in the commensurability of historical moments, even when their distance in time and differences in habits and outlooks were apparent to the historian and novelist, is the result of the author's own situation 'at the time of transition between... [two] ways of looking backward', namely, 'Enlightenment uniformitarianism and Romantic historicism' (Fleishman 25). These were not simply philosophical positions; they also influenced historical writing between the end of the eighteenth century and the beginning of the nineteenth. Scottish philosophers and historians, in particular, argued that

> [o]ur most fundamental character as human beings...even our moral character, is constantly evolving and developing, shaped by a variety of forces over which we as individuals have little or no control. [...] At the same time, they also insisted that these changes are not arbitrary or chaotic. They rest on certain fundamental principles and discernible patterns. (Herman 54)

The combination of these two attitudes towards history and human nature results in the perception of a 'quality which, regardless of period, makes a particular stretch of time unique to itself', while also preserving 'the features common to human nature at all times', both of which are mediated by the awareness of 'the necessary failures, the imperfection of human knowledge and its transmission' (MacQueen 1). Consequently, Scott's view of history and of his own practice as a historical novelist accepts the 'particular concept of historical time developed in the Scottish Enlightenment [...]. [This] entailed the idea of movement and change which was at least partially unpredictable, and of contrast between one era ... and another, even when the two were closely adjacent' (MacQueen 7). However, the appreciation of difference does not result in a contemplation of the past in itself, but of its significance for the present: where examining a specific historical moment in isolation leads to an emphasis on radical difference, its study and representation in relation to what followed implies the existence of retraceable stages of change: 'The recognition of the past as past can lead to a sense of history as process' which also encompasses the present (Shaw 27). The difference between moments in time may still be apparent, but it becomes historicised.

That Scott's engagement with the period and the materials that would form the subject of his novels takes on a specific national tinge is especially important. Not only did his approach to the past rely on a strand of Enlightenment thought articulated and developed within the national boundaries of Scotland and somewhat in contrast with eighteenth-century philosophy's otherwise 'smug contempt for the past' (Herman 261) in the name of reason and civilisation. The evidence of the impact of modernity on traditional cultures was also especially apparent in the contrast between the declining social systems of feudal patronage of the Highland clans and the commercial capitalism of Edinburgh and Glasgow. Similarly, contemporary historical novelists in Britain are confronted with a specifically national predicament. Even as they find themselves in a postmodern climate which is, almost by definition, cosmopolitan, supra-national and sceptical towards such closed entities as the nation (hence, for instance, Linda Hutcheon's unproblematic discussion of British, American and post-colonial works under the all-encompassing heading of historiographic metafiction), the retrospective dwelling on the past that is required of them as historical novelists and that past's uncertain transmission and ideologically bound representation inevitably leads these authors to a reflection of the particular national experience that shapes the present's relationship to the past. For Britain, that experience is the Empire and its loss, in the aftermath of which the national climate corresponds to what Tim Gauthier calls 'the growing sense of "declinism"' in a Britain 'generally perceived as having relinquished its position as a global and economic power' (3).

The genre that seemed to embody the epistemological and representational concerns of postmodernism in fact exposes the limitations of its transnational assumptions. The ensuing nostalgia is not, contrary to the assumptions of theorists such as Fredric Jameson, an expression of postmodern a-historical dimension but rather its opposite – a consciously deployed form to counter the pervasive presence of postmodernism's unthinkingly homogenising traits. Indeed, John J. Su identifies nostalgia as 'a central feature of novels written in England', describing it as 'the longing for lost or imagined homelands' (119) (to which could be added the longing for cultural forms perceived to have been lost), and argues for a recognition of its role in envisaging the contemporary nation.

The internal contradictions of postmodernism become clear when one considers that the 'main focus' of this 'current of contemporary debate' is 'the representation and analysis of a perceived breakdown in the universalizing and rationalist metanarratives of the Enlightenment: those grand theories which have grounded modern Western politics, knowledge, art and ethics, for the last two hundred and fifty years' (Waugh 87), and yet the outcome of its efforts has been the presumption of an equally universalising position that transcends the particularities of history and geography. The rise and popular success of the historical novel in Britain signals a correction of this position and indeed an ironic revisiting of the very circumstances of its initial emergence as a genre influenced precisely by the Enlightenment ideas of history and human nature that postmodernism so vociferously rejects. Thus, in the early nineteenth century Scott's initial interest in the culture and society of the Highlands arose precisely from the awareness of its progressive vanishing, so that his work functioned simultaneously as a historical account of the forces of modernity as they impinge indiscriminately on eager and reluctant participants, on the one hand, and as an antiquarian operation of archival gathering and preservation of an irretrievable past, on the other. In late twentieth-century Britain, as Suzanne Keen suggests,

> the experience of decolonization, the crisis of Suez, the spasms of patriotism stirred up by the Falklands War, the transition to a postimperial condition, and the concomitant rise of the post-colonial novel in English come together to make the archive an

especially vivid emblem of what remains when the Empire is no
more. (15)

That archive is plundered by the works I discuss in this book, in
search of the moments that show the process of national decline
(arguably the process of history *tout court*) in action. Yet at the same
time, as was the case for Highland society in Scott's novels, the
recording of those moments grants them a significance that transcends history and functions as a symbol for what once was and has
now been lost.

The value of Scott's example for an understanding of contemporary historical fiction, then, is not confined to the realisation that the
formal features and representational approaches which have been
identified as recent innovations, shaped by supposedly new attitudes
towards reality, knowledge and texts, are in fact defining characteristics of the genre from the start. A comparison of the cultural and
contextual conditions of the early nineteenth century with those of
the late twentieth reveals interesting points of contact, among them
the closeness between historiographical and fictional practice, the
exploitation of divergent approaches to the past, and the significance
of the retrieval of the past for an understanding of the nation in the
present.

Scott's engagement with the events of Scotland's past drew impetus
from a combination of the practice of Enlightenment historiography,
on the one hand, and the practical work of archaeological recovery
of the antiquarian movement, on the other. Similarly, the interest in
re-imagining and representing the past on the part of contemporary
writers is shaped by the theoretical and historiographical work of
Hayden White, while also taking place in the midst of what is the
essentially anti-historical political and economic promotion of the
notion of heritage. The parallel between past and present conditions
is not exact, and the interaction between the elements listed above is
complex and shifting; nevertheless, some patterns do emerge.

In the first place, there is a degree of tension between the principles
of Enlightenment historians and the antiquarians' attitude towards
the past they helped to bring to public attention. The former recognised the difference between the past and the present, but implicit in
this perception was an element of comparability between the two, in
so far as they both involved a manifestation of human nature, whose

presence was continuous even when its traits were not constant. It is a small step from this to the study of the individual, with all its timeless human qualities, caught in the unfolding of the historical process which is the subject of Scott's novels. The antiquarian attention to the detail of life in the past, from habits to artefacts to accurate information about episodes from legend or history, gave Scott access to a specialised knowledge that complemented and countered the tendency of contemporary historiographers to generalise in the name of abstract absolutes. The so-called local colour that makes Scott's novels valuable documentary records of geographically and historically delineated circumstances is largely a product of Scott's association with the antiquarian movement. At the same time, however, in such parodic paratextual creation as the Reverend Dr. Dryasdust, Scott condemns the antiquarians' underlying outlook: their emphasis on the uniqueness of their findings and on the curiosity value of the information retrieved about the past served to detach the detail of that past from the perception and experience of the historical process. The result is a piecemeal past, enshrined and even fetishised for its own sake, rather than as a conduit to historical understanding: '[T]he cult of the material persistence of...history' promoted by antiquarianism is ultimately 'a cult of the dead' (Dennis 93).

In the late twentieth century, the respective positions of postmodern historiography and the heritage industry with regard to the past reflect comparable divergences. The approach outlined by Hayden White and other contemporary theorists of history towards the representation of the past insists on the role of narrative in shaping our understanding of it. Thus, what were single events connected by a coincidence of time and space (they took place, that is, contemporaneously and in the same location) become an intelligible and satisfyingly explanatory sequence when they are granted meaning and significance by their position in a narrative, a form which, by its nature, provides 'real events' with 'the coherence, integrity, fullness, and closure of an image of life that can only be imaginary' (White 1987: 24). Not only does this perspective on historical representation suggest a reliance of historiography on the techniques of fictional narrative which neatly reverses and complements Scott's own exploitation of the historiographical positions of his time, thus confirming the borderline nature of the discourses of history and historical fiction equally, but the centrality posited for narrative and for the historian's use of it also reasserts the sense of a process that joins past and present together, formally as much as substantively. As a form, in fact, narrative connects past and present in a complex network of correspondences between the prospective unfolding of events and their retrospective understanding. The result is a representation of the past which depends, for its coherence, on the knowledge of the consequences of that past, of what followed the events narrated: something which can only be attained in the future. In turn, it is the historian or the historical novelist, working in the present, who engages in the process of retrieving the past, establishing connections between events, and shaping these into an intelligible and explanatory (because coherent) narrative. It is worth pointing out that, not unexpectedly, the notion of process has shifted from the domain of the historical real (the sequence of events and their effects as perceived in the course of time) to the realm of historical representation (the sequence of events as they are articulated in narrative and their effects as perceived in the unfolding of that narrative). While acknowledging this change in emphasis, Louis O. Mink (1987) rejects the suggestion put forward by critics of postmodernism that the philosophy of history and historiography 'have abandoned substantive problems for methodological issues'; instead, he argues that 'it may be said that these problems have resurfaced as methodological issues' (119). The historical novel, as I have shown above, is the genre most suitably placed to respond to the altered perspective Mink describes.

However, there is widespread evidence that at least in one version, with considerable popular appeal, the suggestion that the past is a reality reproduced and recreated (as opposed to a represented one, an enterprise with methodological and philosophical implications) in the present as pure surface is indeed valid. This is the commodification of the past that goes under the name of heritage. In *The Heritage Industry: Britain in a Climate of Decline* (1987) Robert Hewison argues that the proliferation of museums and other visitor attractions that generally come under the economic heading of 'leisure' in Britain since the 1970s is the political and popular sign of 'a country obsessed with its past, and unable to face its future' (9). The particular kind of industry heritage sustains 'is expected more and more to replace the real industry upon which [Britain's] economy depends' (9), in accordance with the more general economic shift towards late forms of capitalism: what the heritage industry produces is, in this view, not a tangible item of identifiable value but rather an infinitely repeatable – and indeed infinitely replicated – experience of something (the past) whose original is by definition lost. This description points to a certain antiquarian pleasure in reconstructing the exact detail of specific objects or habits from the past, as 'landscapes, buildings, art objects, religious ceremonies, even the weather can be part of the heritage' (Keen 103), without however acknowledging their existence in time, or the process that has translated them from their original context to the present one, offering them instead for mass consumption as if the history they were once part of and are still supposed to embody in the present was over. Heritage sites are evidence 'of a cherished past – preserved, restored, and defended' (Keen 103), all attitudes signalling that the past has been enshrined in its difference from the mundane present and functions as a contrast to it, without being granted any power to intervene on the present. The reverence for the past manifests itself as nostalgic contemplation.

The underlying assumption that the present can neither compare with the intensity of the past nor contribute to a (changed) national environment by becoming historically significant in its own right militates against an appreciation of the historical process. It is also further evidence that heritage develops and gains predominance in a cultural context that takes for granted the decline of the nation, whose perception it exacerbates by pitting the completed and incomparable achievements of the past (even in its less salubrious aspects) with the fragmented, unsatisfactory, ultimately unheroic present: '[H]eritage, far from compensating for present discontents, either as a spiritual or crudely economic resource, quietly increases them, by holding before us the contrast between a decaying present and an ever improving and more appealing past' (Hewison 141). What this operation conceals is the eminently historical notion of hindsight, or retrospection, namely, the fact that the past gains its completeness, intelligibility, even aesthetic coherence from the fact that it can be considered from the perspective of its future; in other words, that the past was once as confusing as the present seems now and, conversely, that the present will one day lend itself to comprehensive and persuasive representation.

The omission of retrospection, which as I argued earlier is a function of historical narrative, is significant. The anti-historical attitude

Hewison pinpoints as defining heritage, which privileges the 'emotional experience [and] the symbolic recovery of the way we were' (21) over an understanding of past and present in relation to one another within the workings of a variously articulated entity called 'history', has much in common with a widespread perception of postmodernism as characterised by an emphasis on simultaneity and on the disconnected moment rather than on diachronicity. Indeed, Hewison's labelling of the reproduction of the past in the present as 'recycled imagery' (133) as well as his contention that in contemporary recreations of the past 'a self-referring consciousness of medium is all' (133) implies not only a lack of historical perspective but also, more gravely, the inability to perceive that lack at all, hence the author's reference to 'surface...appearance, not content' (133).

There is no doubt that contemporary historical fiction, including the 13 examples examined in detail in this study, emerges in this climate of 'widespread perception that Great Britain has suffered a decline in economic well-being and global status' (Keen 103) favourable to the proliferation of heritage as a substitute for history which Hewison describes. The suspicion of the genre's complicity with the assumptions, means and aims of the heritage industry is fostered by the prevalent setting for contemporary historical novels, the Victorian period, conveniently near enough the present in time to be emotionally appealing, yet different enough not to impinge on the readers' preconceived attitudes towards it. The mid-nineteenth century has been made familiar by the numerous costume dramas and adaptations of classic novels for the screen, both of which pride themselves in the accuracy of their reconstruction of the period in all its details (objects, clothes, manners, speech) and therefore emphasise its static value as a completed, teeming, exhaustively investigated whole. The plots of contemporary historical novels are primarily concerned with individual lives and loves, and only incidentally with the historical events impinging on them. This is perhaps inevitable, in so far as a focus on the individual in his or her interaction with his or her social, geographical and historical surroundings is almost by definition what the novel as a genre is concerned with. However, in seeking to engage the reader in an emotional response to characters and events, the historical novel appeals to its consumers in similar ways to heritage reconstructions. Nor can the charge of escapism frequently levelled at the genre, which offers a convenient way out from having to confront the difficulties of the present or even attempting to actively intervene in it, be fully dismissed, particularly when the historical setting is combined with the traditional recreational genres of detective, romance and adventure. And yet, despite their participation in the perpetuation of heritage attitudes, the historical novels I consider in the chapters that follow do not conform to the a-historical premises of the commodification of the past Hewison describes. Rather, they seek to probe the roots of the perceived irretrievability of the past as part of an ongoing history which underlies its nostalgic recuperation as heritage reconstruction and to find ways to engage anew in an exploration of the historical process over the reproduction of finite and unconnected moments or places in history. Three related aspects mark the difference between the reproductive aims of the heritage industry and the representational enterprise of contemporary historical fiction: the latter's awareness of history as both text and process; its dialogue with the Victorian realist tradition; and its examination of the competing models of the nation offered by the example of the past.

It is a given of postmodernism in all its forms, and one which has seeped into a widespread contemporary understanding beyond academic circles, that our experience and understanding of ourselves and the world is always already mediated by texts, and indeed that texts largely replace the reality of both the world and the experience of it. This dictum acquires particular significance for historical novels, in so far as it is literally true for their experience and representation of their object: not only, in fact, is the past only available through its textual remains, it is in turn reconstituted for the readers as another text, the novel. However, in spite of this double textual dimension that appears to confirm and conform to the strictest postmodern premises, and contrary to the still reproduction of the past for public fruition of heritage, the historical novel reinserts the element of time and process in its representation purely by virtue of the form that representation takes, narrative. In other words, even though the past is apprehended synchronically by the novelist, in the collection of texts at his or her disposal, it is presented diachronically in the unfolding of the plot and the structure of the narrative. The act of piecing together the remnants of the past and shaping them into a story becomes itself historical, displacing the notion of process from the sequence of events in history to the stages of their representation in fiction. The novels I discuss in Chapters 2 and 3 are particularly concerned with questions of textual evidence and textual representation: not only do they include various examples of texts in their narratives, they also make their decipherment and ultimate use a central component of the plots. For *The Chymical Wedding* (1989), *Possession* (1990) and *Ever After* (1992) this strategy opens the way for an exploration of the discontinuity between past and present made apparent by the former's physical remains and leads to the search for the narrative means to overcome it. *The Map of Love* (2000), *English Passengers* (2000) and *The Rising Sun* (2000), on the other hand, shift their attention to the ideological function of texts in the shaping and understanding of national and individual identity, particularly when confronting the otherness of an alien land and culture.

Among the texts contributing to the representation of the past in contemporary historical fiction the novels of the period when its stories are set are especially influential. Thus, historical novels whose action unfolds in the nineteenth century explicitly refer to the writers of the time, either claiming them as models or regretting their distance not only in time but also in achievement, immediacy of representation, innocence of experience. The example of Victorian fiction is celebrated at the same time as it is deemed unrepeatable; the result is an approximation of it by means of pastiche or by self-conscious contemporary re-writing of notable instances of nineteenth-century realism. The awareness of the weight of the literary tradition on contemporary historical fiction is shared in varying degrees by all the novels I discuss, but it holds particular prominence for the texts in Chapters 1 and 4. The intrusive presence of a self-conscious omniscient narrator in *The French Lieutenant's Woman* (1969) is an attempt on Fowles's part to revisit Victorian narrative from a contemporary perspective, emphasising its desirability while also acknowledging that the representational self-confidence that characterises it is no longer tenable at a time of literary, philosophical, and representational scepticism. The narrative self-consciousness of *The Siege of Krishnapur* (1973) manifests itself in Farrell's parodic cannibalising of the Victorian genres of imperial adventure and imperial romance, while the evocation of E.M. Forster's imperial experiences in *Heat and Dust* (1975) points to the novel's rejection of a unified and coherent representational form to represent the reality of the colonial space of India. For James

Robertson and Philip Hensher in *Joseph Knight* (2003) and *The Mulberry Empire* (2002), on the other hand, the influence of an unquestioned literary tradition of representation of Scotland and the Empire, respectively, is something to be confronted and challenged in its persistent perniciousness. As was the case with the novels in Chapter 3, here formal concerns foreshadow reflections on the ideology of narrative and representation.

The engagement with the realist novel that is common to all the works in this study is not confined to reverence for its form and regret at its present impossibility. At the basis of realism was, as Lukács argues, the representation of the present as part of history's unfolding, an aim achieved by constructing plots that show the individual caught in the historical process, whether it be changes in social configurations or recognisable historical events, and reacting either in accommodation to it or in vain strife against its tyranny. This pattern of locating the present in and as history results in a wider exploration of the common experiences and goals of a number of representative individuals constituting the nation as a textual and narrative construct. Contemporary reflections on the example of realism similarly embrace an assessment of the viability of a national narrative articulated by means of a correspondingly viable representational form that joins past and present in a continuous perception of history. This operation proves all the more urgent in the context of the contemporary resigned acceptance of national decline: once again, what appeared to be mere literary nostalgia for the achievement of a form whose strategies prove irrecoverable in the context of present literary practice is in fact revealed to have substantive implications for the ways in which the present understands itself and articulates its experience of history. All 13 novels under consideration put forward and explore models of the nation variously located in physical spaces, literary artefacts, actual communities, oral transmission of stories, or elusive imagined refuges from an unstoppable history. Ronan Bennett's *Havoc in Its Third Year* (2004) and Gregory Norminton's *Ghost Portrait* (2005), however, are especially interesting in so far as they situate the productive tension between individual aspiration and historical necessity respectively at the moment immediately preceding, and in the aftermath of, England's most obvious historical conflagration, the Civil War. The move away from the canonically inflected nineteenth century for their setting arguably signals the authors' programmatic distancing from the earlier novels' formal preoccupation and the intention to delve into a representation and explanation of the historical process which, paradoxically, aligns them precisely with the Victorian models they eschew narratively.

The trajectory of the genre this study traces, then, is one of progressive consolidation of the experiments with form and narrative voice which first signalled the resurgence of the historical novel as a 'serious' genre in the decades following World War II; these, in turn, give way to an ever keener and more openly displayed interest in the representation of the past as a component of the historical process, without however being fully abandoned even in the most recent and politically engaged examples of the genre. The four chapters that follow are arranged in broad chronological order, aiming to provide an informed survey of the subtle changes (I hesitate to use the heavily connoted 'Victorian' term development) in the forms, substantive concerns and representational aims of the contemporary historical novel from the last quarter of the twentieth century, to either side of the millennium, and finally into the twenty-first century. Chapter 1, 'Tradition and Renewal', situates the success of early contemporary examples of historical fiction in the context of a narrative and critical reflection on the state of the nation in the aftermath of the loss of the Empire. The novels are shown to provide only contingent and unsustainable national models, which correspond to the uncertain allegiances of their narrative forms. In Chapter 2, 'The Romance of the Past', contemporary historical fiction's preoccupation with narrative form takes centre stage, and is examined in the light of the postmodern articulation of theoretical positions on representation. These make their way openly into the novels' plots, and their possibilities are explored and exhausted before being discarded in favour of the representational framework provided by romance. With the potential representational *impasse* largely resolved, the novels in Chapter 3, 'Empire and the Politics of Representation', redeploy the formal strategies of earlier works to political effect, applying them not to the relative safety of national boundaries but to the ideologically fraught matter of the representation of colonial territories and of the imperial enterprise more generally. The ideology of articulating a national identity by means of its imperial counterpart is subjected to close scrutiny, with the congenital weaknesses of the resulting national models exposed in the unfolding of the plots. Finally, Chapter 4, 'Political Engagement and the Romance of Withdrawal', identifies two tendencies in the probing of narrative images of the nation: the first two novels in the chapter reflect on the exhausted model provided by the literary tradition when applied to an imperial context; the remaining works, on the other hand, seek to locate the inherent limitations of a national identity articulated by narrative means before any systematic national imperial expansion to the period of the English Civil War and the establishment of the modern state, if not of a unitary nation. While there is a degree of linear unfolding in the story the chapters tell about the genre of the historical novel in its contemporary incarnation, of equal importance is the web of correspondences between the 13 novels that emerges in the course of the analysis, in themes, attitude towards their object of representation and the representational enterprise itself, narrative strategies, recurrent tropes, even incidental details. This network of cross-references will be assessed in the Conclusion to this study, 'Fictions of the Garden', which raises the question, firstly, of whether they amount to a consistent attempt to put forward a model of the nation in the present, evidence therefore of the contemporary relevance of the past and of its representation in the genre of the historical novel, and secondly, of whether, if that is the case, the picture they assemble is a coherent one.

1
Tradition and Renewal

As Ronald Binns acknowledges in his study of J.G. Farrell's fiction, the historical novel was not 'a genre which ... held much appeal for British novelists' in the aftermath of World War II (14). He traces the decline of the genre to its very origins, the work of Sir Walter Scott, whose influence manifested itself on the 'popular historical romance' rather than on the 'serious novel' (14). In separating the two, Binns replicates a set of specious distinctions – between entertainment and ethical purpose, self-conscious irony and seriousness of artistic aims, accessibility and philosophical depth – that John Fowles's *The French Lieutenant's Woman* (1969), J.G. Farrell's *The Siege of Krishnapur* (1973), and Ruth Prawer Jhabvala's *Heat and Dust* (1975) seek to undermine. The popular and critical acclaim of these three novels (two were made into successful films, two won the Booker Prize) 'helped to reverse the declining critical fortunes of the historical novel' (Kaplan 89). That they needed reversing seems beyond doubt. Bernard Bergonzi, among the most influential critics in the decade of the novels' publication, fails to discuss the historical novel at all in the first edition of *The Situation of the Novel* (1970); he belatedly adds a chapter on 'Fictions of History' in the revised edition (1979), but the label seems to apply indiscriminately to any work engaging with history either as past events or as historical process (214–37). Several years later, even Allan Massie's *The Novel Today* (1990), a work aimed at the wider reading public and suspicious of 'unhelp-fully restrictive' terms like 'the literary novel', nevertheless confirms that 'dull and conventional practitioners' of the historical novel 'have endangered the critical validity of the genre' (39). Interestingly,

Massie also suggests that, in the right hands, the genre may still regain its prestige, 'if only because so many of the greatest novels in the nineteenth century fell into that category' (39). This mention of the Victorian novel in relation to contemporary examples of historical fiction explains the genre's critical neglect; at the same time, it points to a fruitful direction of enquiry when examining its revival.

The novel as a literary form, by which commentators seemed to mean the realist novel, was being declared no longer viable in Britain at the time of the publication of *The French Lieutenant's Woman, The Siege of Krishnapur* and *Heat and Dust*. Gasiorek lucidly divides the sources of the pressure on the genre in the immediate post-war into aesthetic, broadly cultural and specifically historical (1). The War, the Holocaust in particular, defied the available narrative forms and called for a representational approach that avoided naturalising the historical event and instead preserved the horror inherent in it. Literary culture more generally was in competition with television and other media, which, critics were keen to point out, were supplanting the novel as a supposedly unmediated means of representation. Finally, when compared with French and American fiction, the British novel was declared provincial in subject, its concerns insular, the reliance on long-standing representational conventions derivative: the novel, unable to provide what its name demanded (novelty), had lost its raison d'être. Nor did the experimental novel fare much better: after the achievements of modernism, further manipulations of the form seemed to Bergonzi cerebral and sterile (11–34; see also Hayman 1976). Bergonzi goes so far as to envisage a time when novels will no longer be published. What he and other commentators lamented was the contamination of the literary novel by elements of genre fiction, which made the novel 'about life, but scarcely about life in a wholly unconditioned way; the movement towards genre means that experience is mediated through existing literary patterns and types' (26). Despite the rather naïve belief that such a thing as unconditioned representation is possible, Bergonzi unwittingly identifies the attitude to their narratives of Fowles, Farrell and Jhabvala. Not only do these authors acknowledge the influence of literary genres in our understanding of the past, a subject for which no claims to unconditioned representation can possibly be made; they also exploit the shared ground generic conventions grant them – a territory shared with readers, of course, but also with the novelistic tradition whose demise appeared so imminent. The tradition with which they engage is, I suggest, a specifically national one, and the forms of that engagement respond to a particular perception of the situation of the nation in the aftermath of World War II.

The seemingly parlous state of the realist novel in the post-war period was not purely the result of a literary *impasse*. It revealed a deeper unease with what the tradition of realism had seemed to promise: a homogeneous, intelligible representation which stood for equal intelligibility and homogeneity of the world it represented. This world was, in turn, imagined as a nation: as Benedict Anderson suggests, the realist novel provided the 'technical means for representing the *kind* of community that is the nation' by virtue of its formal construction of continuity in the narrative and the unfolding of the plot in a homogeneous time, 'a precise analogue of the idea of the nation... moving steadily down (or up) history' (25–6). Timothy Brennan confirms that '[i]t was the *novel* that historically accompanied the rise of nations by objectifying the "one, yet many" of national life, and by mimicking the structure of the nation, a clearly bordered jumble of languages and styles' (49). The imagined community thus constructed by literary-narrative means was oblivious to its internal contradictions, which went similarly unquestioned in critical discussions of the novel until the late twentieth century. First among them is the slippage between 'English' and 'British' as the apt national adjective for the realist novel, which elides the contribution of Scottish, Welsh and Irish writers to the form by claiming their work for a homogeneous national entity. The historical novel since its inception shared in the incongruity of these definitions, in so far as Sir Walter Scott presented the Scottish material in his novels as an irretrievable past submerged by the forces of progress, modernity – and Britishness. It seems appropriate that in the post-war period the same genre should signal that such national and literary uniformity is no longer tenable.

The second, related contradiction refers to the relationship between realism, the nation, and empire. Ian Baucom has shown that imperial expansion posed unforeseen challenges to Britain's understanding of itself as a nation, in conditions that test its 'command of its own narrative of identity' (3). The reassertion of a uniform national identity against the potentially centrifugal effect of the accumulation of disparate territories relies on a range of symbolic practices, among which literary representation is paramount. The spread of the study of English literature, which gradually replaced the classics as the repository of a liberal education (a fact which contributed greatly to the shaping of a literary-national tradition), was closely related to the colonial enterprise in India. It aimed to instil in the departing colonial administrators a clear sense of the national character they would embody and represent to the natives as well as fellow Britons abroad. The representational strategies of realism, resting on the conventions of homogeneity and intelligibility, were mobilised in an imperial context, producing imagined communities of Britons in the colonial territories to be consumed by those actively involved in Britain's imperial expansion as well as by the wider public at home, ensuring that 'British men and women distant from one another in space' would see each other as 'fundamentally alike' (Baucom 20). Anderson notes the coincidence of dates between the rise of the idea of the nation, on the one hand, and the emergence of the novel as a distinct and recognisable literary form, on the other, while Brennan traces the need for a clearer definition of 'nation' to the assertion of imperial aspirations. These historical considerations are drawn together by Booker, who emphasises 'the contribution of literary representations of empire ... to the British cultural identity from the nineteenth-century days of rapid imperial expansion to the late-twentieth-century days of imperial aftermath' (1997: 2). He further identifies a paradoxical degree of continuity in the progressively more forced attempts to apply to an alien reality the epistemological and representational parameters of a familiar one, in order to achieve the sense of cultural, spatial and historical continuity. The reliance on literature to understand both empire and metropolis 'already suggests the limitations of this epistemological approach' (6). When representational form and represented reality are no longer commensurable, and the latter exceeds the formal constraints of the former, the ensuing sense of crisis is of a literary as much as a politico-ideological kind: after World War II, the historical novel becomes the genre that reflects upon the rupture in the British sense of the nation and enacts it in its narrative choices and in the unfolding of events in its plots.

Fowles, Farrell and Jhabvala are especially valuable examples because they set their novels at key moments in the history of Britain as a nation that understood itself as being culturally homogeneous.

By placing their narrators in the future of the events narrated, all three novels also exploit the ambivalent power of retrospection, which both establishes historical continuity and allows, in hindsight, to perceive the seams in the construction of that continuity. The narrator of *The French Lieutenant's Woman* takes every opportunity to remark on the historical significance of 1867, a year at the cusp of social, cultural, ideological and political change: shortly after the dissemination of Darwin's ideas on evolution and natural selection and shortly before Marx published the first volume of *Capital,* this was also the year of Mill's failed attempt to extend to women the right to vote. These are events of which the characters, though contemporary to their taking place, are aware in a partial way, if at all. Charles Smithson, the protagonist, 'called himself a Darwinist, and yet he had not really understood Darwin' (53), while he 'knew nothing of the beavered German Jew quietly working...that very afternoon in the British Museum library' (18). His fiancée, Ernestina, 'giggled at the previous week's *Punch*', showing 'a group of gentlemen besieging a female Cabinet minister' (115). Only the historical understanding acquired with the benefit of retrospection, and shared by author and readers at the expense of the characters, can grant full appreciation of the ideas of the time.

The Siege of Krishnapur adopts a similar stance with regard to the intersection of prospective unfolding of the plot and retrospective gauging of the significance of events. The meaning given to the Indian Mutiny of 1857 in its immediate aftermath greatly differs from the understanding of it at the time of the novel's publication, when all but a handful of British colonies had gained independence. The successful quashing of the rebellion seemed to confirm Britain's invincibility and 'became a source of intense national pride to the Victorians, inspiring...a whole generation of minor artists and lesser poets to dizzy flights of patriotic fantasy' (Strobl 193). From a twentieth-century standpoint, however, the same events are emplotted in the novel to show that the imperial solidity was constructed rather than real. The novel tugs at the readers' knowledge of the loss of the Empire to cast an ironic light on the certainties of 1857 and confirms the greater understanding conferred by historical knowledge: in 1947, 90 years after the Mutiny, India gained independence. When the Collector 'feebly tried to imagine 1957' (158), the date is resonant of the Suez debacle a year before, the event which, while not literally marking the end of Britain's colonial power, psychologically signalled that things had changed utterly, and in the space of barely a century, from the confidence of Victorian colonialism. Farrell 'singled out the decline and dissolution of the Empire as the important event of his lifetime' (Crane 13), the same Empire that had officially come into existence in a national sense with the Mutiny, since it was only as a result of the events of 1857 that India was removed from the control of the East India Company to become a British possession.

The effect on post-war Britain of the loss of the Empire was 'a disturbance of its sense of historical belonging and coherence' (Connor 3). The continuity of the nation, reflected in the homogeneous time constructed by realist narrative, was ruptured, with the result that 'a certain pressure has been put upon the powers of historical narrative to organise the world' (3). The collapse of the accepted sense of the nation is reflected in the crisis of the means for its formal imagining, the conventions of realism. Thus, in the immediate post-war 'the Victorian novel appeared ... as a vast and orderly genre reflecting a coherent society, which had since broken up, leaving its surviving relics in an uncertain world' (McEwan 1981: 18). Bergonzi joins novelistic and national decline when he reminds his readers that 'in literary terms, as in political ones, Britain is not a very important part of the world today' (57). The historical novel holds particular significance in the process of re-imagining the nation. Its backward look had once performed the welding of the present with a past made meaningful by being re-cast as a national beginning, thus exploiting 'the authenticating force of historical origins in a narrative of Englishness' (Connor 49) to 'guarantee that the nation's past, present, and future would be fundamentally alike' (Baucom 20). In the decades of decolonisation, on the other hand, the same backward look dwelt on the structural weakness of the historical joints and showed the ease with which they would come apart. The narrative structure of *Heat and Dust* enacts this sense of historical rupture. The novel's plot unfolds over two separate timeframes set in India in 1923 and 1975, dates poised at near-equal distance from the key event, which goes unrepresented, of Indian independence. The protagonists are, respectively, Olivia Rivers, wife of the Assistant Collector of Satipur, and a young unnamed Englishwoman (granddaughter of Olivia's husband by his second wife) who is also the novel's narrator. It is only by the conscious effort physically to retrace the events of the earlier woman's life that her modern follower can establish a connection with the past, as there is no imaginative continuity between the two periods, nor is there a sense of belonging to a shared community moving in history. Only the narrator's diary, with a date at the start of each entry, in which present events are recorded and Olivia's story is told, frames experience by containing it in a visible chronology and sequentiality. The contemporary protagonist-narrator thus imposes a textual order whose artificiality is immediately apparent and which, even when successful in shaping links between past and present, never allows them to be perceived as natural.

The three novels under consideration foreground a range of narrative strategies that aspire to the formal and substantive achievements of realism, while acknowledging that such an aspiration cannot be met given the weight of historical awareness resting on the shoulders of the contemporary historical novelist. *The French Lieutenant's Woman, The Siege of Krishnapur* and *Heat and Dust* posit a Victorian novel 'pastoralised as a place Edenically unaware of its own conventionalisation, awaiting ... that *felix culpa* of a Fall into Modernity which will enable it to start to know itself' (Conradi 19). Conradi's appeal to the story of the Fall to articulate the place of contemporary historical fiction is particularly interesting, since it redeploys metaphorically and at a formal level what Anderson describes as a literal '[d]isintegration of paradise', namely the 'ebbing of religious belief', which changed the substance of the perception of individual life and made nationalism possible (12). Once again, there is a correspondence between the novels' concerns with literary-traditional form and their substantive engagement with the perception of national-historical fracture. While recuperating 'the usable elements of nineteenth-century realism', these novels do not conceal the fact that what that form articulated as a 'smooth filiation between past and present' is in fact better figured as a 'broken lineage' (Conradi 61–2). Jhabvala's modern heroine, whose relation with her colonial counterpart is precisely *not* one of linear genealogical descent, embodies the acknowledgement of discontinuity.

If these novels show contemporary authors coming to terms with the disjuncture of form and content, representation and reality, in realism, they also deploy the armoury of its opposite narrative form, romance. Romance, which comprises adventure and the gothic, consistently lends Fowles, Farrell and Jhabvala its conventions: among the stock situations exploited are the dangers for a young woman travelling to an exotic country in *Heat and Dust,* the pluck of the besieged of Krishnapur even when all seems lost, *The French Lieutenant's Woman*'s depiction of the lure of forbidden love in the conventionally socialised setting of Lyme Regis. The 'generic and stylistic diversity' (Ferns 131) exhibited by the three novels in this chapter finds an illustrious precedent in the politically inflected co-existence of representational modes in Scott, where '[t]ragedy or romance ... are the narrative modes of the defeated – realism is a luxury available only to the victors' and marks the 'political, economic, and cultural hegemony of Great Britain' (Ferns 132). It is no more than a continuation of the representational strategies at the origins of the historical novel that, with the loss of Empire, the adequate means of narrating Britain in the post-war period should be romance, a genre that signals the 'dissolution of a ... highly structured view of reality' (Costantini 155). As Diane Elam has argued, romance holds a 'troubled relation to both history and novelistic realism' (3) because it exceeds 'the boundaries imposed by the continuous, chrono-logical ordering of historical periodicity' (11). Excess, in both histor-ical and aesthetic terms, is also the signature of the gothic, a genre characterised by '[a] particular attitude towards the recapture of his-tory' and 'self-conscious un-realism' (Punter 4; see also Botting 1 and 6). Adventure, in Martin Green's seminal study, equally emerges as a genre that articulates a wish to trespass the boundaries of what is recognisable as civilisation, even when the trespass is conducted in its name (4).

The elements whose stability romance, the gothic and adventure upset (periodicity, continuity, chronological sequence) are, in Anderson's description, the conditions for imagining the nation; the novels' introduction of generic and narrative elements that cannot be limited within exact confines therefore exposes the nation's fra-gility. According to Cannon Schmitt, these genres 'problematize [the] two preconditions of the modern nation' in so far as they pre-sent 'indecipherable, illegible, or unspeakable' milieus and, in the presentation, 'return over and over to moments of slowed or stopped time' (12). The formal and generic jostling of realism and romance in *The French Lieutenant's Woman, The Siege of Krishnapur* and *Heat and*

Dust is analogous to the questioning of the accepted sense of the nation. This is, in turn, reflected in the novels' plots, where the characters' preoccupation with categorising and classifying is motivated by the very unwieldiness of the material being ordered. At the centre of this negotiation between representational modes are texts. They appear in the novels under the guise of letters and diaries (*Heat and Dust*), bureaucratic reports alongside poetry and science (*The Siege of Krishnapur*), and the canon of nineteenth-century literature interwoven with commentaries on the socio-historical context of its production (*The French Lieutenant's Woman*).

The array of materials deployed in the three novels both fulfils and undermines the attempt at a comprehensive representation of the past. While their range appears to cover all the facets of the reality of 1867, 1857, and 1923, the fact that authors and narrators stress the amount of research they have undertaken and foreground the textuality of their subject-matter makes it clear that any approach to the past is always mediated and already encoded. As Victor Sage suggests in relation to the work of J.G. Farrell, these texts' function 'is not "verisimilitude" or "authenticity", but...the opposite' as they 'make the reader witness the congealing process, the entropic decline of full and living truth into dead narrative' (180). The recreation of the past, however convincing, is the product of erudite study and not immediate apprehension. In fact, the persuasiveness of the representation rests on the contemporary reader's prior familiarity with the texts of the period: as McEwan perceives, '[o]ur sense of how fully [the characters in these novels] belong to their own time is stronger than could have been achieved in a Victorian novel', since 'the nineteenth century is intimately known to us because of its novels' (1981: 31). If, collectively, the interpolated texts project a sense of unity, continuity and comprehensiveness of representation analogous to the construction of the nation, they also carry an inherent danger of the construct breaking up into irreconcilable multiplicity (the many, not one, to reverse Brennan's definition). Even when united by period, subject, discipline, aesthetic allegiance, texts do not relinquish their separateness from one another. Indeed, taken individually, they confirm the fragmentary nature of any knowledge of the past, whose gaps are papered over by the (distorting) power of historical narrative. Thus, in making their engagement with both the realist literary tradition and its romantic 'Other' explicit; in devising plots concerned with taxonomic arrangements and exposing their limitations; and in exploring the elements that transcend categorisation, Fowles, Farrell and Jhabvala reproduce the textual operations for the imagining of the past and explore their shortcomings in the light of an understanding of the post-war British nation.

1. John Fowles's *The French Lieutenant's Woman*

Romance, realism, and the respective national models they propose are closely examined in the display of texts and the deployment of intertextual references in *The French Lieutenant's Woman*. The characters understand themselves and one another through texts. To Ernestina, the Cobb in Lyme is a place experienced through her reading (' "These are the very steps that Jane Austen made Louisa Musgrove fall down in *Persuasion*" ' [14]), a reference which grants her entry into a world of romance she, and even the worldly-wise Charles, considers lost. His suggestion that there is '[n]o romance' (16) in provincial life reprises her earlier declaration that '[g]entlemen were romantic ... then' (14). In both cases, romance is displaced in time or space, preventing it from disruptively intruding into the couple's engagement, whose foundations lie on the exchange of a substantial marriage portion for a title and country estate. As Conradi suggests, this union would 'fulfil not merely the plot of many of the period's novels but one plot too of nineteenth-century British history' (63–4). The conjunction of literary resolutions and national-historical change is especially relevant in the light of Fowles's dismantling of the conventions of realist closure in a conciliatory marriage. The flippant omniscience of the first ending in chapter 44, where the narrator reviews all the characters and apportions to each their deserts, is, on a purely metafictional level, a parodic rejection of the form of Victorian realism that underlies the genre of the condition of England novel. Beyond the author's dissatisfaction with the genre, however, is a substantive resistance to the kind of convenient resolution it offered: it is not realism *per se,* as a set of representational conventions, that is at stake in the novel, but the ideological implications of those conventions for the national community they project.

Fowles's commitment to unearthing and displaying these implications surfaces in two strategies. The first consists of having a disproportionate amount of epigraphs excerpted from Hardy's poetry.

Appearing alongside the story of Tina and Charles's engagement, and pre-empting its genteel telling given their position before the events in the chapters are revealed, the epigraphs offer a short-hand reminder of the limits to realist representation, which excluded the treatment of a sexuality that exceeded the bounds of propriety and threatened the bounds of property defined by the marriage contract. If Hardy's rejection of the novel because the expectations of the form could not sustain his chosen themes is alluded to in the epigraphs, his preoccupations find their way into the main text of *The French Lieutenant's Woman*, under the guise of intertextual echoes and explicit literary-historical commentary. Claiming to have 'come under ... the very relevant shadow, of the great novelist who towers over this part of England' (262), the narrator proceeds to expand on Hardy's life and love for his cousin Tryphena. The earlier writer's ghostly presence in Fowles's novel had already been intimated in the outline of Sarah's early life, whose schooling beyond her social class was the result of her father's 'obsession with his own ancestry' (58), a circumstance identical to Tess of the d'Urbervilles. There is also a more sustained engagement with Hardy's *A Pair of Blue Eyes*, whose plot 'is hauntingly similar' to that of *The French Lieutenant's Woman* (DeVitis and Palmer 91), revolving as it does around a love triangle marred by social expectations of female sexuality, propriety and property and featuring fossils as a central motif. The epigraphs thus use the knowingly self-referential device of intertextuality to unmask the repressions operated by realist representation.

The second strategy consists of pitting in the same chapter a domesticated version of romance against its untamed counterpart. Thus, among Tina's favourite reading material is *The Lady of La Garaye*, a poem presenting a conventionalised romance, where surfeit of love is purified by suffering and renunciation. When she tries to share the poem with Charles, he falls asleep, proof that the dangerous edge of romance has been neutralised both in the poem and by the situation, as the couple are ensconced in a genteel room complete with Axminster carpet, while their time together is sanctioned by their host. If Charles is not susceptible to the safe romance offered by Tina's poem, he finds the lure of Sarah irresistible precisely because it is not framed by the conventions of polite conduct. From her look, far removed from the one favoured by the age, 'the demure, the obedient, the shy' (16), to the wildness of the place where their meetings take place (Ware Common with its reputation for impropriety), to the fact of their meeting at all, every aspect of the French Lieutenant's Woman, starting with her appellation, speaks of the trespassing of social acceptability. Sarah's romantic status is directly associated with her refuting the model of national community proposed by Lyme society, the same model that Fowles rebuts with the formal disruptiveness of his metafictional interventions. Her crime in the eyes of the town is compounded by the fact that she gave herself to a Frenchman; Charles himself confirms that the echoes Sarah's eyes rouse in him 'were not English ones. He associated such faces...with foreign beds' (119). Travel abroad, for Charles, signals the freedom of romance, which began with the loss of sexual inhibitions in Paris. He returns to the subject elsewhere in the novel, firstly to bemoan the fact that if once '[h]is future had always seemed to him of vast potential...now suddenly it was a fixed voyage to a known place' (129), and then again to articulate his dissatisfaction with the social impositions of Lyme as a desire for travel, 'sailing...through the Tyrrhenian; or riding...towards the distant walls of Avila; or approaching some Greek temple' (173). The social alternatives that are foreclosed to Charles in England are projected onto other lands; similarly, the literary options unavailable to Fowles within the confines of the representational conventions of Victorian realism are pursued in the metafictional gestures towards French theoretical positions.

It is not surprising that Charles and Dr. Grogan believe that they can explain Sarah with reference to two French texts. The first is Flaubert's *Madame Bovary,* a novel Charles had read 'very much in private, for the book had been prosecuted for obscenity' (119). The secret reading, and the reasons for it, function as a counterpart to the secrecy of his meetings with Sarah, and mark the woman's distance from the tameness of Ernestina's example of romantic text, and from its publicly validated reading. The difference between the two texts is not simply their literary quality; it resides in the degree of self-awareness they display. Where the English verse romance, although set in France, tells a straightforward Victorian story with clear moral overtones 'of pain, sorrow, love, duty, piety and death' (114), the French novel tells of the dangers of reading romances and shaping life to conform to them. The text is unsettling in its 'proto-modernist textual self-consciousness' (Wells 33) and exceeds not only social propriety but literary decorum too. By referring to Flaubert's novel Charles allows for Sarah's complexity to a degree denied by the other inhabitants of Lyme; nevertheless, he presumes to reduce and confine her to a comprehensible model. In other words, he denies her the prime feature of romance (exceeding conventional boundaries) even as he identifies her allegiance to the genre.

The second text supplied as a means of understanding Sarah co-opts the discourses of medicine and the law to enforce that confinement. It is the account of the trial of Émile de La Roncière, a French Lieutenant accused of sexually assaulting the daughter of his regiment's Captain. It reveals the woman at the centre of the affair to have been hysterically delusional. There are several interesting elements in the story and Grogan's use of it. Despite flaws in the young woman's account of events, the Lieutenant is condemned 'by social prestige' (226). As is the case in Lyme, the rules of social behaviour are enforced at the expense of truth, so that all the versions of Sarah's story are attempts to blunt the disruption that her presence alone performs. For Mrs. Poulteney, her employer, Sarah ought to conform to the role of the repentant sinner, whose abjection is a form of expiation; similarly, Mrs. Talbot, from whose employ Sarah fled to join the Lieutenant, casts her as the heroine of a romantic tale whose shame may be cancelled by self-destruction. The combination of legal argument and medical evidence, as well as the fact that it is written in a foreign language (the doctor hands over the text with the question, ' "I think you read French?" ' [221]), make Grogan's text more sophisticated than either the Bible or adolescent romances. The complexity does not, however, conceal the fact that the barrage of discourses serves an identical purpose to the simplistic approach of the two women, namely, to contain Sarah's indecipherable being into a scheme which not only makes her intelligible but confirms the intellectual superiority to the rest of the town of the men who devise it, even though the need for such an array of discursive approaches to explaining Sarah confirms the difficulties she poses. The text of the trial is one ground on which Charles and the doctor meet, the other being their acceptance of Darwin's ideas. In both cases, however covertly or inadvertently, the taxonomic system employed is diverted to signify social stratification and enforce social control.

Booker identifies 'the Victorian mania for taxonomy and classification and the Victorian obsession with scientific description and explanation' as the attempt 'to try to contain, delimit, and circum-scribe the [Romantic] sublime in any way possible' (1991: 181). Thus, the effort of categorising exists in direct competition with romance's threat to exceed or nullify boundaries, including the limits of intel-ligibility. The taxonomy of fossils is a counterpart of the attempted categorisation of Sarah according to possible explanatory narratives. Fossils function intertextually to signal *The French Lieutenant's Woman's* dialogue with the Victorian novel (and specifically Hardy's work); at the same time, they are made to convey Fowles's preoccupa-tion with a viable national model, and to act self-referentially in tra-cing Charles's relationship with Ernestina and Sarah. At the start of his stay in Lyme, Charles participates in the commodification of fos-sils, by purchasing some specimens in a local shop; the framework of this transaction domesticates the items and confirms the buyer's place in an ordered society and capitalist economy: having handed over his cash Charles owns the pieces outright. When the next trans-action occurs, however, it is fraught with obligations, and involves him in a situation for which his social understanding is inadequate, as Sarah gives him two specimens of tests (a fossil not available in the shop and therefore, like its giver, not placed in a system of social exchange) in Ware Common, a location socially out of bounds. From being a mark of his social identity and intellectual status, fossils become the instrument of Charles's exclusion from the society of Lyme and the source of mental confusion. Fowles explores the impli-cations of taxonomy by relating Charles's allegiance to Darwinian ideas and his interest in fossils to social change. The character finds 'an immensely reassuring orderliness' in the classificatory impulse, particularly in so far as it ultimately identifies 'the fittest and best, *exempli gratia* Charles Smithson' (54). It is only when he loses the pro-spect of inheriting his uncle's estate that he realises that evolution will not conform to comfortable social patterns, so that although '[t]he abstract idea of evolution was entrancing' (278), 'its practice seemed fraught with ostentatious vulgarity' (279). The perspective is clearly that of a specific class specimen, the leisured gentleman.

In the sudden understanding of the forces of social change that follows the loss of his inheritance, Charles perceives the true import of the theories of evolution and natural selection and initially con-veys his position within the framework of science, reflecting on 'the enormous apparatus rank required a gentleman to erect around himself ... like the massive armour that had been the death warrant of so many ancient saurian species' (281). However, instead of pursuing this new insight and its historical implications, Charles re-encodes his situation in mythical terms, as a retelling of the loss of Eden, precisely what had been heralded by Victorian discoveries in the fields of biology and geology. The choice is, implicitly, a rejection of the science of the age, but as such it is congenitally undermined by anachronism. Surrounded by the lusciousness of nature, yet unable to enjoy it after being cast out of Winsyatt, Charles 'felt ... excommunicated. He was shut out, all paradise lost ... – he could stand here in Eden, but not enjoy it' (234). Charles's sentiments are worth pursuing because they form a significant part of the narrator's broader tracing of the relationship between place and national identity.

At the start of the novel, while the characters indulge in the romantic associations of place through literature, the narrator's glance dwells on the fact that Lyme is 'redolent of seven hundred years of English history [and] ... is a superb fragment of folk-art' (9). This approach is not immune from the temptations of romance in its nostalgic incarnation, as the narrator muses on 'a town that had its heyday in the Middle Ages and has been declining ever since' (10). The introductory historical account succumbs to the otherness of its opposite narrative mode as the town's vicissitudes are emplotted as romance. So are the events of Charles's longing for, and ultimate loss of, his family's ancestral home. The difference is that where Lyme witnessed the encroaching rituals of polite society, its visits and concerts and walks in order to see and be seen, representing one path towards national identity which, like Charles and Tina's marriage, is rightly rejected for its lack of authenticity, the Smithson estate appears to be the longed-for place to which the questing Charles is denied access and which takes on the value of the nation and of paradise at the same time. In his last fateful visit to the family estate Charles associates the landscape with an 'ineffable feeling of fortunate destiny and right order which his stay in Lyme had vaguely troubled' (190). Crucially, his attitude repeats what he felt in relation to evolution. The land and house (a 'piece of England' [190]) stand, in Charles's eyes, synecdochically for the nation itself, whose 'centuries-old organisation' (190) grants continuity and resilience, traits exemplified by the fact that no taxonomic operation is necessary within the confines of Winsyatt. Thus, the estate can support and accommodate the collection of 'everything under the sun' (18) because it is not subject to the pressures of history, or the capitalist and historical demands of the clock: 'green todays flowed into green tomorrows, the only real hours were the solar hours' (191). Charles, in other words, perceives the order as immutable because it stands outside history and modernity. Fowles exploits the irony inherent in the fact that the moment of this realisation coincides with Charles's loss of Winsyatt as a result of his uncle's impending marriage. He dispels Charles's a-historical vision of the place and shows it for the class-determined and pre-capitalist perspective it in fact is: what the character is envisaging, by his own admission, is 'real possession' (190) of the estate and the workers that come with it. As he leaves, '[t]hose lawns, pastures, railings, landscaped groves seemed to slip through his fingers as they slipped slowly past his eyes' (211), the words suggesting once again an underlying desire for physical possession. If, on a superficial level, this casting off is encoded as a loss of paradise, it is in fact marred by the implications of the generic structure that underlies it, the pastoral. The genre envisages an immutable system of 'benevolent and divine' (191) social stratification based on birthrights and paternalism, but its immutability runs counter to the nation's diachronic understanding of itself, confirming that, however attractive, this is not a viable replacement for the repulsive national model of Lyme.

The alternative to the class-based pastoral world of Winsyatt is the Undercliff, of which Ware Common, where the meetings between Charles and Sarah take place, is a part. This 'English Garden of Eden on such a day as March 29th, 1867' (71) proposes a national (it is English) and historically specific (because dated) paradise, a combination that is subversively paradoxical, particularly in view of the introductory description of the place, which stresses the 'botanical strangeness... rarely growing in England', and makes it 'the nearest this country can offer to a tropical jungle' (71). The Undercliff's proximity to Lyme provides a contrast of landscapes that reproduces the contrast between national images, while the unregulated and unrestrained growth of the vegetation is in direct opposition to the systems of control deployed in the town – systems which signally fail to achieve their aims. Whether Ware Common is still a viable metonym for the nation in the present of the novel's writing remains, however,

doubtful: 'in 1867 there were several [cottages], lived in by gamekeep-
ers, woodmen, a pigherd or two', while today 'there is not a single
cottage in the Undercliff' (71). Indeed, '[t]he cottage walls have crum-
bled into ivied stumps, the old branch paths have gone; no car road
goes near it, the one remaining track that traverses it is often impass-
able. And it is so by Act of Parliament: a national nature reserve' (71).
Two related elements in the articulation of a specifically English 'form
of belonging' (Baucom 176) are apparent in this description. The first
is the equation of the possibility of national plenitude with something that has been lost, so that in the present the imagined community is united by that loss. Proof of this is the second remarkable
aspect of national identity, the preservation of the loss by official
means. The wildness of Ware Common has becomes institutionalised
and its national value normalised, arguably neutralising any remaining potential to stand for the nation subversively founded on romantic excess and transgression. Fowles's meditation on the nation is
ultimately nostalgic, in so far as the loss of the true national paradise,
which is articulated as resembling a state of nature, is sanctioned by
the further reach of the institutions of the state and, itself, becomes a
foundation for national identification.

This paradox finds a counterpart in Booker's description of '*bovar-
ysme*' (1997: 8) in relation to Britain's colonial experience. The term
refers to the fantasies of romantic exoticism in the descriptions of
India by those responsible for the propagation of the institutions of
the British state to the colony, which, if successful, would deprive
those fantasies of their territory by 'civilising' it. Booker consequently
argues that the production of literary images of the colonies is
informed by a pre-emptive sense of loss for something that had not
yet even been conquered. This suggestion draws a parallel between
the national and the imperial model of national identity. The
attempts to uphold the image of the British nation in India (and the
failure of those attempts) are the subject of J.G. Farrell's *The Siege of
Krishnapur*.

2. J.G. Farrell's *The Siege of Krishnapur*

Farrell's novel opens with a collection of ruins, the remains of the
once mighty British presence in India, which now promote curiosity
and tourism. Like the abandoned cottages of Ware Common, change

and loss have been preserved for national consumption as the unnamed traveller evoked in the early pages of *The Siege of Krishnapur* is clearly British, as are the values that colour his experience of the approach to the former imperial quarters. The congruence in aims and means between *The French Lieutenant's Woman* and *The Siege of Krishnapur* has not escaped critics. Fowles and Farrell are the only authors Bergonzi mentions whose work belongs to 'historical fiction proper' and is marked by 'conscious realism' (225 and 228). Binns identifies pastiche and irony as the point of contact between the two novels (65), while Chris Ferns places 'Fowles's meditations on the impossibility of recovering ... the narrative certainty of the great practitioners of nineteenth-century realism' alongside Farrell's 'demythologising of Empire' (1999: 276). Farrell's telescopic approach to the events of the Mutiny at the opening of the novel resembles Fowles's, and indeed, as was the case in the earlier novel, a literal telescope follows the main characters at key junctures in the plot, as if to replicate within the text the operation performed by the author with respect to his subject, but the insistence on the distance between the omniscient and retrospective narrator and the events foregrounds the constructed nature of the representation. The limits of representation are posited in the first page of *The Siege of Krishnapur,* a close re-writing of E.M. Forster's *A Passage to India.* This establishes a third temporal referent (the early twentieth century) and a further representational stance (that of Modernism) to the nineteenth-century subject of the novel. The strategy is comparable to the use of Hardy's poems in *The French Lieutenant's Woman*: where Hardy stood at the moment when Victorian literary and social conventions came under fire, Forster's intertextual presence alludes to the difficulties of representing India in a coherent narrative form.

This dialogue with tradition is pervasive. As Farrell makes clear in his Afterword, the novel is made up of 'actual events taken from the mass of diaries, letters and memoirs written by eyewitnesses' (314). Daniel Lea has traced the novel's engagement with the imperial sub-genre of the Mutiny romance, suggesting that the latter 'had a talismanic importance to the British ..., for it placed on display all the qualities which they believed defined the greatness of their national character' (67). Farrell's parodic re-creation of the stock elements of the genre dismantles its underlying assumptions about national identity, and shows them to have been 'a romantic idealisation' shaped by textual models, rather than 'a genuine reflection of actuality' (Lea 67). Part I of the novel, preceding the outbreak of the Sepoy rebellion, establishes the parameters of a conventional romantic plot, as George Fleury is smitten by the fair beauty of Louise Dunstaple and has to compete for her approval with the dashing Lieutenant Stapleton on occasions such as picnics and balls. In the eyes of the Collector, the character on whose thoughts Farrell dwells most consistently, these social rituals are crucial to the colonists' sense of identity. At the height of the siege, he remembers the 'many enjoyable garden parties' in what had once been a 'lawn, green and well-watered' but is now a 'parched brown desert dotted with festering animals' (171). The scarlet of the uniforms of the military band performing on those occasions, against the green of the garden, 'seemed to him the indelible colours of the rightness of the world, and of his place in it' (171). This nostalgic image conjures a territory tamed to recreate the equivalent space in Britain so successfully that its guardians do not need to perform their roles but can instead indulge in entertainment. The rightness of the world is equated with an indelible superimposition of British customs on India and it is only in the context of these premises that the Collector understands his position in India. The siege shows up the true characteristics of the land and forces the soldiers to take up their real function if their presence is to continue and the colonists' understanding of themselves is to be preserved. This is part of a pattern in the novel that exposes the ways in which the performance of British culture and customs conceals colonial domination in the country, but also hints at the colonists' investment in those social practices as a marker of their identity as Britons. Even when the siege has stripped the British residents of all their social niceties, the Collector insists that '[i]f [social conventions] don't matter, then nothing does' (227). What is under threat is not just a specific community in a foreign land but the very principles that are acknowledged as defining Britishness.

Like romance, the conventions of adventure are used to underscore Harry Dunstaple and Fleury's actions early in the novel. The young men's 'adventure together' consists of hearing 'what had sounded mighty like a musket shot which, although not *very* near, might or might not have been fired in their direction but, they decided, probably *had* been' (94). The sequence of conditionals makes clear that, in the telling, the trivial episode is being modelled to fit the parameters of adventure; this emphasises the role that narrative and representation more generally perform in transforming the real into a recognisable and therefore controllable pattern. Harry's fellow soldiers, caught up in the slaughter at their barracks, 'seemed to be having trouble telling ... what it had been like' (94). Their 'involuntary glimpse of the abattoir' (95) cannot be made to conform to the structures of adventure stories, which guarantee that the protagonists emerge bravely unscathed however dangerous the situations; as such, it cannot be related. Farrell's critique is not confined to imperialism but encompasses 'the kind of entertaining fiction about empire that [he] is imitating' (Rignall 24).

The novel's ending performs the final undermining of the generic conventions appealed to at the start of the novel. No 'rousing cheer' (308) accompanies the entrance of the relief force into Krishnapur. The new arrivals still abide under the misapprehensions of the codes of adventure and romance. Lieutenant Stapleton 'had made a point of wearing [Louise's] lock of hair ... on his own chest' (307), but when he finally reaches her Louise is not the creature he had imagined to find, 'lovely, well dressed, and as sweet-smelling as he remembered her', but a dirty, ragged, and smelly version (308). Fleury's victory in the romantic stakes comes from the fact that he can 'get closer to Louise without discomfort ... because he stank worse than she did' (309). General Sinclair's description of the siege, in the schoolboy language of imperial adventure stories, as a 'sticky time' (310) is laughably inadequate. He considers the survivors 'a pretty rum lot' (310) and envisages a depiction of the relief in a conventional painting where he would take a heroic posture 'in the foreground', confining those who had undergone the siege to 'an indistinct crowd of corpses and a few grateful faces, cannons and prancing horses' (311). The suggested arrangement contributes to the enduring perception of the Mutiny as an arena for heroic action, and provides implicit metafictional commentary on the novel's divergent representation. It is also one of the many instances in the novel of taxonomic arrangement of reality, even if only along the co-ordinates of foreground and background, to generate ideologically desirable meaning. By deploying the generic codes before showing their underlying mystifications, Farrell does not simply question a misguided understanding of the colonial environment and the British presence in it; he also responds to the principal culprits in the dissemination of that understanding. *The Siege of Krishnapur* does not deny individual acts of courage, but these do not conform to the patterns perpetuated by the literature of colonial adventure as the defining qualities of the national character; rather, they occur against the background of the crumbling of social niceties and customs that bound together the British residents in the name of 'an ideology, a culture, a whole *system* of values' (Ferns 1994: 283 my emphasis).

The mention of a system is crucial, as the central theme of *The Siege of Krishnapur* is the failure of all attempts at cultural and administrative taxonomies. These practices are represented in the novel by the Great Exhibition of 1851 and the collation of an imperial archive in Krishnapur's vernacular record room. While the official title for the Collector refers to his role in excising tax for the East India Company, it also defines him by his abiding passion for the Crystal Palace Exhibition, from which he brought back to Krishnapur several models of exhibits. As Paul Greenhalgh (1988) makes clear, the Great Exhibition was conceived as a show of national achievement designed to engender nationalistic pride across the classes, in order to forestall potential social unrest. These aims were pursued by emphasising the meaning produced by the collection in its entirety, rather than the peculiarities of the individual exhibits, which were to be understood not in themselves but in relation to the twin banners of technological progress and moral advancement, weaving together 'national pride, imperial glory, the mastery of history, the progress of technology and the free operation of the market' (Pearce 136). The relationship between nation and empire is relevant to understanding Farrell's use of the Exhibition. The latter's conflation of economic, nationalist, and moral discourse reflects the position of the British in India on the eve of the Mutiny: they are employees of a commercial institution (the East India Company), but what unites them in their eyes is their allegiance to the British flag (whose symbolic importance is acknowledged in the Collector's efforts to ensure its defence throughout the siege) and their civilising mission towards the natives, which they articulate as a national duty. Talk of progress and Britain's imperial destiny abound at the Collector's table, but the high-minded views on moral purposes and abstract humanity are always in danger of being exposed for the glossy cant they are with every mention of the exploitative activities that underlie them and fund the colonial presence, particularly opium production. The prominent display of the models from the Collection seeks to ensure the same combination of awe for British superiority and intimidation of its possible antagonists that the government had successfully employed in the Exhibition against the threat posed by the working classes. In other words, the Collector deploys 'a complex of hegemonic practices involving subtle strategies of cultural manipulation' (Booker 1997: 6) to supplement and ideally replace the real need for actual military and coercive control, while also concealing the materialistic reasons for the British presence in India.

As was the case for the social ritual of the garden party with its military band, this cultural operation is the means for the colonists' understanding of their place in India. The grandeur of the Residency at Krishnapur (complete with columns and Greek marble statues along its perimeter) aspires to the architectural model of the English country estate, which is further reproduced in its rich furnishings and the division of its rooms. The British community's flight towards the refuge of the building at the outbreak of the rebellion has symbolic significance, while the fact that their arrival signals the end of the orderly use of those rooms and makes the upkeep of the building impossible intimates its rhetorical, rather than actual, value in the assertion of identity. The objects that give the interior its British character (particularly the models form the exhibition) become important when that character is challenged: in a rather unfortunate metaphor given the tendency to flooding of the plains around Krishnapur, the Collector muses that '[p]ossessions are surely the *physical* high-water mark of the *moral* tide which has been flooding steadily for the past twenty years or more' (125). Lars Hartveit suggests that at the height of the siege 'the[se] objects and possessions become elements in the concept of identity which holds the garrison together' (463). That identity is specifically cultural and national, but its reliance on pre-existing systems of classification harbours its own dangers, quite apart from the outside challenge by the Sepoys. A collection is an assortment of disparate objects 'endowed with a common set of secondary values' to produce a meaning that transcends and re-inscribes the individual nature of the exhibits (McLeod 126). Any weakening of the principles of organisation and display may result in the foregrounding of the heterogeneity of the objects and the consequent loss of their ideological function. Paradoxically, it is the Collector who sets in motion the process of dissolution of the function of the collection. By selecting only some of the objects for transportation to Krishnapur he undermines the significance of the exhibits as a totality and reinforces their value as single items; he then compounds this by removing the models from their original context: in India they become part of another, idiosyncratic, collection that includes antlers, books, marble statues and scientific curiosities and are valued for their peculiarity rather than for their general significance. Thus, the Collector owns a contraption exhibited at the Crystal Palace for producing effervescence in the mouth when drinking soda; although the experience of trying it is unpleasant, he 'admired its ingenuity and had grown fond of it, as an object' (88). The suggestion that the individuality of the model is paramount deprives it of its taxonomic place and any secondary value. Something similar occurs with the nearby 'model of a carriage which supplied its own railway, laying it down as it advanced and taking it up again after the wheels had passed over', which has the Collector reminisce on 'those ecstatic summer days, now as remote as a dream, which he had spent in the Crystal Palace' (88). The nostalgic tone runs counter to the image of progress the 1851 display aimed to project, conceding that the prototype was effective only at a specific time and place (in the past and elsewhere); no corresponding real machine has ever been produced. In the colonial context, this object acquires new, and unwelcome, metaphorical meanings, as the ephemeral railway that can be uprooted without leaving any trace is uncomfortably similar to the transitory quality of colonialism.

In the course of the siege, all the objects are put to individual and practical use, marking the end of their taxonomic value and confirming their repressive function. The same possessions that had been envisaged metaphorically as a moral flood find themselves shoring up the mud embankments during the torrential monsoon rains, while the last Sepoy attack is repelled by using as ammunition all the implements which early in the novel had defined the Collector's ideal of social intercourse (silver forks, allegorical statues, a violin). Objects thus reassert their materiality and literalness over any imposed secondary metaphorical value. The disaggregation of the collection under pressure from the resisting forces intrinsic in it parallels the break-up of the colonists' understanding of themselves as a national community when the social rituals that fostered it have become empty of meaning.

The Collector's efforts to project Britishness taxonomically are accompanied by the attempts to achieve a classification of India by means of extensive gathering and storing of data in the documents that make up Krishnapur's imperial archive. Thomas Richards has theorised the relationship between the Victorian faith in facts and the range of imperial cataloguing enterprises upon which 'knowledge-producing institutions like the British Museum, the Royal Geographical Society, the India Survey, and the universities' embarked (3). The archival project acquired national overtones, in so far as '[c]omprehensive knowledge was taken to be a nationalist project, initiated within national institutions..., pursued by state functionaries... and like state sovereignty itself, presumed to be evenly operative over a legally demarcated territory (such as British India)' (Richards 111). The Collector's attitude towards statistics, which he describes as 'the leg-irons to be clapped on the *thugs* of ignorance and superstition' (173) is representative of the age, but his naïvely moralistic view conceals the fact that the collecting and collating of information aimed to establish power over the colonial territory, while the mass of its findings was envisaged as a weapon against the enemies of Britain. Farrell sets out to show both the weaknesses inherent in this reliance on data to exercise control and the ideological mystifications of presenting the pursuit of data as disinterestedly scientific or benignly progressive rather than what it in fact was, another form of imperial domination.

The 'objective facts' (173) the Collector summons to support the thrust of his metaphorical reasoning are not only irrelevant to the context of India and of little use to the colonists' situation; they also refuse to yield any meaning that transcends their specificity. In other words, they fail to perform the 'ordering of a chaotic universe' (173) which the amount of data produced promised. When that aim is projected onto the future by the Collector's reflection that '[i]f mankind was ever to climb out of its present uncertainties, disputations and self-doubtings, it would only be on such a ladder of objective facts' (173), the displacement is equal and contrary to that nostalgically operated in relation to the Great Exhibition, suggesting that taxonomic comprehensiveness and meaningful coherence can never be achieved in the present.

The archive's parallels with the Collection are extensive. The information gathered from the district are taxonomically arranged according to a colour-coded system in the vernacular record room, a building which, like the Crystal Palace, 'looked like a greenhouse' (100), so that it is no surprise that the Collector should feel 'very safe indeed' lying on the documents (158). However, the intended outcome of the classification cannot be guaranteed, as local conditions, in this case the white ants, take over; at the same time as documents are destroyed, the room is in danger of being overwhelmed by the quantity of papers, just as the once noble proportions of the Residency were with the clutter of possessions. Equally, the Collector's final realisation that his ideological investment in the Crystal Palace display had prevented him from noting the significance of '[t]he extraordinary array of chains and fetters, manacles and shackles exhibited ... for export to America's slave states' (300) forges a linguistic connection with the suppressive dimension of the archive.

The archive fulfils its real purpose during the Sepoys' decisive attack, as the rebels are thrown into disarray by the 'providential snowstorm' (216) of paper from the booby-trapped vernacular record room, just as the possessions, finally understood as objects, inflict death. The climax to the attack in both cases makes apparent the literal aspects of the British cultural and administrative representational strategies; at the same time, the dismantling of the coherence of the collection and the comprehensiveness of the archive in favour of their fragmentary and partial elements opens a metafictional dimension in Farrell's representation of the siege. Thus, the novel's extensive pastiche of non-fictional texts documenting Victorian debates and eye-witness accounts of the Mutiny gestures towards referentiality and, in its seeming pursuit of realism, risks complicity with the positivist underpinning of the imperial archival project. At the same time, however, the characters in the novel are shown to be unable to perceive themselves and India other than through preconceived notions, making any claim to objective testimony suspect, while the countless drawn-out controversies on religion, medicine, science, culture are not only laughably inappropriate to the situation of the besieged but also inconclusive. The exploding of the archive puts forward, in concentrated form, the novel's consistent attitude towards its own enterprise: the irony that pervades *The Siege of Krishnapur* 'effectively highlights the basic ridiculousness of the idea of British colonial rule in India' (Sage 180), just as 'the ... inappropriateness of the tone of the book makes a point about the inappropriateness of that rule' (Booker 1997: 110), whose failure the novel attributes to the inability to acknowledge the randomness of events and their basic uncontrollability. This is the Collector's final realisation, 'that a people, a nation, does not create itself according to its own best ideas, but is shaped by other forces of which it has little knowledge' (313). Borrowing Fowles's penchant for natural history, Michael Thorpe sums up this epiphany: 'the evolution of truth and historical insight, in time, is as slow – and unpredictable – as biological adaptation, rightly understood' (185). This philosophy confirms the substantive link between Farrell's novel and *The French Lieutenant's Woman*.

3. Ruth Prawer Jhabvala's *Heat and Dust*

In *Heat and Dust*, the Nawab's Palace at Khatm has an underground storeroom that holds a heterogeneous array of disparate European objects, including 'camera equipment … still in its original packing […,] some modern sanitary equipment and an assortment of games such as a pinball machine, a croquet set, a miniature shooting gallery, meccano sets, and equipment for a hockey team' (86). These items are defined by their incongruity both with their context and with one another. They were never intended to be a collection, and cannot be made into one, nor are they publicly displayed as an example of cultural uniformity. Where the insistence on the potential for disaggregation in Farrell's collection metafictionally pointed to the fragility of identity and historical representation, Jhabvala's denial of the very possibility of taxonomy pre-empts any attempt by the novel's characters to understand themselves in relation to cultural markers and, equally, undermines the validity of the modern protagonist's efforts to narrate the past. The novels' respective uses of the trope of collecting to articulate their attitude towards the relationship between past and present can be examined in the light of Susan Pearce's discussion of the analogy between collecting and historical representation.

Pearce identifies two approaches to the past which are comparable to two principles of engagement with objects: the first stresses 'Sameness', which 'supposes that there is a real and direct relationship between one set of events and the next, so that history is not really a random set of occurrences but a living web of cause and effect', its structures 'recognisable and intelligible' (311). This approach corresponds to a faith in the secondary value of a collection superseding the individual (and potentially heterogeneous) identity of its components; it also presumes the continuity between, and commensurability of, past and present predicated by realist historical narrative. The second attitude is founded on 'Otherness', and refuses to concede that past and present can in any way be subsumed under comparable principles of understanding (or, in the case of collections, classification and organisation), instead putting forward 'the notion that the past is indeed a foreign country and everything is different there' (Pearce 311). *The Siege of Krishnapur* traces the trajectory leading from one approach to the other, espousing an omniscient narrative voice only to explode the referential principles on which it rests, while illustrating a concomitant dissolution of taxonomical meaning. The opening page of the novel is a travelogue entry aimed at '[a]nyone who has never before visited Krishnapur' (9), whose effect is one of metaphorical displacing of temporal onto spatial distance, as the traveller is urged to 'look closely and shield [his] eyes' (9) to gain entry into the place and with it into the past, so that the exact historical moment 'towards the end of February 1857' (10) can be conjured.

Heat and Dust, on the other hand, turns the representational enterprise of its narrator into a literal journey to an India that is radically other from its past as part of the Raj. While, in fact, the narrator initially envisages this displacement as having temporal, as well as spatial, value, soon she has to acknowledge that India is '[n]ot what [she] had imagined at all' because 'everything is different now' (2). Thus, all that remains of the exotic treasures of the palace of Khatm, which 'had never been catalogued' (99), are 'some pictures', incongruously kept in the London flat of the Nawab's descendants, Karim and Kitty, and showing 'princes and princesses': the former 'looked like Karim', the latter 'like Kitty' (99). With this formulation, which anachronistically reverses family resemblance from the present to the past, Jhabvala questions the basis of historical narrative (prospective unfolding from a retrospective viewpoint) and instead admits to the inevitable reading of the past through the lens of the present. The journal where the modern protagonist records her experience of India appears as a chronicle untainted by retrospective recollection and ordering, but simply arranged by date, both the most objective and least revealing taxonomy. The novel operates similarly in relation to its narrative models. The liberal ghost of Forster is evoked by Olivia's assertion that '[p]eople can still be friends ... even if it is India' (103), but her story serves to deny the accuracy of that statement, while there is little reliance on the modernist representational strategies of *A Passage to India*. This rejection of the canonical text on India is all the more apparent as a character closely modelled on its author features prominently in the novel, a 'plump, balding Englishman called Harry something who was a house guest of the Nawab's' (15). The situation and the character's actions, including his homosexuality and his impatience with the British, follow Forster's account of his stay with the Maharajah of Dewas in *The Hill of Devi*, but there is no hint of literary talent to Jhabvala's character, and *Heat and Dust* sharply diverges from the earlier author's portrait of India. As Richard Cronin has demonstrated in his sustained analysis of the relationship between the two texts, the former 'shows how a relationship based on power may be superseded by a relationship founded on love', while the latter 'responds with a picture of a princely state in which love, power and race are inextricably entwined' (176). Jhabvala presents a relationship complicated by the intrusion of gender into the power dynamics of colonialism, finding existing literary codification of colonial power inadequate to encompassing gender from anything other than a patriarchal and paternalistic perspective: the British administrators 'had that little smile of tolerance, of affection, even enjoyment ...: like good parents, they all loved India whatever mischief *she* might be up to' (58).

Formally, therefore, Jhabvala rejects the 'High Bloomsbury polish' (Strobl 228) of the modernist model, just as she had eschewed the temptations of realist retrospective continuity, and instead replaces it with a deliberately flat, unimaginative and inelegant prose. The discomfort and inaccuracy of impression the narrator's style reveals, coupled with the artificial arrangement of events in an intermittent journal, reflects the fact that she cannot avail herself of the modes of colonial representation (even those, like Forster's, that question the legitimacy of the British presence) to relate the experience of an India that is no longer colonial. The resulting narrative is episodic, following the modern young woman's journey in search of a past whose reality proves beyond reach and which is available only as a tourist attraction with occasional remains of an earlier time. Her task is impeded by the intrusion of a contemporary India with which she has to interact, making the past recede further: the curtains in the Nawab's palace are 'dead and mouldering' (13), while the changes wrought by its current keeper (including constructing a Hindu shrine in what had been the residence of a Muslim ruler) indicate that the wish to preserve the past intact is limited to the British visitors. As Inder Lal, her landlord, puts it, 'who cares about that now? All those people are dead, and even if any of them should still be left alive somewhere, there is no one to be interested in their doings' (12). The novel suggests that India as an independent nation founds its identity on being modern (hence Inder Lal's fondness for cars and refrigerators), while the British quest for the past has nostalgic connotations.

What Jhabvala questions in her formal juxtaposition of past and present, journal entries and descriptions of the events of 1923, is the contemporary projection of some form of wholeness onto the earlier period. In the British cemetery, the narrator reflects on the damage wrought by time on the angel marking the grave of an infant: it had been 'new and intact – shining white with wings outspread and holding a marble baby in its arms', whereas all she can see is 'a headless, wingless torso with a baby that had lost its nose and one foot' (24). At one level, this is a commentary on the essential impermanence of colonialism, despite the durability of its material remains, as indeed it is their resilience that marks them as foreign. In this respect, the changed grave reprises the opening of *The Siege of Krishnapur,* where the bricks and marbles that stand out in the barren landscape and which a visitor may recognise as 'an essential ingredient of civilisation' (10) belong to a cemetery, whereas no trace remains of the mud huts that are erected and inhabited each year after the floods. Yet the section that immediately follows this episode in *Heat and Dust* shows that these sentiments of loss were already at the basis of the colonial administrators' understanding of their role in India. The graves that occasion their reflections on the past are those 'dating from the Mutiny when a gallant band of British officers had died defending their women and children' (25). To Douglas Rivers, Olivia's husband and 'a boy who read adventure stories and had dedicated himself to live up to their code of courage and honour' (40), they represent an ideal of heroic masculinity that the conditions of his presence in India make unattainable. In the pacified colony the closer the administrators come to upholding a romantic code of heroism is in dealing with the persistence of suttee. The attempts to enforce the laws that banned the practice of widow-burning can in fact be encoded within a paradigm of colonial adventure, with the 'civilised' representative of British compassion coming in defence of an Indian woman for whose protection he is responsible and who is under threat from the 'barbarism' of her own culture. In so far as this conduct can be articulated as saving India from herself (the gendered connotations of the colonial enterprise are once again at the forefront) it conforms to colonial discourse and is indeed supported by 'a rich store-house of memories that went back several generations and was probably interesting to those who shared it' (57–8). The narratively transmitted nature of these identity-defining collective memories confirms that, despite being physically in India and having direct experience of it, the British characters understand it through preconceived models. Thus, even Major Minnies, arguably the most sympathetic of the characters to India, can only replicate Orientalist statements of incommensurable otherness between a gendered exotic country and its conquerors: 'it is all very well to love and admire India...but always with a virile, measured, *European* feeling. One should never, he warned, allow oneself to become softened (like Indians) by an excess of feeling; because the moment that happens – the moment one exceeds one's measure – one is in danger of being dragged over to the other side' (171).

It is precisely the female, exotic, and romantic excess invoked in these words that disrupts the sanctioned understanding of both suttee and the British response to it. The situation, a formal dinner at the table of Mr. Crawford, the Collector at Satipur, recalls the social rituals that punctuate *The Siege of Krishnapur* and serve to define the colonists' identity, so that Olivia's defence of suttee in the name of romance ('to want to go with the person you care for most in the world' [59]) acts as a challenge to the moderation the Major identifies as proper for the British character. In his seduction of Olivia, the Nawab exploits both the conventions of social intercourse and Olivia's own penchant for a romantic reading of her actions: mimicking a 'hearty English greeting' (56) he appropriates the very behaviour that Douglas uses to mark his difference from Britain's native subject, implicitly undermining British pretensions and identity. He then issues a series of invitations for Olivia to go to his palace, replicating the round of calls and visits that, as Lyme showed in *The French Lieutenant's Woman*, formed such a part of British life. It is at this point that gothic elements disrupts the seeming familiarity and intelligibility of the situation, as the labyrinthine building hides unseen eyes as well as unseen riches and that eminently British social event (the picnic) becomes the occasion for crossing the boundaries of propriety. The secluded spot where the Nawab takes Olivia is an 'oasis' in the parched landscape, and the Nawab explicitly links it to 'Paradise' (132). The apparent familiarity of the situation and the cultural frame of reference, however, are soon disrupted by the sinister appearance of men who 'looked like mediaeval bandits' (133) and seem to be on friendly terms with the Nawab; the paradisal spot is further sullied by the Nawab's tale of his ancestors' bloody deeds. He gives Olivia the kind of exotic experience that she (echoing Forster's Adela Quested) may well identify with the real India, and she is so caught up in the romantic understanding of her relationship with the Nawab that she elides the reality where actions have political implications and social consequences. Ironically, it is as a result of her transgression that an episode from Mutiny lore can be re-enacted, and it is that re-enactment of the historical moment so admired by Douglas that finally explodes the ideals on which the British perception of their role rested. Appropriately, it is also articulated with reference not to the actual events of 1857 but to their representation: Olivia's arrival at the Palace after abandoning her ties of marriage and race reminds Harry 'of a print he had seen called *Mrs. Secombe in Flight from the Mutineers*' (172). This pre-encoded reading of Olivia's actions confirms the Mutiny's role as the framework of interpretation for the British, making this recent re-enactment with a difference (the flight in 'in the opposite direction' [172]), like the Nawab's mimicking of British behaviour, all the more subversive.

The narrator's repetition of her predecessor's actions, going so far as to become pregnant by her landlord, is not fraught with the same social and national dangers, nor does the India she experiences conform to the high-flown romantic, adventurous, and gothic elements of Olivia's story, even though the potential for a gothic reading of modern India is intimated at the narrator's arrival, when a missionary ('paper-white, vaporous – yes, a ghost' [4]) discloses a hellish vision of European loss of identity in an alien world. The gothic elements are confined to the Europeans, while the narrator's extensive intercourse with Indian people reveals them to be unthreatening. It is only in relation to the fate of her quasi-ancestor that the narrator resorts to literarily identifiable conventions, as is apparent from the description of Olivia's last residence, a room complete with 'embroidery frame stand in a window embrasure' (175) which envisages her inhabitant in the fateful mode of the Lady of Shalott. The even, plain and matter-of-fact narrative that accompanies the modern protagonist's actions, on the other hand, is a wilful refusal to emplot events sensationally and this divergence of style heralds a divergence of choices: the young woman does not abort her unborn child and, literally and metaphorically, travels further than Olivia as her account ends with her decision to join a mountain religious community. On the one hand, both style and final choice are an assertion of identity outside national, racial and even gender parameters (the narrator stresses on several occasions her lack of conventional femininity), particularly as we have no sense of who or what she was in England and she only defines herself in relation to a past that is not her own. On the other hand, the very detachment of her narrative risks going from disinterested to callous, particularly when describing the life of Inder Lal's wife Ritu, a woman unhappy in her submission to her mother-in-law and prone to hysterical fits. The narrator describes the horrific attempt at 'curing' her with hot irons applied to her body without comment or intervention; she becomes friends with Inder Lal's mother and her fellow widows, even while stating that their presence is oppressive to their daughters-in-law. In her desire to avoid the preconceived cultural notions of her British counterparts in 1923, she does not find an ethically viable form that allows her to intervene compassionately without reproducing the colonial attitude towards suttee.

At the journal's end, the ethical impasse becomes a representational one, as the narrator is unable to describe a landscape where 'everything remains hidden' (180). The dissolution of the referentiality implied in the journalistic style that otherwise characterises her writing suggests that a neutral piecing together of information, if attempted coherently, leads to a dehumanised perception. Until the end, the narrator is '[u]nobtrusive, anonymous, even unnamed ... a voice, almost disembodied' (Sucher 102). Instead, her identity is asserted when 'unable to see' the natural features of the landscape around her because of rain and mist she 'imagine[s] mountain peaks higher than any I've ever dreamed of; the snow on them is also whiter than all other snow – so white it is luminous and shines against a sky which is of a deeper blue than any yet known to me. That is what I expect to see' (180). At the close of the novel and at the very moment when retrospection is made impossible as Olivia's story is left unsettlingly unfinished while her own 'moves towards an as yet invisible and unscripted future' (Newman 48), the narrator appropriates for herself the possibilities of the romantic imagination. The novels discussed in the next chapter posit the irrecoverability of the past from the start, and dedicate themselves to unearthing and deploying those possibilities.

2
The Romance of the Past

In their foregrounding of the textuality of the past and in the pervasiveness of traceable intertextual references to realist and Modernist representational modes that characterises their narrative re-encodings of that past, Fowles, Farrell and Jhabvala raise a problem of referentiality which is pursued from a consistently theoretical angle in the three novels discussed in this chapter, Lindsay Clarke's *The Chymical Wedding: A Romance* (1989), A.S. Byatt's *Possession: A Romance* (1990) and Graham Swift's *Ever After* (1992). Theory, whether it be a recognisable academic discipline, as in *Possession,* or philosophical and individual instability more generally, as in *The Chymical Wedding* and *Ever After,* is at the basis of these novels' approach to the representation of the past and their recuperation of a sense of the nation in the context of millennial anxieties. The novels examined in Chapter 1 metonymically invested physical locations with the task of providing models of national identity in reaction to the tendency towards disaggregation produced by the novels' reliance on texts. The novels under consideration here, on the other hand, pursue the implications of acknowledging the textual nature of the past and articulate a representational model that situates the nation in the very texts which seemingly fragment it, attempting to reconstitute it by an act of the imagination and through the narrative mode of romance.

This complex engagement with the question of accessing, appropriating and representing the past relies on a rigorous deployment of theoretical positions on narrative and representation that confirms these novels' alignment with postmodernism, in its specific association with 'telling stories' which become 'indistinguishable from what was once assumed to be knowledge' (Waugh 1). At the same time, their positing of an ultimately representational goal in spite of their discursive self-awareness suggests an enduring allegiance to the Victorian project that figured so prominently in Fowles's novel. *The French Lieutenant's Woman* is indeed the ancestor to Clarke, Byatt, and Swift's reflections on the relationship between representation and reality, the Victorian literary tradition and its post-structuralist theoretical foil (see Byatt 2000: 65–90). In particular, it is the canonicity of the mid-Victorian period that the novels in this chapter take as their starting point and propel, as a continuing awareness, into the present, a historical moment which defines itself, rightly or wrongly, as that period's epigone.

These two elements have formed the basis for critical discussions of Clarke's, Byatt's, and Swift's novels, which have been variously included in surveys of 'postmodern', 'neo-Victorian', 'retro-Victorian' or 'post-Victorian' fiction. Postmodern historical novels, Frederick Holmes (1997) suggests, reveal a coincidence of methods and aims between postmodern literary and historiographical theory, on the one hand, and the formal choices and thematic concerns of the novels' fictional practice, on the other. The novels' self-reflexive comments on the methods by which we know the past and the uses to which we put that knowledge are what distinguishes them from 'traditional historical novels, [which] sustain throughout the pretence of supplying direct access to the past in all of its fullness and particularity' (Holmes 11). While its broad terms remain unchanged, with the use of 'neo-Victorian' and 'retro-Victorian' Shiller (1997) and Gutleben (2001) shift the emphasis of their discussions to the novels' close and occasionally contradictory relationship with the Victorian realist tradition, which is foregrounded in the nineteenth-century setting of the plots as well as in the intertextual allusions to notable works in that tradition. Thus, 'neo-Victorian novels are acutely aware of both history and fiction as human constructs', but do not wholly relinquish their representational aspirations; rather, they propose a version of informed realism, exploring 'the ground between writing as though there are no persisting truths ... and writing as though there is indeed a recoverable past' (Shiller 540 and 541). In so doing, they participate in 'the resurrection of the Victorian tradition', whose prior perceived absence 'is expressed in terms of loss – loss of a feeling subject, loss of authenticity, loss of aesthetic integrity' (Gutleben

160 and 198–9). Finally, the hybrid 'post-Victorian' is used by Sadoff and Kucich (2000) to 'convey the paradoxes of historical continuity and disruption' between postmodernism and the nineteenth century (xiii).

This final definition is especially valuable in that it points to the element of paradoxical temporality in Clarke's, Byatt's and Swift's novels, a trait they share with, and explore by means of, romance. Romance, in fact, is the narrative mode whose characteristic paradox and anachronism offer 'a way in which to rethink narrative and its relationship to the legitimation of historical knowledge [...,] upsetting our ability to recognise the past as past, challenging the way we "know" history' (Elam 12). For Fowles, Farrell and Jhabvala romance in its broadest terms provided a set of generic elements that disrupted repressive social conventions and unmasked the oppressive cultural practices of colonialism. The novels in this chapter, on the other hand, engage more narrowly and theoretically with romance as a medium for the representation of relationships (between past and present, reality and representation) that cannot be encompassed within a linear, mutually exclusive, rational and realist narrative. Romance thus satisfies what Mark Currie (1998) identifies as the postmodern novel's 'rebellion against two major laws of philosophical logic': these are, firstly, 'the law of non-contradiction, which says that an argument is flawed if it contradicts itself'; and secondly, 'the law of cause and effect, which organises not only philosophical argument but the events of a novel, the relation of the novel to criticism, the relation between modernism and postmodernism, or personal and historical experience ... as a linear sequence' (64).

What emerges from the analyses of contemporary historical fiction detailed above is a particular understanding of postmodernism as an attempt to recover a viable narrative form for the representation of the past in the awareness that the historical, cultural, and literary conditions of late twentieth-century England prevent the unquestioning reliance on Victorian realism. *The Chymical Wedding, Possession* and *Ever After* posit the Victorian period as the postmodern present's other, not only philosophically and conceptually, but also narratively and nationally. This sentiment is reflected in the structure of the three novels. Their plots unfold in parallel over two independent timeframes, one set in the Victorian past and one, of comparable weight, set in the present of the authors' writing and detailing the search for the very past narrated separately as the nineteenth century story. The two periods are inescapably divided by a narrative chasm evident in the alternating timeframes, with the novels exploring the underlying substantive foundations of this formal separation. This formal arrangement displays, comments upon, and enacts the relationship between the remains of the past in documentary form and the progressive shaping of the fragmentary evidence into a narrative with representational claims. In the process, *The Chymical Wedding, Possession* and *Ever After* articulate the narrative conditions whereby the representation of the past may be achieved. The representational aim at the basis of the split-time form points to the fact that the self-reflexive aspects emerging in both past and present timeframes are not primarily parodic in their knowingness, but more urgently substantive: '[t]hese are not really novels which contemplate *themselves* so much as novels which contemplate the logic and ideology of narrative in the act of construing the world' (Currie 68). They demonstrate a preoccupation with seeking and putting into practice the narrative mode that will allow the past to be represented in such a way that it is apparent that the authors' objective is to emulate the achievements of the Victorian realist enterprise, without however denying the postmodern position of belatedness with respect to it which makes the unproblematic adoption of a realist narrative mode impossible. Such a move strives to reach beyond documentary evidence or methodological constraints to a fully realised historical vision. As Wells (2003) notes, the novels' 'internal project' consists of 'working out the terms of a new representational stance for contemporary narrative that allows for mimetic reference despite textual self-consciousness' (16).

Precisely because it is seemingly unavailable, realist representation, which in these novels is equated with a narrative innocently untainted by self-conscious disclaimers, becomes the object of a pervasive nostalgic desire. In turn, that desire is expressed as longing for a lost state of wholeness which, in an identifiable postmodern gesture, becomes conflated with a coincidence of language and things – or, reality and its representation. The contemporary characters in *The Chymical Wedding, Possession* and *Ever After,* all of whom are skilled literary interpreters, locate this unity in English novels of the mid-nineteenth century, a historical moment which becomes 'the point of originary purity and self-presence', while the contemporary state is one of 'fall' (Currie 82). *The Chymical Wedding*, *Possession* and *Ever After* all adopt the image of a physical Edenic garden invested with metafictional attributes to articulate the sense of belatedness that pervades their contemporary timeframes and the impossibility of return to a prior state of representational fullness. The latter is also the site for a comparable moment of imaginative national unity. In effect, the specificity of the literary tradition appealed to, Victorian realism, points to the national dimension of the novels' engagement with postmodernism; indeed, it arguably signals an English approach to postmodernism (countering the cosmopolitan and supra-national nature of this phenomenon and of the conceptual apparatus accompanying it) which equates the canonicity of the mid-nineteenth century with the summit of the nation as an imaginative and imagined community, and interprets the derivativeness and belatedness of its late twentieth century counterpart as a symptom of the threat to its unity.

The identification of the Victorian period and its literary production as the desirable site of representational and national unity entails, at the time of the novels' publication, a confrontation with the contemporary appropriation of the same historical moment for political purposes. The Thatcher and Major governments of the 1980s and early 1990s, in fact, reacted to the irrecoverable loss of empire (arguably the originary event for the perceived present national fragmentation) by reinforcing the nation's presumed collective memory of the nineteenth century as the period when Britain was great: the political rhetoric of the time echoed its Victorian predecessor in equating national power and influence with the upholding of a set of 'traditional' values traceable to the mid-nineteenth century, including 'industry and hard work [...], the imagery of Victorian diligence and prudence' (Brannigan 93). At a time of steady economic decline and diminished global influence this appeal to the past 'was closer to wish-fulfilment, and national myth, than reality' (Stevenson 51). Nevertheless, its conservative force and proven success in terms of electoral results, as well as the contemporary widespread denigration of this return to the past on the part of politically engaged authors and critics, posed a specific ideological challenge to Clarke's, Byatt's and Swift's projects, since their novels find themselves implicated in, if not complicit with, a reactionary deployment of the very attitude at the centre of their narrative negotiations. *The*

Chymical Wedding, Possession and *Ever After* do not, as this chapter shows, wholly eschew the charge of sterile nostalgia, of 'taking refuge in images of a mythic past' or reducing the past to 'agreeable playgrounds' (Brannigan 94). In particular, their persistent articulation of the denouement to the romantic quest as something that leads to personal fulfilment but does not change the often limiting circumstances in which the search for the past was first undertaken is open to the charge of rejecting the opportunity for political engagement. Yet the novels' emphasis on the discontinuity between past and present and their suggestion that the outcome of the bridging enterprise is always uncertain or, even if felicitous, is precariously dependent on particular unsustainable and irreproducible circumstances, undermine the simplistic understanding of history pandered by conservative discourse, by denying that a national return to past grandeur is in any way possible.

The novels' double enterprise (theoretical and representational) is reflected in the double narrative and dual temporal dimension. These, in turn, are more explicit and self-aware instances of the co-existence of times common to historical novels *qua* historical novels, negotiating in their generic features the productive dichotomy of the time of the setting and the time of the writing. In his discussion of historical fiction, Steven Connor makes a valuable distinction between 'historical' and 'historicised' fiction (Connor 142). The former

> seems to assert in its form and language the capacity of the present to extend itself to encompass the past, either in a twentieth-century language which confidently assumes its adequacy to the task of historical representation, or in an ensemble of different historical languages which nevertheless speak in one voice, as it were, and thus enact the translatability of past and present into each other. (142)

The latter, on the other hand, 'seems to highlight the difficulty of this translation, by displaying the lack of fit, or ironic incompatibility, between past and present viewpoints and languages' (142). Historical fiction, in other words, in Connor's definition closely resembles the narrative operation at the basis of imagining the nation, namely, the establishing of seamless continuity and commensurability between different stages in the national history and the reliance on a common language to articulate the sense of belonging and mutual interrelationship of individual members of a nation. Historicised fiction, however, questions the unproblematic assumptions inherent in the national model, and instead concedes that the univocal identity of the nation can only be achieved by suppressing the elements that do not conform to the model or refuse to accept its comprehensiveness. The project of historicised fiction is the recuperation of these disruptively ex-centric (or, as in the earlier chapter, excessive) elements and holds clear political and anti-hegemonic significance.

The Chymical Wedding, Possession and *Ever After* participate of both directions and offer a contradictory engagement with the question of national identity. The chronological discontinuity enforced by the split-time form is an instance of the nation's failure to imagine itself in relation to a traceable past but, while they acknowledge the chasm between past and present and the narrative negotiations it imposes, in their contemporary protagonists these novels aspire to the comprehensiveness of vision of traditional historical narrative, with its related unified sense of the nation. At the same time, that past can only be imagined through the narrative mode of romance, the form, that is, of excess and disruption of precisely the features of historical (and national) narrative.

The sense of coming late that informs the modern characters' every action replicates the novels' attitude towards their nineteenth-century model: they long to recapture the feelings of their predecessors (indeed their very being) while at the same time conceding that what they are, purely as a result of living in the late twentieth century, makes the wish unachievable. They participate in what Lawrence Lerner, in a study of Renaissance pastoral, has identified as 'the paradox of articulateness' (49), or the fact that the desirability of a state (in this case the past over the present, or representational over self-reflexive goals) is only apparent to those who have experienced its counterpart, and only after the experience. Inherent in the recognition is the impossibility of return, but it is that impossibility, inextricable from the moment of recognition, that makes the prior state desirable. Lerner's conceptual paradox mirrors Northrop Frye's description of 'the quest romance [as] the search...for a fulfilment that will deliver it from the anxieties of reality but will still contain that reality' (193). Frye's exploration of narrative and generic models illuminates the terms around which this chapter revolves, in so far as his contrast between the modes of romance and realism is conveyed as the difference between 'the analogy of innocence' (151) and 'the analogy of experience' (154). The subtitle to two of the novels considered here (*A Romance*) thus acquires a programmatic relevance, as does the explicit association with the formal, thematic and linguistic conventions of romance in the title *Ever After*, while the poles of innocence and experience offer productive standpoints from which to examine the novels' engagement with postmodern positions on representation.

This chapter argues that although Clarke, Byatt and Swift articulate such postmodern positions in the formal shape of their novels, in the unfolding of their plot, and in the reflections of their characters, the resulting examination leads not to an endorsement and validation of postmodern epistemological and representational uncertainty, but rather to an attenuated perception of its impact and a questioning of its specificity. By the end of their quests, the protagonists of the contemporary plots have negotiated the basis for a form of historical referentiality which, while inevitably self-conscious, fulfils the characters' and novelists' desire for representation, without, however, concealing the ethical and political compromises necessary to ensure a successful quest for knowledge of the past. The regaining of an Edenic garden, whose presumed unattainability serves metafictional functions in the novels, is once again at the centre of this negotiation. The trope of the garden, echoing *Richard II's* Garden of England, implicitly connects the modern characters' attempts to re-establish continuity between past and present to the reappropriation of the nation's cultural patrimony. Far from resulting in merely stylistic reproductions of the past that confirm the postmodern 'loss of historicity' (Jameson x), the discursive nature of these novels' engagements with the past is a particularly appropriate means to approaching a national past that is itself a discursive entity equated with its cultural artefacts. Thus, what initially appeared to be formal concerns with the representation of the past are recast as substantive reflections on what constitutes the national past and on who has the right to divulge it.

1. Lindsay Clarke's *The Chymical Wedding*

The difficulties inherent in the relationship between the Victorian and the contemporary are summed up by Connor's pointed remark that 'identification is not identity, and the very desire to recall the nineteenth century is a mark of the unclosable gap between the conditions and potentialities of narrative between the nineteenth and twentieth century' (138). In *The Chymical Wedding* the perception of that gap is recognised, but its reality is called into question by one of the protagonists, Edward Nesbit, an ageing former poet and seeker after the secrets of two Victorian alchemists. The figures from Victorian culture he mentions in his summary of the age are Marx, Lyell, whose 'principles of geological dating had knocked the bottom out of a literal interpretation of Genesis', Darwin, and finally Freud, who 'would...darken counsel by dragging the sexual skeleton from the closet as though it explained everything' (172). The terms in which Nesbit describes the Victorian crisis leading to modernity (which forms the subject of *The French Lieutenant's Woman*) encompass modes of reasoning founded on dichotomy, on the scientific observations that made the world irreducible to human time or morality, and on theories of the unconscious that made the human mind unknowable to itself. They can be seen to question the claims to mediatory power, commensurability of the world, and reliability of psychological understanding made for realist narrative, thus intimating the need for a different representational mode. The lucidity with which a contemporary character traces the seeds of the general loss of intellectual stability and psychological security to the nineteenth century grants it a degree of self-awareness not dissimilar from that of Edward's own time. This mention of 'the century's intellectual giants' (172) continues the uneasy codification of the Victorian period 'as the origin of late twentieth century modernity, its antithesis, or both at once' (Kaplan 3) that had begun in *The French Lieutenant's Woman*. There, Darwin, Freud and Marx provided the majority of the non-literary epigraphs to its chapters. If in Fowles's novel their uncertain status with respect to a narrative voice firmly rooted in the present, on the one hand, and an action wholly confined to the past, on the other, is confirmed by their position in the textually liminal space of the epigraph, in *The Chymical Wedding* they are part of a narrative whose ultimate aim is to reconstitute a relationship between past and present that allows Marx, Darwin and Freud both to be historically situated in their time, and to belong anachronistically to the present.

Edward's quest in the novel is for a stage (represented by Henry and Louisa Agnew's alchemical explorations) within a larger post-lapsarian endeavour which, for him, shapes human history itself, namely, the search for the means of regaining a form of the earthly paradise, variously identified as the moment where human consciousness was whole, or when language and things were one. The alchemical project to which Victorian and modern characters in the novel devote themselves and on which they pin their hopes of reconstituting personal and global wholeness is expressed in terms of a return to Eden, to be achieved by the very means that occasioned the Biblical Fall – knowledge:

> [T]he alchemists maintained that mankind had suffered a fall; but this lapse from grace...was a critical moment in the great experiment of Nature. It was the very access of consciousness – life's arrival at the moment where it might contemplate and shape its own existence. But consciousness comes at a price, and the price is banishment from the Garden. [...] The alchemists maintained that through the correct disciplines such a return might be made. If one knew how to go about it the Fall was reversible (222–3).

Paradoxically, this description of the alchemical quest historicises the desire to escape the linearity, sequentiality and irreversibility of historical time. As Lerner suggests, Eden is a way of 'refusing history [whereby] the ideal version of man's life is placed outside ordinary time' (72). The 'flagrantly anachronistic' (Elam 12) temporality that emerges as the signature of the alchemical project is shared by romance as a narrative mode and a literary genre, both of which are evoked by the subtitle to Clarke's novel. In the progressive convergence of what initially seem parallel events confined to their own time, the split-time form of *The Chymical Wedding* participates of the anachronistic tendencies that the novel's plot describes.

Henry Agnew's and his daughter Louisa's project is to make the secrets of alchemy available to the world as an antidote to the confusion of their age: the novel is set in 1848, the revolutionary year that saw political and social unrest throughout Europe and, in Britain, a radical threat to the institutions of the state. It is carried out in the shadow of their illustrious ancestor Sir Humphry and, in ways not dissimilar from that of their contemporary counterparts, is motivated by the desire to recapture an earlier age and reveals the nostalgic tendency to identify the moment of wholeness with a time receding ever further into the past. The attempt, however, suffers from the inevitable dichotomy of words and deeds. As Louisa labours on her *Open Invitation to the Chymical Wedding* she is keenly aware that she is describing a sensual union of which, as an unmarried woman, she has no direct experience; and that, conversely, in writing she is only distancing herself from experiential reality. Only the latter can grant 'a knowledge that is no longer pale intellectual *idea* but he very quickness of ... touch' (404). Knowledge thus acquires a primarily sensual dimension, which is fulfilled in her illicit love for married clergyman Edwin Frere. For Louisa '[t]he words had proved an exact analogue of experience; and not of experience past, but that which – when the words were written – was yet to come' (404), so that the power of alchemical writing manifests itself in the anachronistic inversion of the sequence of experience and its representation. The disruption of the chronological sequence is, in turn, imagined with reference to the Fall, as Louisa 'had been shown the gate of the Garden even as it closed before her' (406). In order to regain Paradise and live the co-existence of times that characterises the temporality of romance as well as the goal of alchemy, Louisa and Frere must consummate their romance: it is then that the clergyman embodies 'an Adam shown the garden after his own fall. Yet, astoundingly, the gate stood open' (430).

However, the romance cannot last, as the couple's trespass begins to impinge on Frere's conventional conscience. He begins to perceive his action not in a Biblical and mythical framework ('he had thought [the Garden] Paradise' [469]) but with a Christian and historical frame of reference ('he knew now that its true name was Gethsemane' [469]). The element that replaces love in this new understanding is death. Not only is this further reference to the expulsion from Eden, following which the prospect of death entered human experience; it also suggests the intersection of consummation and death in which finds culmination the narrative desire that drives the modern characters' quest for knowledge of the past in *The Chymical Wedding*, *Possession* and *Ever After*. Reality reasserts its prerogative over romance in Frere's drastic attempt to extinguish sexual desire by self-castration. What replaces the romantic intensity of alchemical experience is an epistolary correspondence, a poor textual substitute, which Louisa burns before her death. These flames are only a smaller, more private version of the fire that had earlier burnt all the copies of her book, in an act that marked a ritual destruction of her attempt to make experience and words one. The result is that she becomes her book, and it is a silent one, so that if the secret is to be recovered it cannot be done by conventional historical documentary means.

The contemporary characters' quest for the Victorian story and the alchemical solution it contains is informed by this silence and participates of the same tension between language and experience. It is made more urgent by the personal circumstances of the three protagonists and the wider political situation in the last quarter of the twentieth century. Edward, Laura and Alex's investigation takes place under the threat of nuclear annihilation, underlined by the drone of military jets taking off from a nearby NATO base, while meetings of CND, demonstrations, earnest political talk punctuate the novel and the protagonists' researches. The remote rural corner of Norfolk where the action of the novel takes place becomes the epitome of a nation that has lost its former influence and finds itself 'colonised' by the power with whom 'it [had] had to enter into partnership ... to promote its national interest' following the loss of its empire (Finney 3–4), while the fact that the modern characters' epistemological enterprise is funded by the owner of a country house, a descendant of the Agnews, suggests that their search is inextricable from a potentially nostalgic and unviable socio-political position. As is the case in all the novels in this chapter, concerns with national identity are voiced as narrative negotiations. The division of the world into two irreconcilable and mutually exclusive ideologies renders the search for the lost source of unity (for this is what the alchemical secrets consist of and promise) all the more pressing, and, by foreshadowing the end of time, affects the perception of history itself. What destruction by the atom bomb heralds, in fact, is the impossibility of the retrospection which is at the basis of historical thinking, historical investigation, and historiographical composition, as well as of realist narrative. Once again alchemical desire is associated with a paradox: the anachronistic possibilities of alchemy are needed in order to guarantee the historical understanding that denies such anachronism is possible. Narratively, this manifests itself in an unresolved tension. On the one hand is the absence of an overarching narrative voice that would relate the story of the Victorian lovers to that of their modern-day counterparts in their respective historical periods, within a 'homogenous' medium that makes them 'measurable' and therefore commensurable, knowable, while also maintaining their difference and specificity (Ermarth 20). On the other hand are the growing parallelisms and coincidences between past and present, some consciously sought by the contemporary characters, others of which they remain unaware, perceived only by the readers in the unfolding of the stories in alternate chapters. The accumulating echoes across the narrative divide of the split time create correspondences that serve to increase the novel's undermining of the linearity and periodicity of history and to make past and present irreducible to their respective times, since '[r]epeating patterns … provide an endless series of textual metonymies: *patterns* themselves suggest previous repetitions even before *repeating* repeats them again' (Hennelly 21). The tension culminates and finds resolution in the final chapter, where past and present overlap and converge in the key moments of the burning of Louisa Agnew's papers containing the alchemical secrets and the revelation of those very secrets to an Edward newly restored to life after a near-fatal heart attack. The novel's climax thus suggests that knowledge is contingent upon defying the limitations on individual retrospection inevitably imposed by death. Both plot and narrative conform to the promise of the novel's epigraph, '[r]eality favours symmetries and slight anachronisms', while also fulfilling Diane Elam's definition of romance, excess, as '[b]oundaries, whether temporal and generic, fail to maintain control over that which they are intended to delineate' (Elam 12). In other words, romance transgresses the boundaries within which a historical understanding may attempt to confine it, whether they be the strictures of periodicity or the structure of the novel. By the end, *The Chymical Wedding* approximates alchemical wholeness, a state that accepts paradox, refusing *'our distinction of things into the* either *and the* or' and instead *'embrac[ing]* both *this* and *that – however paradoxical the conjunctions'* (445).

The contemporary protagonists start their quest from the 'fallen' condition of no longer having access to a language that is intrinsically related to things: Alex Darken's description of his 'journey across England' to Norfolk as 'a banishment' (9) evokes the Biblical loss of Eden, while locating the experience within a specific national context. His is also a narrative quest informed by a postmodern linguistic understanding of the Fall, whereby 'the sign ... can be circulated, repeated and used without the thing to which it refers being present. Interpreting the sign then becomes a process of working backwards to the originary and mythical moment when the sign and the thing were unified' (Currie 82). The loss engendered by this literal, metaphorical and mythical Fall is made personal in the fate of the two male protagonists, Alex and Edward, poets who find themselves unable to write. Its relevance to the alchemical endeavours is apparent from the start, when on arrival to the village of Munding Alex notices that Louisa Agnew is described on her tombstone as 'a silent book' (25). Poetic language is specifically the medium that can counter the effects of the devaluation of the sign into a currency with no gold to support its value, its role made clear by Louisa in another instance of the perceptiveness of the nineteenth century: '[I]t is of the nature of truth to deplete in the telling and ... only poetry can offer sufficient resistance to such depletion' (130).

Alex and Edward initially deal with the loss of presence differently, although both their approaches involve a version of a pastoral world. Alex sees 'a rudimentary promise of renewal' in the figure of the Green Man, 'this clumsy, feral creature sired sometime in the dark between the Fifth Day and the Sixth, and neither man nor beast' (13). His description gropes towards a formulation of an intermediate state that defies the either/or dichotomies by which the system of language functions and on which linguistic understanding rests; at the same time it intimates the recognition of the importance of sensuality in the recovery of a meaningful speech. This echoes Edwin Frere's dream of wholeness ('the possibility of an innocent nakedness' [368]) as a 'realm' where 'the only speech was sensual speech' (368), which is briefly fulfilled at the consummation of his love for Louisa. Alex is initially admitted to the alchemical project being pursued by Edward and Laura on the strength of his linguistic training, which allows him to work on the Latin texts in the Agnew library. However, in what is further proof of the inadequacy of conventional historical research to gleaning the truth of the past, the archival research proves inconclusive, 'for all the significant events had happened *outside* this library' (346). The contemporary romantic engagement with the past moves beyond the archive and into the garden: Alex's first glimpse of Edward and Laura is of the couple 'pale and naked ... clasped in each other's limbs, tussling and rolling in a hollow where the glade banked into mixed woodland' (14). Aware of the limitations of documentary examination, which presents a past already encoded in depleted language, they are engaged in an effort at communion with the past, by reproducing the symbolic alchemical joining in actual sexual union at the very place where Louisa's book was burned and her secret lost. Yet this literal rendering of the imagery of Eden marks a depletion of the metaphorical power of Louisa and Frere's consummation, as the garden contains 'not the true serpent's tooth at all' (15). Equally, Laura's literal firing of a pottery kiln is a paltry thing when compared to the insubstantial but pervasive fire of Louisa's and Frere's passion for knowledge and for each other. Both may be potentially uncontrollable, but only the latter has the power to create and destroy. Even the modern dangers seem at first to consist of no more than petty betrayal in a clichéd love triangle, and a prosaic death from heart attack.

However, when Alex and Laura experience their only sexual encounter as 'closer to a state of possession' by the past (334), in which they momentarily lose their modern, divided self and hear and speak words that are not their own, they do gain unarticulated knowledge of the past. Their feelings defy expression and give substance to the opposition between being and saying which, starting with the epigraph ('[p]roclaimed, it were but a word; kept silent it is *being*'), runs through the novel and which it is one of the aims of the alchemical project to resolve. For the same reason, they also escape a transmissible meaning. Understanding of the secret is, nevertheless, granted to Edward and knowledge of it becomes inextricable from the paradoxical experience of death as the moment of ultimate yet impossible retrospection. The reality of an anachronistic return from the dead manifests itself in terms of a co-existence of irreconcilable states: 'Though all the seven deadly sins had left their evidence across those windrow features, it seemed also that a kind of innocence had been resumed' (538). It is a trait Edward shares with Louisa, whose portrait reveals 'innocence and experience ... brought to gentle reconciliation.' Both '*were* what they knew, and in that identity was no distinction such as words must seem to make' (538). In his silence Edward has become a living version of the silent book evoked by Louisa's tombstone. In his paradoxically experienced innocence he has made real the anachronistic temporality of romance.

The success in the private enterprise comes, however, at a public cost. The political aims foregrounded by the novel in its initial definition of the alchemical quest as a response to the threat of nuclear annihilation recede at the same time as the urgency of the modern protagonists' quest for the secrets of the past intensified, so that even when Edward has become the repository of the elusive alchemical knowledge, that knowledge's beneficial divulgation is deferred indefinitely. Nor does Louisa and Frere's earlier transgression lead to a reforming of the political reality of their time: the subversive potential of romance, in their case, operates only at a personal level and while they defy conventions (a choice that does not go unpunished), their actions fail to undermine the system that upholds those conventions. The contemporary narrative concludes with the image of a pastoral fête in the grounds of Agnew Hall, with '[e]state-workers and their families, children scampering about among the bushes, and old friends' (520). The contemporary world under threat by technology is eschewed in favour of a retrenchment into the familiar, benevolent but limited confines of the country house and, in its association with an old order that will have no continuation into the future (Ralph Agnew, the present incumbent of the title, is unmarried and homosexual), the proposed model is both politically suspect and practically unsatisfactory. The novel's ending is as historically sterile as it is generically happy.

2. A.S. Byatt's *Possession: A Romance*

As the epigraph to *The Chymical Wedding* suggests, Clarke's novel is pre-eminently concerned with the romantic dimension of reality (its 'symmetries and slight anachronisms'); it therefore offers only incidental comments on the narrative implications of the choice of romance as a representational mode. Although magic permeates the unfolding of past and present stories, these are represented in what is a largely unproblematic realist narrative: few documents are reproduced *verbatim* and the spectre of representational impasse raised by the anachronistic doubleness of the plot is circumvented by resorting to the pregnancy of silence. *Possession*, on the other hand, demonstrates its awareness of romance's potential as a mode to represent the past from the start. In its epigraph, it quotes Hawthorne's well-known definition of the genre, which highlights the 'latitude, both as to its fashion and material' that romance grants the author with respect to the strict adherence to plausibility, 'which he would not have felt himself entitled to assume, had he professed to be writing a Novel.' By further relating romance to 'the attempt to connect a bygone era with the very present that is flitting away from us,' the epigraph anticipates the aims of the novel. Thus, the parallelisms, coincidences and anachronisms to be found between past and present plots, however implausible, are excused by the initial disclaimer that this is not a novel, but a romance. At the same time, they are justified in view of their successful recovering of the lost relation between the nineteenth and the late-twentieth centuries by that most traditional of romantic devices, the discovery of a genealogical connection which, at the end of the novel, restores the rightful heir to her position in society. In Hawthorne's (and Byatt's) formulation, romance both exposes the difficulties of establishing meaningful connections between past and present and fulfils the author's wish to make them nonetheless.

Romance, in its high and low incarnations, 'unashamedly' permeates all aspects of Byatt's novel (Buxton 212). Contemporary academics Roland Michell and Maud Bailey, their names imbued with literary echoes of the romance tradition from Chrétien de Troyes to Byron and Tennyson, are engaged in a quest for the truth about the relationship between two Victorian poets, Randolph Ash and Christabel LaMotte. Roland and Maud move in a postmodern world of textual (self)consciousness and linguistic hyper-awareness, where, while they realise that 'metaphors *eat up* [their] world,' they cannot but rely on the literary connections metaphors engender, in the hope that 'they held a clue to the true nature of things' (253). The tension between 'the desire for knowledge' (82) and the postmodern scepticism towards its possibility shapes their every action. Interestingly in light of the novel's subtitle, their situation is understood by the characters and articulated by the author in terms of a loss of romance, in the contradiction of 'a time and culture which mistrusted love "in love", romantic love, romance *in toto*' and which nevertheless 'prolif-erated sexual language, linguistic sexuality, analysis, dissection, deconstruction, exposure' (423). The parameters of this description of the postmodern condition, with their reference to what Clarke termed the depletion of language specifically in the expression of love, recall Umberto Eco's famous use of the paradigm of romance to illustrate the plight of the postmodern historical novelist

> as that of a man who loves a very cultivated woman and knows that he cannot say to her, 'I love you madly,' because he knows that she knows (and that she knows that he knows) that these words have already been written by Barbara Cartland. Still, there is a solution. He can say, 'As Barbara Cartland would put it, I love you madly.' At this point, having avoided false innocence, having said clearly that it is no longer possible to speak innocently, he will nevertheless have said what he wanted to say to the woman: that he loves her, but he loves her in an age of lost innocence. (67–8)

In her implicit reference to Eco's exploration of postmodernism (some ten years earlier than *Possession*'s), Byatt engages with a specif-ically postmodern tradition of thinking historical representation. Her aim in the novel, however, is bolder: exceeding the resigned acceptance and exploitation of intertextuality that Eco advocates, she seeks to recapture the innocence he deems impossible, and all without relinquishing the state of experience. In other words, hers is a romantically anachronistic quest for the means of combining the two moments of representational innocence and experience in one form, by removing the mutual exclusiveness imposed on them in the periodicity of history. To achieve this state, she resorts to a double re-writing of the story of the Fall, in the past and in the present, emphasising both its inevitability and its fortunate aspects.

Maud and Roland's quest is articulated with reference to the myth of a lost Eden to be regained, a motif introduced at the start with the description of Roland's basement flat with 'the garden...visible between railings' (17), entry to which is forbidden to him. Roland's world as he begins his quest is a post-lapsarian one, and while he did not himself cause or even experience the Fall (he did not sin, and was not expelled), his mundane relationship with Val and the insin-cere sex that defines it compound the impossibility of return to the

Garden. As was the case for Louisa Agnew and Edwin Frere, in the romantic plot which Roland inhabits only consummation can, paradoxically, restore innocence and reopen the gate. The ramifications of the enterprise are not, however, purely personal: the wall that encloses the garden 'dated from the Civil War, and earlier still ... had formed a boundary to General Fairfax's lands' (18). It therefore represents a historical remnant beyond the archive of proliferating documents from the past. Its conquest promises to grant a connection with one of the defining moments in the national past. The wall points to a solidity in the national history that surpasses the heritage wars that will develop around the Ash and LaMotte correspondence and that, at least in part, counters the discursive understanding of the nation as represented by its cultural products. This experience of the past is supported, if not engendered, by the mythopoeic dimension of the imagination which is still, at this point, a fledgling trait in Roland, but will gain full prominence by the end of his romantic quest.

It is all the more significant that, when a literal casting out of a desired place occurs, it should be evoked with specific references to the iconography of the expulsion from Paradise, with Sir George Bailey intimating ' "You may never come back" ... from behind his lance of light' (85), and that it should be Maud (not Val) who accompanies Roland out of the metaphorical Eden. In turn, this particular version of the Garden is symbolic of the nation with all its tradition and present decline: it is a stately home slowly succumbing to the ravages of time, whose inhabitants progressively retreat to an ever smaller area and which, nonetheless, contains the material remnants of the past (the Ash-LaMotte correspondence) and, potentially, the means for its restoration to glory. By the end of the novel, in fact, the money from the sale of the letters will pay for improvements to the life of Sir George and his wife. The novel's ideological stance with respect to the nation's decline is ambiguous. The apparent conservatism of locating the nation in the ancestral home is undermined by the fact that this version of the Fall proves fortunate, since it allows the two protagonists to abandon the incompatible aspects of their respective upbringing and academic allegiances: a psychoanalytic feminist critic and an old-fashioned textual scholar hardly meet on academic grounds; '[m]oreover, in some dark and outdated English social system of class, which [Roland] did not believe in, but felt obscurely working and gripping him, Maud was County, and he was urban lower-middle-class, in some places more, in some places less acceptable than Maud, but in almost all incompatible' (425). The protagonists' romance is the direct result of being cast out of the enclosed historical security of the Baileys' home. The analogy between theoretical and social divergences underlines the novel's use of academic concerns as covers for national ones.

The ejection from Seal Court immediately follows the academics' discovery of the bundle of letters between the Victorian poets, whose hiding place is revealed by textual clues. There is an interesting postmodern aspect to this version of the Fall, in that it is the exercise of linguistic skills that leads them to knowledge, while the object of their knowledge (the correspondence, or, language) cannot be taken with them into the world. Instead, Roland and Maud engage in a retracing of the steps of the two poets which is romantic in so far as it attempts to overcome not only the historical differences between the past and the present but also the very periodicity of their mutual relationship. Two apparently opposite means allow them to defy periodicity: the first is 'an effort of imagination to think how [Ash and LaMotte] saw the world' (254); the second is the belief in the power of the physical persistence of the past in the spaces where it happened, a persistence that cannot be harnessed into the systems of signification the two contemporary scholars initially resort to to prise open the secret of the past. As John J. Su puts it, '[t]he disparity between their theoretical models and the observable world suggests the inadequacy of the former to explain the motivations of the Victorian poets; more importantly, the disparity also implies that greater attention to material traces might provide the basis for accurately reconstructing the poets' beliefs and attitudes' (693).

The sequence of interlacing events in which Roland and Maud are involved is summed up in the terms of a romance towards the end of the quest, when all the characters find themselves together. Not only is Euan's appearance as the *deus ex machina* described as 'magic' (481); the fact that each recollected episode is introduced by the conjunctions 'and then', with no attempt to review the sequence retrospectively nor to establish causal connections between events, further strengthens the novel's aim to escape the fetters of historical time and its corollary periodicity. Indeed, the genealogical link unearthed at the end of the quest 'unifies the narrative [...]. The plot thus comes full circle [and] making the ending itself a point of origin, these previously hidden ties of kinship are a pointedly anachronistic device for providing closure' (Holmes 21).

If Maud becomes herself a material remnant of the past, proof that the romance between the Victorian poets exceeded its textual confines and historical boundaries and leapt into the reality of their direct descendant, Roland fulfils the promise of a connection with the past by means of the poetic imagination. The discovery of a poetic voice is initially shaped by a desire to counter the depletion of language advocated and practised by postmodern critical theory. Language, however, even poetic language, if detached from cultural and historical referents is not enough, and Roland's rebirth as a poet (a kind of return to innocence from the fallen state of theory) begins following a rereading of Ash's poetry that engenders recognition of his own experience, rather than vicarious analysis of the verse. The realisation is Adamitic, since it concerns 'the words that named things' (473) and, appropriately, coincides with his entry into the forbidden garden of his flat. Its historical associations are reiterated by the mention, once again, of 'the ... wall which had once bounded General Fairfax's Putney estate' (474), celebrated in one of the poems Roland composes. The re-enactment of the myth of the Garden thus allows for an imaginative recuperation of the national past. This, in turn, establishes a connection with the Victorian poets, as in one of his letters Ash tells of a vision he had while riding in Richmond Park – of a hind that was '*a solid poem*' (183) making the Elizabethan period present to the nineteenth century. The Victorian period and the Civil War thus become intermediary stages in the sewing together of national history.

The Biblical overtones of the modern plot culminate in Maud and Roland's sexual consummation of their now fully grown love, described as taking 'possession of all her white coolness, so that there seemed to be no boundaries' (507). The co-existence of wholeness with the exceeding of boundaries encapsulates the inexhaustible nature of romance, whereby the attainment of the desired object only serves to reveal the impossibility of its containment. It is an act that does not herald banishment from Paradise, but rather its regaining by experience, as '[i]n the morning, the whole world had a strange new smell. It was the smell of the aftermath ... which bore some relation to the smell of bitten apples. It was the smell of death and destruction and it smelled fresh and lively and hopeful' (507). The academics' progress from language to being (to maintain the terms of the opposition introduced by Clarke) finds a counterpart in the novel's own representation of the past: the 'realistic' congeries of scattered, incomplete, or unavailable documents that forms the remains of the Victorian poets' story and provides the clues to the academics' quest gives way to a third-person, omniscient representation of what was not preserved. Thus the past itself exceeds its representational confines to reveal its romantic status and provide 'coherence and closure' (422). In the process, it acquires a significant anachronistic tinge.

That an anachronistic moment of sexual consummation should conclude the quest and mark the boundaries of Maud and Roland's story is a testimony to the pervasive presence of romance in the contemporary timeframe. However, that those boundaries should themselves be exceeded in the 'Postscript' dated 1868 confirms that romance informs the entirety of the novel. The Postscript's appearance beyond the compass of the contemporary characters' experience sheds retrospective light on their enterprise, while disrupting the sense of general chronological sequence and closure by reintroducing past events after the conclusion of present ones. It also calls into question the adequacy or indeed the desirability of a documentary approach to the past: as Steven Connor suggests, the postscript's 'very failure to be gathered into the design [of the novel] is to be read as a mark of its authenticity' (150). It is therefore the historical imagination, of which the omniscient narrator is the repository, rather than a collation of textual evidence, that invests the episode with narrative and historical value and points to *Possession's* representational aims. The mode of the Postscript's delivery, preceded by the claim that '[t]here are things which happen and leave no discernible trace, are not spoken or written of' (508), makes this site the prerogative of an omniscient narrative voice of a distinctively Victorian cast, which, with the two previous interventions in the same mode, refines the novel's definition of romance in a metanarrative direction.

The interventions by the omniscient narrator grant the reader access to the blank spaces between the discontinuous documentary record, to moments innocent of previous encoding. The first is the Yorkshire guesthouse bedroom where Victorian poets Ash and

LaMotte consummate their love and reflect on their own experience of the ever-vanishing present. The second is Randolph Ash's death-bed, with the revelation of his unconsummated marriage through Ellen Ash's recollection of their honeymoon, to which 'there were no words attached' and which 'she remembered ... in images' (458). The third is the meadow where the unwitnessed and unrecorded meeting between the poet and his daughter takes place. Consummation, death and the end of reading are the standpoints from which romance, life and the story itself can be narrated retrospectively, retrospection being in the very nature of a realist narrator. Here Byatt exploits the ironic possibilities opened by introducing narratorial omniscience in a novel which 'consistently works to undermine its characters' assumption that given access to enough documents, the scholar can attain complete knowledge of his or her subject' (Shiller 548). She firstly articulates and then resolves Eco's dilemma: she knows that we know (and that we know that she knows) that realist narrative cannot be embraced innocently in an age of postmodern experience such as it is presented in the contemporary plot of the novel; if she nevertheless wishes to give us everything a realist narrator would, she must tell us that we are reading a romance. The novel's status as a romance ultimately rests in its adoption of realist narrative techniques. If the realist narrator stands, in relation to the narrative, after its end, from where he/she can retell the story *as if* it were unfolding in the present while guaranteeing its retrospective dimension (Brooks 23), *Possession* re-explores this double temporality and seeks to undermine the linearity, chronology and mutual exclusiveness implicit in the *as if* formulation of the relationship. To do so, the narrative must rediscover and re-enter the Edenic garden for the Victorian lovers, as it did for the contemporary protagonists.

The epigraph to chapter 1, from Ash's poem *The Garden of Proserpina*, introduces the elements involved in the narrative of the Fall, 'The Garden and the tree/The serpent ... the fruit ... /The woman' (1). The poets' correspondence, in turn, revolves around notions of a fallen world, which for Ash carries religious and scientific connotations of *'the smutty accretions of our industrial cities, our wealth, our discoveries, our Progress'* which generates *'speculation and observations ... palimpsest on palimpsest'* (164). If, in the mid-nineteenth century, discoveries and progress intimate Lyell's geological speculations and Darwin's theory of evolution, it is also only a small step from the mention of palimpsests to the bemoaning of the depletion of language, which LaMotte provides soon afterwards when she compares '*what a Poet might be in those days of Giants* [...] *seer, daemon, force of nature, the Word*' and '*what he is now in our time of material* thickening' (169). These reflections, whose substance would not go amiss in the mouths of Maud and Roland, reveal a commonality of thought that belies the perceived specificity of the postmodern period, and indeed suggest that, as Edward argued was the case in *The Chymical Wedding*, the quest for a pre-lapsarian state of linguistic innocence is itself a constant historical phenomenon.

The two-stage operation past and present characters share consists of first identifying an unattainable object of desire and then nostalgically longing for it, in the full awareness that the very articulation of the desire is the mark of the impossibility of its fulfilment. There is, however, a difference between the two pairs of questers. If for Maud and Roland the goal is to recover the past in the present, for Ash and LaMotte it is to attain a-temporal (romantic) status for their own present; and where the means to achieving the former aim is the narrative mode of romance, for the latter it is romance's central component, love, that is indispensable. Throughout the correspondence, and alongside the Biblical and mythical echoes of a pre- and post-lapsarian garden, runs the poets' growing sense of the inescapable consequences of the passing of time against their desire to suspend its flow. After their meeting in Richmond Park, Ash reflects on the impossibility of return from one's actions: '*And I could have taken your hand – or not taken your hand – could I not? Either? But now only the one*' (192). This becomes a poignant commentary on the inescapable thrust of narrative and its relation to the anachronism of romance: the use of the past conditional is revelatory and acknowledges that the co-existence of times is only possible prospectively (in the 'either'), but it is always envisaged retrospectively, which is to say at the very moment when it is no longer achievable. The fall into retrospection, the identifying aspect of historical and realist narrative, also signals the closing of options in a world of realist causality rather than romantic openness. And yet Ash is shrewd enough to unearth the possibilities for re-encoding this seemingly fallen world: '*How shall this be the end, that is in its very nature a* beginning?' (193) Theirs becomes a romance of experience: '*We must come to grief and regret anyway – and I for one would rather regret the reality than its phantasm, knowledge than hope, the deed than the hesitation, true life and not mere sickly potentialities'* (196). It is a fine paradox that, in order to enact the suspension of time this particular kind of romance demands, Christabel must leave the enclosed safety of her Richmond garden, moving from Eden to a geological expedition, as close to its opposite as a Victorian could experience.

In Yorkshire together, Ash and LaMotte can experience the 'world in which the ordinary laws of nature are slightly suspended' of romance (Frye 33). The suspended laws are those of the unstoppable forward movement of time, but the suspension is always temporary. Consequences will not be eschewed and 'the Romance must give way to social realism' (284). Although Paradise has been re-experienced, it has not been regained; when their time together comes to an end, Christabel finds herself pregnant, while Ash returns to the literal innocence of his unconsummated marriage. Expulsion from the Biblical garden introduced death to human experience, and it is at the moment of Ash's death, which coincides with the second intervention by the omniscient narrator, that the paradoxical nature of this re-inscription of garden mythology is further elaborated. It is revealed that the 'Edenic picnics' of the Ashes' honeymoon are accompanied by the 'locked gateway' of Ellen's sexual panic (459). Not only does this suggest that re-entry into paradise is achieved by sexual consummation, thus confirming that the paradise to be regained is one of experience; when examined in the light of Ellen's comments on the non-narrative status of her memories and the silence associated with them, this section also implies a connection of the garden of experience with narrative. Consummation, therefore, is associated with both the fall into history and the regaining of paradise. And it is this association that engenders narrative.

The scene for the 'Postscript' is the 'ultimate romance garden' (Hennelly 455), and the impression of an encounter taking place outside any spatial or temporal boundaries, in spite of the 1868 dating in the title, is reinforced by the vagueness of the references ('[t]here was a meadow,' '[t]here was a child,' '[t]here was a man' [508]) and by the abundance of '[o]ver twenty species of flowers ... all of which, by Byatt's own admission, cannot bloom simultaneously' (Colón 88). If, as Connor suggests, this event is granted a special position of authenticity, then its romantic setting confirms my suggestion that romance in the novel becomes, paradoxically, the mode for realist representation. The divergence between the date of Ash's meeting with his daughter and its position in the novel after the end of the contemporary narrative further disrupts the retrospection granted by omniscient narration. The result in an 'emphatically non-linear' conclusion to a story that finds wholeness in its being constituted 'both in prospect *and* in retrospect *at the same time*' (Melbourne quoted in Martyniuk 283). *Possession*'s split-time form, its genealogical denouement and the anachronistic correspondences between the past and the present undermine the sense of precedence and succession inherent in historical narrative. In its stead, the parallel rewriting of the myth of the Garden in both past and present timeframes establishes a connection between them that does not rely on chronological succession and historical understanding but rather on the epistemological, representational, and mythopoeic powers of romance. If these powers are initially put at the service of a recovery of the personal past, the import of this achievement impinges on the codification of a national past where the documentary record that appears to embody it is progressively replaced (in a move analogous to the novel's shift from textual reproduction to an omniscient vehicle for the historical imagination) by the solidity of its physical structures.

What this affectively and narratively satisfying ending elides, however, is the fact that it is made possible by – and arguably validates – the Thatcherite ideology of social mobility and the definition of the self through the possession of commodities. Euan, whose timely intervention produces the happy resolution, is a yuppie figure (benign because literate) and it is money that influences the competition for possession of the Ash-LaMotte correspondence: Professor Cropper's university's wealth is a threat to his impoverished but 'worthy' British counterpart. Ultimately, the correspondence *is* sold, in what is a prevailing of realism over romance, to pay for the repairs of Seal Court, yet another ancestral home destined to have no issue, and even Roland, the least worldly of all the characters and the most disinterested, is rewarded by lucrative job offers in various corners of the globe. The perpetuation of romance on English soil, it seems, is as impossible in the late-twentieth century as in the mid-nineteenth. Even the potentially conservative, but nationally productive, option of having the epistolary exchange appropriated by its rightful genealogical heir is only toyed with but not enacted. Thus, the imagining of the nation remains, and is only successful as, a poetic endeavour: were an attempt to put it into practice to be made, the risk is that the imagined nation would become an artificially preserved 'simulacrum' (210) whose very authenticity, as was the case for Ware Common, is the mark of a rejection of the anachronistic understanding of history that the novel's narrative and the characters' actions promote. Such is the fate of Bethany, the cottage where Christabel LaMotte lived, and which, restored in conformity with its status as heritage, is now too clearly typical of its time to be true. As Roland puts it, ' "It would have looked older. When it was younger" ' (211). *Possession,* in other words, proposes a form of envisaging national history that is dependent on existing ideological and economic conditions: the fact that they are put at the service of a 'just' cause cannot fully conceal their connivance with the politics of the time.

3. Graham Swift's *Ever After*

In her review of *Ever After,* Anita Brookner draws a direct connection between Swift's novel and *Possession,* remarking that the latter 'has given birth to a genre [in which] a contemporary narrator of a professional, vaguely academic kind, will establish a connection with a Victorian forebear or prototype, and the stories will proceed in tandem' (30). There are indeed serendipitous correspondences encompassing *The Chymical Wedding* as well as *Possession*: the fire of alchemy, with which the characters in *Ever After* are 'consumed' (112), is reproduced in a bonfire of family papers; an enclosed garden 'with its locked gate which only the favoured may open' plays a prominent part in the contemporary action of Swift's novel, where it is variously described as 'the Garden of Eden' and a remnant of medieval romance, 'one of those semi-allegorical gardens into which the Lady of the Castle steals (unknown to her absent lord) to solace some wounded knight errant' (80). Specific echoes of Clarke's novel sound in Swift's, yet the changed note signals that *Ever After* approaches its material from a more thoroughly disillusioned perspective. If at the moment of near-death Edward '[f]rom a place somewhere close to the ceiling... is looking down in mild perplexity' on his unconscious body while 'floating... in such detachment' (Clarke 475), Swift's narrator Bill Unwin emphatically denies 'that famed experience of rising out of my own body and surveying it from the ceiling' (4). Where

Edward's survival coincides with the acquisition of a knowledge that cannot be revealed in words, Bill's failed suicide engenders a narrative that admits to 'a good deal of...imagination' (90) adding to any knowledge. The moments of intersection between the novels are thus accompanied by deeper differences.

Ever After follows its narrator, Bill Unwin, in his attempt to edit the journal of his ancestor Matthew Pearce. Swift's novel thus shares with Byatt's the objective genealogical link between the Victorian past and the postmodern present; it also presents another instance of engagement with the textual remains of the past. The difficulties inherent in the paucity and discontinuity of the records of the past are compounded by the intellectual and affective chasm that separates Unwin from the subject of his research. Both the nature of the Victorian man's spiritual crisis and the rigorous integrity with which he adheres to his beliefs are alien to the spiritually empty world described in the contemporary narrative. In *Ever After* the urgent academic scholarship that drove Roland and Maud, or Edward and Laura's belief in the power of alchemy to reconstitute the damaged wholeness of the modern world, are replaced by the TV-celebrity academic Michael Potter. Even the language to describe that chasm is inadequate: the suggestion that '[t]hey took things seriously in those days' (47) is remarkable only for its blandness. The distance between past and present is epitomised in Unwin's perception of Matthew Pearce's life and times as 'the real thing', in explicit contrast to the derivativeness of a present 'underpinned by plastic' (9). Unwin's enterprise is in its turn complicit with the contemporary reality it indicts. It is the Ellison plastic empire, with Bill's stepfather Sam at the helm, that funds his Cambridge Fellowship, to which he has no rights by any objective academic standards.

The parallel unfolding of past and present narratives is less consistently maintained in *Ever After* than in the two preceding novels. In the course of the narrative, Bill Unwin's role as narrator of both Victorian and contemporary stories becomes more prominent. What takes centre stage as a result is the investigation of the difficulties of piercing the layer of self-conscious reflexivity inherent in postmodern engagements with the past, particularly when romance, which had such redeeming powers in the lives of the modern questers in *Possession*, has itself been confined to the past and is tainted with derivativeness. *Ever After*'s past narrative tells the story of Pearce, a surveyor for the Great Western Railway, who meets, falls in love with, and marries the daughter of a clergyman, living happily until a combination of scientific inquiry (he meets the proverbial fossil) and personal tragedy (the death of his infant son) results in the loss of religious faith and a decision to leave his family behind and sail for America. The trajectory from railways to fossils that encompasses Pearce's personal life stands in metonymic relation to the nineteenth century's own shift from faith in human progress to the loss of religious faith. Further, it also echoes the changing preoccupations of the Victorian novel, from Eliot, Gaskell and Trollope's railways to the fossils in Hardy's novels. Hardy's renunciation of the novel in his later years marks a loss of faith in the form: the crisis of representation this heralds, a symptom of the freshly understood incommensurability of the representational system with the (un)representable reality, is a counterpart to the postmodern crisis of realist narrative. As was the case for *The Chymical Wedding* and *Possession,* contemporary impasses are here shown to be reverberations of earlier Victorian questioning. This strengthens the connections between past and present that constitute the pattern of cross-references in the novel, at the same time as pointing to a persistent undermining of the perceived uniqueness of the postmodern condition vis-à-vis a nostalgically sought nineteenth-century model of representational and intellectual innocence.

It is therefore unsurprising that Swift's narrator should encompass side by side in his framework of references the Victorian articulation of the moment of representational crisis and its postmodern revisiting. This becomes apparent in the double encoding of Matthew Pearce's encounter with the fossil. The narrator nods in the direction of his literary forefather Hardy in *A Pair of Blue Eyes,* as well as of his more recent predecessor Fowles. Thus, *Ever After* shares with *The French Lieutenant's Woman* a geological motif that straddles plot and narrative form, becoming something close to a citation in the description of the episode of the fossil. The mediatory role of Fowles's novel is further confirmed by the knowing common literary setting in Lyme Regis, where 'the very steps that Jane Austen made Louisa Musgrove fall down in *Persuasion*' (Fowles 14) can be found. Another fall provides a counterpart to Pearce's geological experience:

The thing was that he saw an ichthyosaurus...on the cliffs of Dorset in the summer of 1844 (age: twenty-five). I see him lurching, slipping, fleeing down that wet path towards the beach. Everything is chance. It might so easily have been otherwise. He might have gone to the aid of the young woman who even then, as he scrambled blindly by, sat on the damp ground, encircled by a little attentive group, nursing a twisted ankle. [...] And if he had gone with the others to assist, if he had not lingered alone for those few mesmerical moments, his whole life might have been different. He might have married the young woman. What an opportunity missed! There she was, pale, shaken, in need of rescue and obliged to show, for all the fussing of her chaperone, an unaccustomed amount of lower leg. He might have fallen in love with this pretty invalid and lived happily ever after. Instead of which, he chose to stare into the eye of a monster. (89)

Pearce's literal slipping down the path stands for his slipping down the road of religious doubt and functions as the equivalent of Unwin's own postmodern slide into representational uncertainty. Some of the details in the scene, such as the twisted ankle and the consequent showing of the young woman's leg, suggest, at the same time, intertextual awareness (this may be Sarah Woodruff's twisted ankle, and Charles's glimpse of her leg in the guesthouse, leading to desire, consummation and, arguably, a start on the path to redemption) and a lazy acceptance of the clichéd version of a Victorian period obsessed with covering up legs and aroused by their uncovering. Where the former confirms the literary knowingness of the narrator, the latter is always a threat in a milieu where attaining TV stardom seems to be the ultimate academic aspiration.

The possibility of immediate redemption is tantalisingly close. As was the case for *Possession,* the past conditional points to the skeleton of a different narrative, while also, by virtue of the temporal value of the grammatical choice, confirming its impossibility. A similar preoccupation with turning points in narrative and, by extension, in life, was present in the musings of Charles in *The French Lieutenant's Woman,* to whom 'it seemed astounding...that one simple decision, one answer to a trivial question, should determine so much. Until that moment all had been potential; now all was inexorable fixed' (320). This common subject for reflection confirms the impression that at the basis of contemporary historical fiction's revisiting of the

Victorian novel is a sense of representational belatedness that finds its expression in the plots' careful delineation of the desire for a return to a prior moment of potentiality, coupled with the awareness that such a longing is made impossible by its very articulation. Ironically, however, by projecting their contemporary preoccupations onto a Victorian past, the modern characters and their authors weaken the case for the existence of that very chasm on which their enterprises, and the form in which they are conveyed, rest. As one would expect in the kind of self-reflexive works under consideration, the implications of this intellectual knot spill into the novel's treatment of its subject. Unwin, a very literary narrator, weaves a tissue of intertextual references to approach the past, as if to confirm, in true postmodern fashion, that the past can only be approximated by quoting previous representations of it. And yet in the representation thus achieved is also the suggestion that, firstly, however imperfect, this is nevertheless the moment when the narrative, like Matthew Pearce, is confronted with 'the real thing'; secondly, that this encounter cannot be sustained. The moment of Pearce's sighting of the fossil marks for him '[t]he beginning of ... make-belief' (101).

Pearce's reaction to coming face to face with an ichthyosaurus is surprising because, as Unwin points out, these creatures were not uncommon even in 1844 and he may well have seen one himself at the British Museum. What interests Unwin, therefore, is the alterity of the encounter at Lyme Bay, which, despite coming after the knowledge of the existence of ichthyosauri and the experience of that existence in a museum environment, nevertheless is re-encoded as being the originary moment of knowledge. The key element, as was the case in Charles's collecting of tests in *The French Lieutenant's Woman,* is between the contained experience of shops or museums 'safe, orderly, artificial places' (100), and 'the rock from which workers ... were labouring to release it [...]. Here. Now. Then' (101). The last three words point to both the immediacy of experience and its detachment from the framework of interpretation offered by historical perspective. This suggestion acquires metanarrative connotations in the light of Swift's use of natural history to articulate the relationship between the real and the artificial. The workers labouring to release 'the thing itself' (100) trapped where time placed it ('in the pathetically locatable nineteenth century' [100]) to re-place it within the artificial environment of the museum are figures of Unwin himself, excavating the life of his ancestor to re-locate it in a readable context whose parameters of interpretation are already established. Thus, the crisis of faith recorded in the journal Unwin is editing may have been individual to Matthew Pearce, but retrospectively (which is to say, in the knowledge of existing narratives of the Victorian period which trace its philosophical changes) it acquires the typicality and representative value of the confirmation of an already present structure of signification. It is in this guise that the notebooks are sought by the narrator's colleague, as ' "an historical document of enormous value – a testimony to the effects on a private life of ideas that shook the world" ' (49). Pearce's story is deemed important not in its 'thing itself-ness' but in so far as it confirms, supports, and typifies an existing explanatory and representational model. The battle for its possession mirrors the scramble over the Ash-LaMotte correspondence in *Possession* and confirms the value attributed to the ownership of the cultural remnants of the past. Like the correspondence, Pearce's manuscript constitutes cultural capital in the present, and is the means for an attempt to reconstitute national continuity via the textual remnants of the past, an inherently paradoxical enterprise given that texts are themselves by definition discontinuous.

Gutleben argues that positing the Victorian period and the realist tradition of its literature as the representational counterpart of the ichthyosaurus (the thing itself) 'implies the setting up of a specific historical referent – a distinctly realist device' (160). In order to recover that referent, *Ever After* explores the role of the imagination in offering an alternative to historical enquiry. At the distance of several pages and with reference to different episodes in Pearce's life, Unwin urges to 'picture the scene' (101 and 185). In the first occurrence, the exhortation concerns 'pictur[ing] how the world might be … in the eyes of another person. Such a simple, unconscionable thing: to be another person' (101). To be another person is to transgress the same physical and temporal boundaries that separate us from the past; if it is to be achieved, consciousness (awareness) has to be abandoned. And yet, to do so would nullify the fulfilment of a desire which, ultimately, is engendered by the consciousness of the irretrievability of past experience. The recurrence of the sentence puts forward another strategy, namely,

> to reconstruct the moment, as patient palaeontologists reconstruct the anatomies of extinct beasts. If it were not for Matthew's Notebooks, nobody might have known it had happened at all, it might have been as though it never was. So what, on the part of this unforeseen testifier, is a little bit of creative licence? (185)

This formulation entails a recognition of the value of contingency in historical representation. In terms that recall Byatt's introduction to the 'Postscript' of *Possession,* Swift acknowledges the precariousness of the past and the role of the imagination in preserving a record of it. As the would-be narrator of this story, Unwin is initially committed to the factual record, 'the edition [...], the scrupulously scholarly exercise' (49), but he soon succumbs to the same desire for full disclosure of the events manifested by Byatt's narrative voice. He tells us of the meeting, love, marriage, of Pearce and his wife, all of which precede the start of the notebooks and are therefore absent from the documentary material. Unwin abandons his faith in the thing itself and in 'the business of strict historiography' (90), and instead gains access to the deeper truth of personal relations. To this narrator, 'it is the personal thing that matters' (119).

These words intimate an aspect of the quest for the past that becomes progressively clear, that Unwin's research into Pearce's life is itself a substitute for the 'personal thing' that has haunted him since childhood, namely the reasons for his father's suicide. More specifically, he wishes to understand whether knowledge of his wife's affair with Sam Ellison contributed to Colonel Unwin's decision to take his own life. In what is a typical move for a narrative that suggests that recuperation of the past amounts to 'the nostalgia for the nostalgia of nostalgia' (81), a thrice-removed reproduction of the real thing, what had initially appeared as 'the real thing' (Matthew Pearce) is revealed to have been instead a sham replacement for something that had lost its solidity, the biological incontrovertible connection of father and son. This situation places Unwin in a compromised ethical position from the start. A quest that had seemingly been undertaken in competition with, and as refutation of, Ellison's enthusiasm for 'substitoots' (7), turns out to be itself an instance of substitution. In a further ironic parallel, given Sam's status as Claudius to Bill's Hamlet (the narrator's understanding of himself is predictably mediated by literary codes), Unwin's desire for stable origins replicates the older man's 'genealogical investigations' (8). What is withheld until well into the narrative, and what gives its existence wholly different motivations, is the revelation that Colonel Unwin, on whose behalf he sought revenge, was not in fact Bill's biological father. Instead, the real father he will never know 'was an engine-driver... [o]n the main line west' (158).

The discovery of his father's job and its location strengthen Unwin's connection with Matthew Pearce, himself a surveyor on the same railway line, doubly making Bill a descendant of the Victorian man: genealogically, through his mother; ideally through his father. However, the discovery also serves to undermine the stability of origins, and the failure of biology (as Unwin sees it) calls into question the very notion of a real thing as something that can be encompassed by, and which can in turn validate, narrative systems of interpretation. Instead, the outcome of the quest reveals the potential dangers hidden in the factual incontrovertible truths of biology and geology. For Unwin, this means the loss of his father a second time; for Pearce, the loss of religious faith and family. The narrator's loss of faith in the viability and effectiveness of a factual narrative, whether in relation to the ostensible object of the representational enterprise (Pearce) or its true one (Unwin himself), marks the acquisition of omniscience. The subject of Unwin's narrative thus becomes the process whereby the narrator of *Ever After* succeeds in conveying a moment of pure contingency where experience and telling, prospective and retrospective narration, are held in suspense, and which can therefore reproduce the anachronistic co-existence of times of romance. Here it is not love that regains the Garden for the novel's protagonist and narrator but death. From the opening warning that '[t]hese ... are the words of a dead man' (1), deaths punctuate the story, from Unwin's father's to Unwin's wife's, his mother's, her second husband's and, the origin of the narrative encompassing all the others, Unwin's own near-death in an attempted suicide. The novel encodes the connection between the moment of death and the beginning of narrative as one of cause and effect. Unwin's mother 'was never an eager *raconteuse* [...] she regarded reminiscence and tale-telling as ... an avoidance of the central issue of life, which was to wring the most out of the present. [...] Yet at the very end I was treated to a final and, so it seemed, irrepressible bedtime story' (26). In other words, narrative is made possible by, and marks, the abandoning of the immediacy of experience; once again, narrative appears to signal the distance from the real thing. Suicide is the narrator's ultimate attempt at contact with, and experience of, the real thing, yet one that, if successful, marks the impossibility of its retrospective encoding. The result of the intersection of death and narrative is a paradoxical state of experienced innocence:

> The word 'innocence' lodges in my mind. A teasing, fugitive notion, easiest to gauge by its loss. [...] And yet, as I sit in these paradisiacal surroundings, it seems to me, equally, that innocence is precisely what has been rendered unto me, as if my return to life ... has restored me, but without expunging my memories, to a condition prior to experience. (159)

The religious overtones of the references to paradise seem purposefully to undo the fallen state of postmodern representation, whose counterpart earlier in the novel had been Pearce's fall into religious doubt. The Edenic setting for this co-existence of innocence and experience recalls the outcome of Maud and Roland's consummation, while the suggestion that it is near-death that has made it possible reflects Edward's situation at the end of *The Chymical Wedding*.

Crucially, however, death as the condition for an innocent representation is posited and enacted at the start of the novel, rather than at the end. The suggestion is that the entire narrative participates, as a result, of this innocence. As was the case for Byatt, Swift does not stop at the recognition of the constructedness and derivativeness of a realist representational enterprise; his aim is to overcome these aspects and, in so doing, recover imaginatively the 'real thing' that Unwin's earlier attempts at factual narrative had failed to reach:

> You have to picture the scene. How it was then, on a wet August night in 1957, in the days before she was famous. [...] He had not expected ... this frenzy and breathlessness to be unclad. [...] Nor was he prepared for the arresting candour, the simplicity and amazement, of nakedness. And this, you see, is me. And this is me. He was not prepared, either, for the tender and inspired

fluency (as if to complete the candour) with which each one of them offers the other on this indelible night the complete and unabridged story of their lives up to this point. (260)

The moment brings to fruition the desires expressed throughout the narrative: the realisation of two distinct yet inextricable selves accompanies the representational fulfilment of the pictured scene. The recurring sentence that introduces this moment, as it had introduced Unwin's attempts at understanding and representing Pearce's self, is no longer an exhortation, believed in or heeded in varying degrees, but is enacted in what follows it. In the ambiguous phrasing and dilatory syntax of the last sentence narrative and sexual consummation are conflated.

In the light of *Possession*'s articulation of the postmodern predicament in terms of language and love, it is interesting that this moment of consummation should be presented as a breaking of the constraints imposed on Bill and Ruth by 'the official language of love' in 1957, 'a language of engagement rings and kisses at front doors, when university-registered landladies exercised their censorious regimes, and sex and sin were still conveniently alliterative synonyms' (250). Not only does the narrative fluency engendered by consummation exceed, in true romantic mode, the boundaries imposed on the expression of love by the official language; in its coincidence of words and deeds it promises a resolution to the central impasse of Clarke's novel. Whereas in *The Chymical Wedding* the coincidence could only be sustained in the power of silence, here it finds the means for articulation and therefore for narrative action. It is only when romance is recaptured in its prospective unfolding that the derivativeness of the present can be escaped and the authenticity of the past re-experienced, but the romantic anachronism is, by definition, unsustainable.

In *Ever After*, romance is shown largely to have been pervaded by the postmodern reliance on mediatory interpretive structures. Romance is a 'welcome intrusion' in Unwin's life from his birth, 'in December 1936, in the very week that a King of England gave up his crown in order to marry the woman he loved' (57). It is the defining framework for Unwin's life in 'the glorious, the marvellous, the lost and luminous city of Paris' as a child and a ready pattern for his recollections of it:

> I find it hard to separate the city that exists in the mind, that existed even then, perhaps, in my mind, from the actual city [...]. It had never struck me before that Reality and Romance could so poignantly collude with each other; [...] I saw Paris as a palpably network of 'scenes', ... the incarnation of something already imagined. (13)

The structures of romance further permeate the narrative of how Unwin fell in love with, married, and then lost his wife Ruth. The romantic setting of the modest stage on which Ruth performs in soon-to-be-lifted obscurity is compounded by the circumstances of their first kiss: 'I owed it all to a summer storm. The oldest ruse in the book of Romance' (77). Her suicide is re-encoded as the final performance of her greatest role, the quintessentially romantic Cleopatra. The sequence of love, marriage, and loss mirrors Bill's emplotment of Pearce's story, as if to prove his ancestor's value as a precursor and therefore confirm the modern protagonist's quest for a commonality of experience that will 'build a bridge, span a void' (203) between past and present. The genealogical link, whose importance has increased just as Unwin's biological connection with his father has disappeared, is thus validated, as is Bill's faith in the redeeming power of origins, which had been weakened in the comparable search for his father. In both cases, of course, the romance (between Matthew and Elizabeth, Bill and Ruth) is shaped retrospectively and controlled by the narrator: as Unwin readily admits, 'he knew nothing ... at the time' (57) of the romantic associations of his birth. The artificiality of the pattern is what grants it lasting power. Nor are artificiality and derivativeness barriers to experience, as Paris, 'the leaving, breathing rendition of itself' (19) had already proved to Unwin. It is, however, a very specific kind of experience being recovered and a carefully delimited one.

If, in fact, by the end of the novel Unwin has indeed achieved narrative and personal redemption by confronting the death of the man he thought was his father and that of his wife, redemption does not lead to a renewed engagement with that contemporary world which, at the start of the novel, was described as pressing threateningly on

the walls of sheltered academic institutions. For all the national significance of the moment of his birth, Bill plays no part in any political event in the course of his life, nor does he confess to any political
opinion. Indeed, the final narrative and emotional climax takes
place against the background of 'the first Aldermaston marchers
[embarking on] their pilgrimage of protest' (249). His position is all
the more damning as Aldermaston is the town where his biological
father came from: the novel is arguably Bill's narrative and entirely
private pilgrimage to the place. The potential difficulty caused by
wilful political disengagement is obviated not only by this act of
posthumous and retrospective contrition but also, from a narrative
point of view, by having a statement of love's a-political dimension
precede the imaginative recreation of consummation. Any doubt
about the ethical validity of Unwin's choice disappears in the representational and sexual fulfilment of the final page. This eschewing
of commitment on anything other than a personal level is a consistent feature of the novel. Unwin's description of the English landscape, a 'living palimpsest' (199) on which the intersection between
past and present can be traced, fails to lead to a reflection on change.
As Unwin admits, he 'should have been struck by some prescient,
elegiac pang at the sight of those great expresses steaming only to
their own oblivion, and taking with them a whole lost age' (199). The
cry 'O England!', however, is raised only to be dismissed. While nostalgia suffuses the narrative, it is never nostalgia for a national past,
only for a family and personal one. World War II itself 'occurred ... off
stage' (199). Even the discovery that a possible motive for his father's
suicide may have been horror at the implications of nuclear research
for military purposes and at his role in promoting it does not result
in greater attention to the world as opposed to the self. It is left to the
novels in the next chapter to modify this imbalance between private
and public concerns, introducing an element in the past that is con-
spicuously missing here, empire.

3
Empire and the Politics of Representation

Suzanne Keen discusses *The Chymical Wedding* and *Possession* as examples of what she calls 'romances of the archive', a contemporary genre which responds to 'the postmodern critique of history with invented records full of hard facts' (3). Keen relates this desire to confirm the accessibility of the past through documentary evidence to the widespread turn-of-the-century concern 'less [with] academic history than [with] British heritage' (5). Heritage, in this context, is the version of the past popularly available and popularly conceived. Judie Newman, in turn, equates the notion of national heritage in the popular perception with the commodification of Empire 'as a marketable entity, based on nostalgia for a past never-never land' (29). The mid-Victorian period that so preoccupies Clarke's, Byatt's and Swift's contemporary characters coincided with organised (governmental, exploratory or missionary) imperial expansion, but this element is barely discernible in the three novels and, even when performing a relevant role in the events, the Empire leaves no trace into the present and does not, therefore, appear in the reconstructed representation of the past by the contemporary characters.

The Chymical Wedding offers the clearest example of this tendency to marginalise the presence and influence of empire in a heritage-inflected national history. Edwin Frere's suitability as Louisa Agnew's alchemical partner, in fact, is a result of a sojourn as a missionary in India, where his conventional faith is first challenged by his witnessing of religious practices founded on sensuality; he will subsequently face (and rise to) a similar challenge in his rural Norfolk parish. While Frere's understanding of the colony is at first predictably coloured by Orientalist binary thinking, whereby sensuality marks India's otherness to the visiting Englishman and threatens to unsettle his understanding of his identity, his later experiences challenge the stability and security of the implied dichotomy. Thus, on his return to England he discovers comparable sexual explicitness in an ancient carving at the entrance to Munding church. This detail seems to suggest a connection between distant places which is founded on an immediate (as opposed to a socialised) understanding and experiencing of life, eventually leading Frere to his involvement with alchemy. The sensual engagement with the past, as the previous chapter argued, is presented in wholly positive terms. However, although the modern protagonists are granted an insight into the importance of sensuality in attempting to establish a connection with the past, the source of Frere's realisation is never gleaned and empire is effectively expunged from the image of the past available to the novel's present protagonists. In *Possession,* the scholars working in the basement of the British Museum, where the manuscripts of Ash's works are stored, have taken over a mythical imperial location, 'a peripheral zone of lost or forgotten knowledge buried deep within the catacombs of the London archive' (Richards 16). The archive now contained there is much narrower in breadth, and of limited usefulness, since it is a combination of physical reiteration and imaginative recreation of the past that guides the protagonists in their quest for the truth of Ash and LaMotte's relationship. Similarly, *Ever After* wilfully limits the geographical scope of the quest into the past by having Matthew Pearce die in a shipwreck just off the Devon coast, when he was on his way to America. His story preserves its Victorian typicality (and its heritage value) precisely because it is curtailed before it can encompass a new nation and a future competitor for Britain in power and world influence.

In *The Chymical Wedding, Possession,* and *Ever After* doomed love, secrets and mysteries define romance, but the genre's potential to unsettle historical, political, and ideological assumptions remains understated if not altogether muted. The linear chronology of historical thinking those novels challenge is nowhere related to the 'linear, progressivist claims of...the major imperializing discourses' (Bhabha 32). The novels examined in this chapter, on the other hand, ambitiously set out to explore the territories beyond English shores, quite literally so since the plots of Ahdaf Soueif's *The Map of*

Love (2000), Matthew Kneale's *English Passengers* (2000) and Douglas Galbraith's *The Rising Sun* (2000) are structured around a voyage out towards the Empire, to Egypt, Tasmania and Panama respectively, also with extensive forays into Scotland, the Isle of Man, France and the United States. The enlarged perspective is crucial not only to the kind of nation these novels articulate but also to their dissection of the means by which national narratives function, and the ways in which the imaginary communities they engender define themselves. From the outset, the works examined in this chapter seem to acknowledge, firstly, that the sense of the nation is founded on 'a pattern of select inclusions and exclusions' (Marangoly George 2) and, secondly, that in order to probe the results of that pattern it is necessary to retrace the process of 'confrontation with what is considered ... foreign' from which the nation gains unified identity, but which is then expunged from the nation's self-image (4). Edward Said describes the process of differentiation and exclusion that establishes a sense of the self (individual and communal) in the following detailed terms:

> A group of people living on a few acres of land will set up boundaries between their land and its immediate surroundings and the territory beyond, which they call 'the land of the barbarians'. In other words, this universal practice of designating in one's mind a familiar space which is 'ours' and an unfamiliar space beyond 'ours' which is 'theirs' is a way of making geographical distinctions that can be entirely arbitrary ... because imaginative geography of the 'our land-barbarian land' variety does not require that the barbarians acknowledge the distinction. It is enough for 'us' to set up these boundaries in our own minds; 'they' become 'they' accordingly, and both their territory and their mentality are designated as different from 'ours'. To a certain extent modern and primitive societies seem thus to derive a sense of their identities negatively. (54)

Soueif and Kneale examine the destabilising effect for the confirmation of national identity of a response from the 'barbarians' that appropriates the original discourse and plies it to their needs. Galbraith, on the contrary, displays the limitations and ultimate failure of a national narrative that attempts to define its subject by

negating rather than affirming difference. In both cases, the resulting picture of the nation is less cohesive and less stable than that
achieved at the end of *The Chymical Wedding, Possession* and *Ever
After*; it is also, however, historically more ambitious.

The historical settings, in fact, mark a widening of the scope
beyond the canonically significant mid-Victorian period comparable
to the expanded geographical reach of the novels under consideration here. So, while the action of *English Passengers* spans a period of
around 30 years culminating in 1857, a moment whose importance
for nation and empire was discussed with respect to *The Siege of
Krishnapur, The Rising Sun* narrates the events on the eve of the Act of
Union between England and Scotland of 1707, the moment when
Britain came into being as a state, if not a nation, and *The Map of Love*
(closest in structure to the works in Chapter 2) proposes two parallel
timeframes at the start and end of the twentieth century respectively, with the death of Queen Victoria programmatically signalling
the desire to resist the equation of the past with the reign of that
monarch. Given the formal similarities with the earlier texts, Soueif's
novel is especially useful in gauging the distance from them. The
past timeframe shows a Britain whose national ideals underlying
imperial discourse have already been compromised by its actions,
while in the present the equivalent political questions are asked of
the United States, as if in recognition that only by involving America
can a worthwhile parallel be made between the imperial past and the
post- or neo-imperial present. Broadly, where the works discussed
earlier are permeated by millennial anxieties, which they counter by
attempting to find a solid established core to individual and national
identity, the novels in this chapter (which, perhaps not coinciden-
tally, were published at the beginning of the new millennium) are
prepared to confront all aspects of the past and to dispute its comfortable heritage dimension.

As the novels' titles further suggest, the wider concerns variously
encompass romance, nationalism, and empire. Soueif applies the
colonising act of mapping, with its intrinsic use of knowledge and
representation to exercise power, to an entity, love, that defies clear
boundaries. On the one hand, then, *The Map of Love* evokes

[t]he exemplary role of cartography in the demonstration of colonial discursive practices...implemented in the production of the

map, such as the reinscription, enclosure and hierarchization of space, which provide an analogue for the acquisition, management and reinforcement of colonial power. (Huggan 125)

On the other hand, by suggesting that what is being mapped is a notoriously protean feeling, the novel also presents the paradoxical task of enforcing onto a reluctant entity 'the procedures, and implications, of mimetic representation' which constitute 'a further point of contact between cartography and colonialism' (Huggan 125). As was the case with *The French Lieutenant's Woman* vis-à-vis the socialised model of the nation, in *The Map of Love* a questioning of the mimetic practices of realism by means of romance entails a critique of colonialism. The process of unsettling received notions is continued in the plot, which emphasises the inevitable hybridity – cultural, biological, or both – of the nation, against and despite rhetorical attempts in both nationalist and imperial discourse (the two are revealed to be disturbingly similar) to present it as uniform and homogeneous. The title of Kneale's novel foregrounds the national dimension of its characters but also their limited agency (they are passengers rather than seamen), while the plot places them in a situation where identity confronts difference, with unexpected results. This strategy is doubled up with the introduction of the competing national narrative of an aboriginal Australian, Peevay. He is the son of a native woman and a white escaped convict who raped her: he embodies the complex and violent history of the continent and, through a process of cultural hybridisation to supplement his biological hybridity, Peevay provides a potential narrative of the nation that challenges the colonisers' discourse of territorial expansion and cultural homogenisation. Once again, hybridity, as the starting point for mixed-race Peevay, is inevitable if not desirable, and offers the only viable form of national identity. Finally Galbraith's optimistic (and ultimately deeply ironic) title reflects the rhetoric of national romance, while the novel itself probes the consequences of the genre's adoption for the representation of Scotland as a nation. It concludes with the acknowledgement that Scottish independence, while romantically satisfying is, for that very reason, historically untenable, and with the acceptance of the new hybrid identity that is Britain. *The Rising Sun* thus disputes the outcome of a romantic understanding of the nation and stresses the genre's potentially pernicious impact on the survival of the nation in the face of actual historical economic conditions.

This concern with hybridity marks a departure from the linear genealogy of *Possession* and *Ever After,* in so far as it implies that there is no univocal origin from which a descent is generated and preserved, because the starting point for the story is already doubled. Indeed, in *The Map of Love* the Anglo-Egyptian family at the centre of the story acquires further hybridising traits in time (initially French and American, and finally Arab-American). There is no guarantee that the linear genealogical links can be retraced through time, and they need to be reiterated and re-established for each successive generation and horizontally in the present. Hybridity also calls into question the reliance on rightful inheritance, transmission, and ownership in the denouement of the earlier novels. These elements are imbricated in the rhetoric and practice of the imperial enterprise. As Anderson explains, '[c]olonial racism was a major element in that conception of "Empire" which attempted to weld dynastic legitimacy and national community' (151). In order legally and discursively to justify 'their interloper status' in the colonised territories, the Europeans made use of the principle of 'the legal inheritance and the legal transferability of geographic space' (174). The process whereby an act of conquest was enshrined in law involved the reconstruction of what Anderson dubs 'the property-history of their new possessions' (174), in other words a quasi-genealogical retracing of the history of 'specific tightly-bounded territorial units' with the aim of providing a validating 'political-biographical narrative' of that territory (174). The spurious linear descent thus created makes the imperial power the rightful owner of a territory it had already annexed, and the means for the creation is, once again, the map, this time in a chronologically sequential arrangement. Discursive articulation and actual appropriation are mutually supportive.

Taken together the three novels trace a reverse trajectory of imperial and national enterprises and question the assumptions on which these are founded, in particular the idea of racial, ethnic and cultural differences and the hierarchy they entail: from being established and accepted (and therefore needing to be contested) in Soueif, these ideas are shown in the process of being articulated by Kneale, who in the character of Anglo-Saxon supremacist Dr. Potter ridicules the *ad hoc* nature of racial theories, while Galbraith finds that difference is already at the heart of the fledgling unified Britain at the beginning of its sustained imperial expansion. The discursive and political needs of the imperial power foster a sense of national uniformity in the colonists' communities and in the imperial metropolis, as the 'other' in the colonial encounter is articulated in terms of difference from the white Briton, but in fact, as Young points out, the very reassertion of the 'fixity, ... certainty, centeredness, homogeneity' (2) of national identity as 'something unproblematically identical with itself' implies the desire and need to quash 'a counter-sense of fragmentation and dispersion' (4).

The destabilising attitude towards the received perception of the past intimated by the novels' titles, whether it be the experience of the British empire or the position of Scotland with respect to it, is confirmed by the multiple texts that make up the novels' structure and the narrative self-consciousness that emerges in those texts. In this respect, the novels discussed in this chapter continue the engagement with the past as a documentary record that was so prominent in *The Chymical Wedding, Possession,* and *Ever After.* The archive Soueif, Kneale and Galbraith consult and (re)produce, however, is a specifically imperial one. Consequently, although the representational strategies of the novels in the two chapters are comparable, there are notable differences between the respective uses of chronological discontinuity, self-reflexivity and romance. If, therefore, these novels rely on 'the accidental, the apparently contingent, the less (or more) than logical, the fact refusing to be contained, the fortuitous occurrence, the "random" event, the unplaceable object (in time or space)' (Griffiths 153) to articulate what escapes the strictures of realist parameters of representation, they do so to undermine not the realist tradition *per se,* but rather its ideological complicity with colonialism. As a result, the use of a romantic mode of representation, to which the traits listed above belong, aims to upset the assumptions of colonial discourse, without however operating the mediatory function that Clarke, Byatt and Swift granted it. So, romance, particularly in *The Map of Love,* does have the power to redeem the truth about the past and the individual's experience of it; it is not, however, a restorative tool that mends the break between the past and present. On the contrary, the novels in this chapter resolutely refuse to grant univocal imaginative access to the past in the manner of *Possession* or *Ever After,* displaying instead, even at the end of their narratives, the persisting discontinuity between times and between the fragmentary textual remains of the past.

The latter is apparent in the abundance of authors narrating an event from different, competing and frequently irreconcilable perspectives, in languages that are not always mutually understood, in forms that vary from the imaginative to the factual to the official. The former is emphasised by the fact that, contrary to the works in the previous chapter, *The Map of Love, English Passengers* and *The Rising Sun* appeal not to the historical imagination (and the literary tradition) but to the historical record, with all its limitations and partiality, but also with the power of referentiality it evokes. These novels 'retain ... a mimetic or referential purchase to textuality' which allows for 'the positive production of oppositional truth-claims' (Slemon 5) in dual resistance both to the textual hegemony of colonial discourse and to the uncertain status of reality in works privileging the imagination as the means for recovering the past. Thus, in Soueif's and Galbraith's novels history, including contemporary events, is woven into the plot, with several identifiable episodes and characters making appearances, and debates from the periods of their settings are reproduced extensively. Kneale, on the other hand, provides an unexpected move from fictional to historical frameworks at the very end, when, contrary to the narrative strategy employed throughout, he takes on the mantle of the historian to condemn the ideology that underpinned colonialism and to produce a real document from the archive which, placed side by side with the fictional ones in the novel, implicitly validates them. The move is equal and contrary to Byatt's concluding 'Postscript': where this addition to the plot was granted a greater degree of authenticity because it was not bound by the 'actual' material remnants of the past, Kneale's invented record of settlement, colonisation and exploitation is invested with historical weight by the concluding 'Author's Note'.

The abruptness of the transition from fiction to fact confirms the author's desire to avoid the consolations and mystifications of seamless connections between events, narrative strategies and historical periods as they are operated by an overarching imaginative reconstruction. It further mirrors the violence of the colonists' appropriation of Tasmania by dragging it into (their) history. The result is that these are much more overtly and confidently political texts, which revisit the past not to find consolation in it, but to expose the elements that are sidelined or erased in the process of producing a version of it for general nostalgic consumption as heritage. They do so without abandoning the narrative negotiations upon which *The Chymical Wedding, Possession,* and *Ever After* (not to mention the even earlier texts discussed in Chapter 2) embarked, but rather by exploiting their potential for subversion.

1. Ahdaf Soueif's *The Map of Love*

In *Orientalism* (1987), Edward Said uses at some length the example of Egypt '[b]etween 1882, the year England occupied [it] and put an end to the nationalist rebellion of Colonel Arabi, and 1907' (35) to discuss the intersection between knowledge as perpetuated by a range of pseudo-scientific academic disciplines, colonial discourse and actual occupation and annexation of territories during the period of imperial expansion and beyond. Egypt, according to Said, is 'not just another colony' but holds a paradigmatic significance as 'the vindication of Western imperialism; it was, until its annexation by England, an almost academic example of Oriental backwardness; it was to become the triumph of English knowledge and power' (35). He goes on to examine the narrative and representational strategies whereby a pre-existing conception of the Orient, based on its essential and irreversible difference from the West, is enforced and reinforced by travel writers, scholars and colonial administrators regardless of the actual reality of the land and people they were supposedly describing. What makes Said's work especially resonant with the political and narrative project of *The Map of Love, English Passengers* and *The Rising Sun* is his insistence on the discursive nature of Orientalism, whose textual production accounts for a significant part of the imperial archive, and his concomitant insight that these writings contributed to the acceptable face of the colonial enterprise in so far as they applied benevolent (Western) rationality to domesticate the unknown but, at the same time, reaffirmed its otherness to scholars and readers alike.

Soueif's novel, in particular, re-imagines the situation posited by Said but redefines, at least in part, his pessimistic outlook on the very possibility of meaningful interaction between the West and the Orient in two ways. She probes *Orientalism*'s monolithic depiction of both visitors to Egypt and the consumers of their writings in Britain and she adds a contemporary Egyptian reader, translator and inter-preter, Amal al-Ghamrawi, who provides the Orientalist materials of the nineteenth-century story with a dialogical dimension. The novel's own dialogue with Said's seminal text is extensive. There is a corres-pondence of time and place, as the past timeframe of Soueif's split-time novel is set between England and Egypt in the period from 1896 (stretching back to the notorious Sudan expedition of Gordon and forward to Kitchener's) to 1913. Lord Cromer, British governor of Egypt, features prominently directly and indirectly in both texts, while in the contemporary timeframe the character of 'Omar al-Ghamrawi, a charismatic musician of Egyptian Palestinian origin disparagingly dubbed '[t]he "Molotov Maestro"' and 'the "Kalashnikov Conductor"' (17) because of his political activism and a disillusioned member of the Palestinian National Council, is modelled on Edward Said himself. The dissection of the Western attitude towards Egypt on the part of Sharif al-Baroudi, one of the protagonists of the past timeframe, echoes the theory of colonial discourse in *Orientalism*:

> Put simply, the East holds...[a] Religious, Historical, Romantic attraction to the land of the Scriptures, of the Ancients, and of Fable. This attraction is born in the European while he is still *in his home country.* When he comes here, he finds that the land is inhabited by people he does not understand and possibly does not much like. What options are open to him? He may stay and try to ignore them. He may try to change them. He may leave. Or he may try to understand them. (481)

Where Said explores in detail the first three options, *The Map of Love* concentrates on the final one. In its past narrative it records the pro-cess of progressive mutual understanding between a representative Englishwoman and her Egyptian husband and family; taken in its entirety, with its careful tracing of historical causes and consequences reaching to the present day, the novel offers the means to facilitating that understanding.

The initial impulse for Lady Anna Winterbourne's (the protagonist of the Edwardian story and, through her diaries and letters, one of the novel's several narrators) decision to travel to Egypt is typically Orientalist. Grieving for her husband, who has returned sick in body and mind from being part of Kitchener's troops avenging Gordon, she finds respite in the paintings of Frederick Lewis. It is his vision of the East, characterised by luminous interiors and intricate architectural detail, that leads her to visit the country on her husband's death. Thus, the idealised and the brutal versions of empire are the very origins of the story and it is important to note that Soueif does not discount the former as unrealistic: understanding the motives for the European fascination with the East is part of the possible peaceful co-existence the novel envisages as desirable (though not necessarily achievable). Anna goes to Egypt armed with the notoriously Orientalist Cook's travel guide, quotes Edward Lane's translation of the Arabian Nights as an early mediator in her experience of Egypt, and, as Amal comments during her editing 100 years later, her first letter is 'a little self-conscious perhaps, a little aware of the genre – *Letters from Egypt, A Nile Voyage, More Letters from Egypt*' (58). She reaches the epitome of conventional attitudes and desires when, at a ball, she spots '*a kind of narrow gallery … around the higher portion of the wall and at the back of that was a curious golden grille, behind which I was told the ladies of the household sat and watched the proceedings if they had a mind to. My interest was naturally immediately captured by this and throughout the evening I found myself glancing up at it*' (93). The Orientalist texts that guided Anna's approach to the country would, as Rana Kabbani (1986) has suggested in a study influenced by Said's work, have used the harem as 'a self-perpetuating *topos*', used to construct 'a definitive edifice of sexuality and despotism [… which] became a metaphor for the whole East' (18). However, the visitor's reactions soon deviate from the norm, as she envisages an identification with the reverse point of view from behind the harem screen: recognising that her '*curiosity about the world behind that screen*' is '*commonplace*', Anna expresses the '*greater wish … somehow to know how we, in the Ballroom, appeared to the hidden eyes which watched us*' (93). The novel affords her the opportunity to fulfil this desire. Thus, hidden under a full black veil that leaves only her eyes visible, she observes from close quarters her fellow Westerners, who suddenly appear as '*bright, exotic creatures*' (195), thus taking on the very characteristics with which 'the classic scene of travel literature' invested the Orient in an 'unexpected reversal of the gaze' (Hassan 762).

Soueif's strategy, then, consists of providing a gendered perspective that complicates the power relations played out in the colonial context (a trait the novel shares with *Heat and Dust*), of offering private documents as additions to the colonial archive that may destabilise its homogeneity, and of arguing for the possibility of individual relations founded on love (real, sustained contact between East and West) that defy the hegemony of colonial discourse. The image used to signify knowledge beyond and against the ideological structures of Orientalism is the view from, rather than of, the harem, made possible by the fact that Soueif's protagonist is a woman. The significance of this choice rests on the fact that the harem occupied a privileged place in the Western imaginary as the epitome of all that is most desirable because forbidden, exotic because socially most different (visibly so, since a screen separates the women's quarters in the public areas of the house) about the Orient. Forays into the harem and revelations about it are acts of discursive as well as actual power, in so far as they are achieved by transgressing a set of boundaries to do with gender, propriety and cultural habits the male Western visitor simply does not accept as applicable to him. Indeed, there is a tradition of literary representations of the harem by male European writers that encodes it within the parameters of otherness and implicitly points to the reasons for the Orient's supposed decline, from which European interventions would rescue it. Thus, the presumed decadent lasciviousness of the women enclosed there, the degeneracy of the eunuchs guarding them, the untold pleasures to be had, all of which are abundantly found in accounts of the harem, discursively operate a gendering of the East that opposes it to the masculine all-conquering Western presence. It is a conquest that starts with (and is symbolised by) entry into the forbidden place.

That this is a conscious rebuttal on Soueif's part is evident from her parodic articulation of the Orientalist view, as in this exchange between Anna and her Egyptian husband, Sharif:

> '[...] Weren't you afraid of me? The wicked Pasha who would lock you up in his harem and do terrible things to you?'
> 'What terrible things?'
> 'You should know. They're in your English stories. Calling in my black Eunuchs to tie you up–' (153–4)

Soueif dismantles this image of the harem by entrusting the narrative in her past timeframes to two women, Layla and Anna, the former belonging to the harem, the other admitted to it and taking up her place there, who together offer a prosaic, even mundane view of this mythically exotic space. In tracing the relationship between Anna and her acquired Egyptian family the novel also suggests that equal and opposite preconceptions were harboured towards the British (a case of 'Occidentalism'): her sister-in-law acknowledges that Anna 'had none of the arrogance or the coldness we were used to imagining in her countrymen' (372). Soueif broadens the scope of Said's work and abstracts its parameters of enquiry, focusing on misunderstandings that are mutual between peoples and cultures, but which can also be overcome at an individual level.

The transition from a mediated to an actual experience of the Orient, from preconceptions to understanding, takes place, subversively, by means of a stock romantic situation, namely the journey to the desert in the company of a 'Pasha'. The mutual attraction, undeniably sexual, and the ensuing love between Anna and Sharif transgresses numerous Orientalist categories, not least those concerned with the gendered understanding of the East and the resulting dynamics of power. There is an interesting ambivalence in the novel with regard to the generic and ideological elements that characterise romance. It can be misguided, as in the case of Edward Winterbourne, Anna's first husband, whose ideals of honour, duty, and manliness are defeated when confronted with the reality of the imperial enterprise in all its indiscriminate violence. It can also open the way to real empathy for Anna and Sharif. The difference rests in the couple's willingness and ability to pierce romance's received notions and accept their experience of '*all that desert and stars business*' (235) as real: she 'penetrate[s] the stereotype; now she is in the painting, she is in the tale' (Muaddi Darraj 103). As was the case for *The Chymical Wedding*, *Possession* and *Ever After*, consummation is the means to imprinting the romance onto reality: it is no coincidence that Anna's first marriage is defined by sexual frustration, which occasions '*stirrings and impulses of so contrary a nature that I was like a creature devoid of reason*' (13), while her relationship to Sharif is underlined by a physical attraction that grants them a level of mutual understanding beyond the difficulties of their different cultures and languages.

However, contrary to those novels, the achievement made possible by romance is not imaginatively represented by an Edenic garden with narratively metaphoric and nationally metonymic significance. Indeed, while Anna is still in England she cannot find solace in her garden during her husband's illness, but is instead soothed by the exotic interiors in Lewis's paintings; her romantic and then real experiences of Egypt take place, respectively, in the desert and in the tiled courtyard of her house. The otherness of the latter's layout is emphasised at numerous turns, while Anna draws inspiration from Lewis's paintings in furnishing her rooms, so that representation and reality become conflated. However, Sharif's attempt to plant and cultivate an English garden for his daughter, and somehow hybridise the house, does not come to fruition: he is assassinated by political opponents before he can complete the project and on his death it becomes impossible for Anna to remain in the country. Only on her return to England does she resume the care of her garden, and it marks the failure to project understanding between individuals from the private to the public sphere. As Layla remarks, Anna 'was not able to bring him peace of mind. It was as though he was angry that his happy private life should exist within public circumstances that he hated. Or as though he longed that his personal happiness should extend to encompass all of Egypt' (373). The incomplete garden stands for the ethical impasse between the impossibility of retrenchment and the intrusion of public life into the private domain.

The unresolved negotiations between textual and actual experience, public and private commitments reappear in the contemporary narrative, to be placed under the scrutiny of Amal al-Ghamrawi. Her role is that of mediator between past and present, East and West, for the benefit of her newly rediscovered American cousin Isabel (Anna Winterbourne's great-granddaughter). The occasion for Amal's mediatory role is an act of translation, in all senses of the word. The physical remains of the past, which consist of 'old papers in English ... many papers and documents in Arabic ... other things: objects' (7) contained in an old-fashioned trunk, are translated like holy relics back to the place where they originated, Egypt. The retracing of the past that the contemporary characters undertake thus begins with a politically significant act of restitution, a recognition that the history whose narration had been appropriated by the West ought to be retold from the perspective of the subjects of that history. The novel also suggests that this benevolent intervention over the past is made possible by the fact that all the main protagonists in the story are women, for whom 'a hundred year – or a continent' make little difference: '[Anna] could have been Arwa, or Deena, or any of the girls I grew up with here in Cairo in the Sixties' (12). Female solidarity, it appears, overcomes difference. Amal is also a suitable mediator because she has experienced cultural difference: married to an Englishman from whom she separated, '[o]nce upon a time [she] lived ... in a house our of a Victorian novel, with stairs and fireplaces and floral cornices round the ceilings, and the sound of passing trains muffled by the lush trees at the bottom of the long garden' (45). The fairytale opening and the textually pre-determined setting imply an analogy with Anna's initial expectations of Egypt and an equivalent experience of cultural otherness for both women.

The papers are then translated in a more literal sense from Arabic into English for Isabel, reversing the situation bemoaned by Anna a century earlier: *'I have come to believe that the fact that it falls to Englishmen to speak for Egypt is in itself perceived as a weakness; for how can the Egyptians govern themselves, people ask, when they cannot even speak for themselves?'* (399) Linguistic mediation in the novel is an important dimension of productive cultural understanding, in contrast with the privileging of sensual, inarticulate experience (the words made things) of the novels in the previous chapter, which was in turn made possible by their projection of cultural uniformity. In the past timeframe, linguistic mediation consists of using French as a neutral means of communication between Anna and her husband, because 'it makes foreigners of [them] both' (157) and forces them to find words that transcend their respective preconceptions, which, as Said and Soueif concur, are linguistically and discursively motivated and enforced. Both Anna and Isabel undertake to study Arabic, and it is in the latter's investigations that the garden, no longer a physical space but a linguistic construct, can be rediscovered: ' "al-Jannah" – Paradise, the place that is hidden –' [...] ' "junaynah", garden, is little paradise –' (492). However, despite the empowering speaking position for Amal, there is little she can do to solve problems that are substantially comparable to those unsuccessfully fought by Sharif. In the contemporary story the novel pits discursive awareness against action: Amal's friends are an intellectual elite who, as one of them puts it, 'sit in the Atelier or the Grillon and talk to each other. And when we write, we write for each other. We have absolutely no connection with the people' (224). This sense of paralysis is brought to the fore by the suicide of one of their group, interpreted as an act both desperate and assertive. Against her powerlessness in the present, Amal finds solace in the past, whose 'beauty' is that '[y]ou leave it and come back to it and it waits for you – unchanged. You can turn back the pages, look again at the beginning. You can leaf forward and know the end. And you can tell the story that they, the people who lived it, could only tell in part' (234). Against her inability effectively to intervene in national affairs, she attempts to influence the village around her ancestral home and land.

In a context where an educated elite strives to understand the appeal of Islamic fundamentalism for the urban and rural poor, Amal's decision to move to Tawasi takes on political significance in spite of the fact that she describes it to herself as a step away from the troubled environment of Cairo. In so far as the villagers in Tawasi are affected personally by the politically repressive regime, but at the same time show resilience and generosity, the remote country province comes to epitomise the nation within a specifically romantic typology of national narrative, which places the people, rather than their political representatives, as both agents and subjects. When the school and clinic, which had been established by Sharif al-Baroudi, are closed by government soldiers, what is being undermined is not simply the optimistic attempt at modernisation but also the social system of near-feudal patronage and paternalism, albeit in 'enlightened' form, of the earlier twentieth century. When Amal takes up residence in the family home, she receives gifts, visits and reports from the villagers as if *she* were the authority there, a role she endeavours to fulfil for their benefit with only limited success. The crisis is resolved only through the intervention of a childhood friend and neighbour, himself a landowner and entrepreneur with influence on the governor of the province and on the central Egyptian government itself. This power, however, is acquired and exercised at the expense of inclusive national ideals, as Tareq, to Amal's horror, is willing to engage a team of Israeli agricultural engineers to improve the productivity of his land. He responds to her shock and accusation ' "I thought you were a patriot" ' (202) by proposing an alternative, pragmatic, understanding of the nation that eschews 'old ideologies' in favour of 'economics': ' "I am a patriot. I do more for my country by strengthening its economy than I would by sitting in a rut and hoping things will take the course I want somehow. [...] [T]his isn't an emotional issue. It's a practical one"' (202–3).

Tareq's stance is supported by a rejection of narrative in the articulation of the nation, accompanied in turn by a refusal to let history (including the question of Palestine) affect action in the present. Amal's reconstruction of the events of a century earlier functions as a rebuttal of this position. On the level of historical events, the documents contained in Isabel's trunk trace the early stages of the increasingly substantial Jewish presence in Palestine and propose some of the causes for the situation in the Middle East at the end of the century. The unfolding conflict between Israeli and Palestinians (and, by extension, all Arabs) in turn punctuates Amal's own life. She was born 'in the year of Nasser's revolution' (117), her mother was a Palestinian who was dispossessed at the creation of the State of Israel in 1948, an event her father fought by leading a volunteer battalion only to be defeated. Amal took part in demonstrations in support of Egyptian forces during the six-day war against Israel, and then against Sadat's peace agreement with what was widely perceived as a national enemy. In both cases she witnessed the defeat of her side, so that her life becomes the story of deflated national aspirations and grubby compromise. On the level of discursive engagement with existing (mis)representations of the East, appropriating her family's narrative, which reveals a national narrative, is an act of personal and political assertion, all the more so as it contrasts with the sense of immobility projected onto Egypt by the essentialist and immutable categories of Orientalism.

Edward Said suggests that there is '[a] conflict between a holistic view of the Orient (description, monumental record) and a narrative of events in the Orient' (240). The former sees the object of its description as static, 'panoptically' (240) available to the scrutiny of the Western observer, and denies it the possibility of historical change, including independent government. The Orient, in this version, is a space – indeed a painting, like Anna's favourite ones – rather than a text. It is no coincidence that in his translation of the *Arabian Nights* Edward Lane uses any opportunity to add notes, glosses and explanations, thus diminishing the narrative thrust of the text in favour of a synoptic arrangement that delays, and distracts from, the unfolding of the stories. The latter, on the other hand, with its inherent diachronicity, 'suggests that history, with its disruptive detail, its currents of change, its tendency towards growth, decline, or dramatic movement, is possible in the Orient and for the Orient' (240). The recuperation of narrative in *The Map of Love* takes as its starting point the unpromisingly spatial trunk, whose contents Amal turns into a love story which is also, in the most traditional sense of the term, history, namely, a retrospective enquiry into the causes of present events, which are traced back to significant moments in the past. Thus, in the novel the details in the present which appear to confirm the static image of the East (the fact, for instance, that in 100 years and in spite of independence little appears to have changed) are countered by a wish to probe the origins of each situation. What neither Amal nor Anna and Sharif before her can achieve, however, is a system, and more accurately a national narrative, that encompasses both public and private, without sacrificing one in favour of the other.

2. Matthew Kneale's *English Passengers*

Isabel's decision in *The Map of Love* to travel to Egypt derives from an intuitive perception of historical time: she wants 'to see what people in a really old country thought of [the millennium]' (19). In her imagination, and regardless of any family ties, going to Egypt is 'like going back to the beginning. Six thousand years of recorded history' (19). When applied to Australia and placed in the mouths of nineteenth-century Englishmen, this attitude becomes the ideological underpinning of the pseudo-scientific and religious expeditions narrated in *English Passengers*. Tony Bennett (2004) describes the operations of colonial discourse in relation to the exploration and appropriation of antipodean territories: 'the placing of the Other in a time different from that of the observer, and the equation of distance from Europe with travelling back in time' (1) served to situate the aborigines within an evolutionary discourse that defined them as a survival from the civilised West's past and, at the same time, to deny them a history of their own. In other words, Australia is predicated as 'a point of origin, still discernible in the present, for evolutionary processes which have their culmination in the modern West', and is, of necessity, 'placed outside of time, at its beginning' (Bennett 137). Matthew Kneale illustrates the European position with respect to Australia in the characters of the Reverend Wilson and Dr. Potter, the English Passengers of the title. In the novel's structure, on the other hand, he challenges the combination of historicist and evolutionary thinking described by Bennett: there are two narrative strands, one, beginning in the 1830s, recounts the early events in the colonisation of Tasmania; the other, in 1857, is concerned with the voyage of the *Sincerity* from the Isle of Man to the antipodes by way of London and Maldon, and with the crew's escape from the charge of smuggling (it is one of the novel's many ironies that the flight from the authorities takes them to the most feared penal colony in the Empire). The two stories unfold towards each other and finally join half-way through the novel, thus not only formally reproducing the colonial encounter experienced by Wilson and Potter, on the one hand, and Peevay, on the other, but also presenting Australia as already part of (Western) history.

Reverend Wilson's belief that the earthly location of the Garden of Eden is to be found in Tasmania is an instance of the more general understanding of the antipodean territories, variously seen as a-historical or pre-historical. It is also affected by the rhetoric of narratives of exploration he reads prior to the journey, which emphasise the strangeness of the land and its timeless quality and either conveniently expunge the presence of the original inhabitants, so that the place becomes a paradise ready to be regained and repopulated, or present them as innocent curiosities, their innocence only confirming the Edenic element in the descriptions. However, the very presence of the European settlers has deprived Tasmania of any innocence: ironically, the Governor justifies the rigours of the penal establishment and their unflinching implementation that extends even to the settlers by denying the possibility of anyone being '*irrevocably innocent* [...] [s]*ince the time of Adam and Eve*' (136). The penal colony is in fact an elaborate parodic reversal of the Garden. The guilty are sent to it for punishment and, more rarely, expiation, a state which, if attained, grants them a reprieve in the form of expulsion from the Garden. God's omniscience becomes the Governor's ambitious creation of '*the most thorough arrangements for the assembling of information yet devised in any land*' (135), while one of the escaped convicts is found out and arrested in the act of having sex with a prostitute. Unsurprisingly, Reverend Wilson is defeated in his attempts to reach the site of the earthly paradise by the place's nature, which is wild, teeming, disturbingly unfamiliar and arguably in its full terrifying manifestation a paradoxical proof of his arguments for locating Eden in Tasmania. It is, however, a paradise that cannot be regained, because it does not conform to the Reverend's anticipation of 'a lush yet ordered abundance, a garden in the wilderness' (15).

This 'civilised' understanding of paradise is, of course, culturally determined and Wilson's vague longings are in fact fulfilled not by what is peculiarly Tasmanian but rather by the recreation of what he has left behind, as on arrival at Hobart he reflects on '[h]ow pleasing it was to find a place, though it lay on the remotest side of the earth, where everything...was unmistakeably *English*. Better still, this was an Englishness of a charmingly old-fashioned kind, that quite took me back to the days of my own youth, before the railways sent everyone rushing so' (317). The sense of recognition is tinged with nostalgia and reflects what I have described with respect to *The French Lieutenant's Woman* as a national identity defined by loss and mourning that is peculiarly English and, in this case, implies a version of the Fall marked by the appearance of the train. It appears, then, that Tasmania functions as a historical Other culturally in relation to England and technology as much as it was assumed to do so scientifically with respect to evolutionary theory and the earth more generally. The authorities even attempt to reproduce this cultural and social model in the aboriginal reservations, where the 'crusade to civilise the blacks' consists of allocating to each a craft 'that they would be required to develop as their own' so that it 'might with time transform them into something like a happy band of English villagers' (244). This is not, however, a purely nostalgic dream: the crafts involve remuneration and, with it, the spending of money, in other words the introduction of 'that most essential pillar of the civilised world, commerce' (244) where none was known. The nostalgic recreation contains what had proved to be the seeds of its undermining in Britain.

If Tasmania ever was a paradise, then, the very presence of those who would recognise the notion of Eden taints it. As was the case for the penal settlements, in the reservations, nominally created for the protection of the aborigines but in fact favouring the dispossession of their land by white settlers, are enacted parodies of the Genesis story. Their inhabitants are forced to wear clothes because their nakedness shames their guardians; they have to undergo a process of renaming – a combination of mock-baptism and Adamic undertaking – by the Europeans, with names drawn from history (Napoleon and Cromwell, for instance), thus providing a system of recognition founded not on individual identity but on a perceived and imposed similarity with personages alien to the aborigines. Indeed, in view of the widespread assumption that Australia is a place without history, in this process of renaming the settlers are imposing on the place and its inhabitants a past which pre-determines their fate: in the 'progressive' manifestation of history as conceived and articulated by the Europeans, in fact, they will always be the losers.

It is in this context that Peevay's own narrative, co-terminus with, yet independent of, colonial textual production, becomes a national chronicle and a narrative of discursive resistance to the cultural and physical impositions of colonial power. On the one hand, the very existence of a written record in English is a mark of the Fall from what Peevay, without any need for further specifications, calls 'the world,' as a result of the colonial encounter that has already happened and cannot be undone. Neither writing nor, of course, the English language existed there prior to the arrival of the first settlers, so Peevay finds himself recording in an alien medium both the oral transmission of stories from the past that constitute a history unrecognised by European written culture and the nomadic life that accompanied it and which, again, is easily re-envisaged by the settlers as further confirmation of the aborigines' backwardness. And yet, concomitantly with this implicit acceptance of defeat of a way of life, Peevay's text also succeeds in recording the customs, traditions and social relations of his people, even making the early sections, concerned with naming the world, an alternative story of the Genesis. It includes the shameful recognition on his part not of nakedness but of difference: when Peevay sees his face reflected in a pond, he realises that he is not like his companions; it outlines temptation in the form of Mr. Robson, who appears to offer the tribe salvation only to enforce banishment from their world, and records Peevay's weakness to those promises, as he betrays his mother and alerts Robson to their position.

The combination, on the one hand, of cultural and linguistic compromise following the colonial encounter and, on the other, of assertion of the prior existence of an indigenous social and cultural system makes Peevay's narrative a form of 'autoethnographic text'. Mary

Louise Pratt (1994) defines this as

> a text in which people undertake to describe themselves in ways
> that engage with representations others have made of them. [...]
> [A]utoethnographic texts are representations that the so-defined
> others construct *in response to* ... those texts. Autoethnographic
> texts are not, then, what are usually thought of as autochthon-
> ous or "authentic" forms of self-representations [...]. Rather they
> involve a selective collaboration with and appropriation of
> idioms of the metropolis or conqueror. These are merged or infil-
> trated to varying degrees with indigenous idioms to create self-
> representations intended to *intervene* in metropolitan modes of
> understanding. (28)

The linguistically hybrid nature of the text, as well as the ambiguity
of its addressees 'both metropolitan audiences and the speaker's own
community' (Pratt 29), is well suited to the biologically hybrid
Peevay, who uses the narrative to articulate the complexity of his
belonging to and difference from white and aboriginal environments
alike. His narrative performs a double function. With respect to the
colonial authorities, it destabilises the assumptions of their discourse;
in relation to the aborigines themselves, it proposes a national chronicle of resistance.

Peevay is perceived as a threat by the colonial authorities. As the
Governor's wife points out, he passes for 'a notorious maker of
trouble' because 'he had learned to mimic the ways of an Englishman
just well enough to be a perfect nuisance [...]' (312). He does not
therefore conform to 'the true aborigines, who showed such a touching resignation as to their lamentable fate' (313). The challenge posed
by mimicry to the coherence of colonial (self)representation is identified by Bhabha (1994) as a rupturing of the surface of identity and
difference: it proposes a colonial subject that is 'almost the same, *but
not quite*' (86). The word itself is semantically and phonetically close
to 'mockery, where the reforming, civilising mission is threatened by
the displacing gaze of its disciplinary double' (Bhabha 86). To counter
the potentially destabilising effect of mimicry, authenticity is conveniently equated with disempowerment, and is further inserted
within an elegiac discourse that inherently deprives the aborigines
of any possibility of historical agency or even survival. Indeed, to

Mrs. Adler they are already a disembodied curiosity indistinguishable in their passive and immobile status from the 'objects of their own manufacture' of which she intends to 'assemble a small, yet perhaps not unimportant collection' which, displayed in her London house would form 'a delightful and also most touching reminder of our time spent upon this faraway shore' (313). Even while they are still alive, therefore, the last surviving Tasmanian aborigines are already envisaged as part of a private museum that will illustrate not their lives but the colonisers' experiences in an alien land: it is fitting that one of Mrs. Adler's tokens should be a photograph of a group of aboriginal women posing with their pipes arranged in their laps in a manner that she considers authentic. The natives are the recipients of a Christian compassion that never stops to consider what their lives mean in an interpretive framework other than the European or indeed that they even had a life before colonisation. This attitude is comparable to Reverend Wilson's conviction as to the early location of paradise. As Walyeric, Peevay's mother, puts it, ' "You say God made Eden Garden long ago? Well, everybody knows God never came here till you white men brought him in your boats" ' (325). She is claiming a past for the land and its people independent of the history imposed on it by the arrival of the first settlers, and with fitting rhetoric identifies the moment of aboriginal Fall with the introduction of the idea of Eden.

But it is Peevay's narrative that challenges the Eurocentric 'division between pre- and post-occupation Australia as one between history, defined in terms of text, writing and documents, and prehistory as the realm of silent and inert objects' (Bennett 152), in so far as it provides that silence and inertness with a voice and a chronological existence in terms that the colonisers cannot dismiss as unintelligible. In borrowing and indiscriminately conflating Biblical rhetoric and demotic expression ('piss-poor situations' alternate with 'tidings of joy') Peevay points to the complicity of missionary activity with aggressive conquest and slaughter. At the same time, he produces a new and compound language that gives expression to the experiences of the aborigines. This aspect of the novel can usefully be examined in contrast with J.G. Farrell's treatment of a comparable character, Hari the Maharajah's son, who received an English education by his tutor but, perhaps because of the formal structure of his learning which discouraged the imaginative appropriation of an other culture, ends up an imperfect hybrid. Hari's habits, which include eating an egg for breakfast while reading *Blackwood's Magazine* and sitting uncomfortably on a hard chair when the native cushions would have been preferable, are, like his ill-fitting suit of Western cut, an unsuccessful attempt at mimicry. So is his tendency to resort to slightly inaccurate and very inappropriate quotations from Shakespeare, another sign that he understands the culture he professes to admire only in part and has not assimilated it to his own. As a result, Hari's forays into English are funny but never threatening, nor can they conceivably form the basis for a national narrative in resistance to and competition with the imperial one.

It is important that Peevay's should be a uniform and unified text as opposed to the scattering of disparate documents that compose the colonial authorities' version of events. Bhabha posits a difference between 'the spirit of the Western nation...symbolised in epic and anthem, voiced by a "unanimous people assembled in the self-presence of its speech"' and 'the sign of colonial government...cast in a lower key, caught in the irredeemable act of *writing*' (Bhabha 93). Somewhat counter-intuitively, he suggests that colonial expansion leads to a disaggregation of national identity. This point is presented in more nuanced ways in *English Passengers*. Although the textual multiplicity that conveys the colonisers' perspective does to an extent prove power and control over the written medium, the lack of a univocal voice suggests at the same time the fragility of their sense of identity and its potential for fragmenting into competing individualities. Peevay, on the other hand, performs in writing the function of the epic and becomes the spokesperson for his people. His narrative stands in contrast with the European version of aboriginal history in that it is ultimately a story of survival rather than extinction: the elegiac tone of the former is replaced by the continuous self-reinvention engendered by the progressive acquisition of discursive ability and the parallel appropriation of its means of expression. Two moments mark the national dimension of Peevay's story. The first is his use of the newspapers to find out information about the events of his people: thus, one of Benedict Anderson's cornerstones of national discourse is co-opted for a different national purpose. What to Peevay had 'once...seemed just white men's stuff' becomes 'mine, too' (346). The power of the medium rests on the fact that events in newspapers 'couldn't be hidden' and on the white men's erroneous conviction that 'our ones [n]ever would see' (346). The second and culminating moment in the national narrative, and what ultimately transforms it from one of death to one of survival, is Peevay's arrival on an island formerly inhabited by seal hunters but now home to a mixed group that includes 'one like a white man ... but there, just beside was another who was dark like Mother. Others were mixed like me' (448). It is a place that has no relics of a past, as the white men and native women that generated the present group are all dead. The peaceful co-existence of this variegated group offers Peevay an alternative paradise to either the Biblical one that is no more than an expression of colonial power or the one he knew as a child and lost with colonisation. His self-appointed task amongst his 'mob' is to 'give them teachings. I tell them writing and laws, white men's tricks and Bible cheating and more' (449). In other words, it is knowledge that preserves this newly gained Eden for the aborigines.

Peevay's intellectual and linguistic abilities are a challenge to the second English passenger, Dr. Potter, who represents the complicity of Victorian science with the imperial enterprise, not only in practical terms but crucially in expounding a coherent racist ideology that justifies Britain's territorial expansion. Modelled on the notorious real-life racial theorist Dr. Knox, Potter's notebooks and completed book, excerpts of which form part of the textual array in the novel, propose a hierarchical gradation of 'races'. At the top are the Saxons, followed by the Normans, the Celts, and then the various non-European races, with the Australian aborigines coming last and supposedly being the least developed, indeed barely human. In common with the historicist attitude described at the start of this section, Potter's views envisage 'immutable categories oblivious to ... historical dynamism' (Suleri 106). In this system, imperial expansion is simply the fulfilment of racial (and national) destiny:

> There is, in truth, no finer manifestation of the destiny of men than this mighty institution of imperial conquest. Here we see the stolid and fearless Saxon Type, his nature revealed as never before as he strides forth in his great quest, subduing and scattering inferior nations – the Hindoo, the American Indian, the Aboriginal race of Australia – and replacing these with his own stalwart sons. Brave yet unseeing, he little comprehends the unalterable destiny that leads him on: the all-powerful laws of the races of men. (280)

Potter's book conflates physiological and psychological characteristics and defines national belonging to a pre-determined and unchangeable objective set of traits, negating both historical development and consensual acceptance as fundamental to the nation. Hybridity, which the ending of *English Passengers* celebrates and proposes as a viable starting position for a new national unit, is of itself a scandal to the system of human classification that guides the scientist.

Peevay's 'mob' at the end of the novel is proof of the limitations and downright blindness of Potter's position, whose strict deductive logic (where the pre-existing theory is applied to any encounter which is then axiomatically made to confirm it) proves inflexible and contributes to his downfall. His voyage to Tasmania is undertaken in order to gather what he euphemistically calls specimens but are in fact aboriginal bodies, skeletons, and internal organs removed without permission or even the knowledge of the authorities, let alone the aborigines. Among the specimens is Walyeric, Peevay's mother, an action for which Potter believes he will go undetected and unpunished because he consistently underestimates Peevay's ability to investigate the events surrounding his mother's death and the desecration and theft of her body. In fact, Peevay succeeds in piecing together Potter's role in the illegal autopsy, in locating his mother's remains, and in exposing Potter's crimes not to the colonial government but to the crew of the *Sincerity*, who, as Manxmen, have equally been the object of the scientist's theories. Not only do they kill him, but, in an ironic twist that is perhaps more telling than death itself, his unrecognisable remains are finally exhibited at a science museum as '*unknown male presumed Tasmanian aborigine – Possible victim of human sacrifice*' (454), persisting demonstration that it is impossible to tell the difference between races according to purely physical parameters and disproving Potter's own beliefs.

3. Douglas Galbraith's *The Rising Sun*

Dr. Munroe, one of the would-be Scottish colonists in Douglas Galbraith's novel, proposes a eulogy to hybridity when he reflects that '[o]ne thing I have learned is that everything strong in Nature comes from mixture. Purity is a perversion to her and she always destroys it in the end' (373). The sentence may be taken as an epitaph to the enterprise narrated by *The Rising Sun* as well as being a pre-emptive acknowledgement of its inevitable failure, both actual and imaginative. Set in the last years of the seventeenth century, the novel revisits, with some liberties as to the historical record, Scotland's attempt to set up a trading empire in competition with its wealthier neighbour, by founding a colony in Darien, on the isthmus of Panama. The story is informed by the retrospective knowledge that this bout of national assertiveness would in fact result in its opposite, namely the Act of Union with England of 1707 and the disappearance of Scotland as an autonomous state, since the failure of an enterprise in which the nation had invested all its meagre resources would result in bankruptcy and the acceptance of England's offer to bail out (or buy out) its neighbour.

This retrospection is replicated in the narrative form, which proposes a variation on the doubling pattern of the novels examined thus far: where split-time arrangements draw attention to the temporal chasm and difference between past and present, and the joining plot strands of *English Passengers* maps the geographical distance travelled by the characters, *The Rising Sun* proposes an internally divided narrative. Its narrator is Roderick Mackenzie, a leading participant in the Darien expedition, whose early labelling of his tale as 'the story of a Britishman' (6) points to the intersection of the prospective unfolding of the story and its retrospective evaluation. The term Britishman, in fact, conflates the type of ship in which the expedition is undertaken, and therefore the subject of Mackenzie's narrative at the start, with the consequences of that expedition's failure, the swallowing of a particular nationality into a generic one (from Scottish to British), thus anticipating the narrator's position at the end of his tale. If the novel traces the events that lead from one to the other, among which are the unsuitable climate of the location for the colonial outpost, the government-enforced competitive advantage of the East India Company over its newly founded Scottish counterpart, and the moral and financial inadequacy of the enterprise's leaders, this initial semantic ambiguity also points to a fundamental congenital shortcoming in the national narrative that accompanies the imperial aspirations, namely, its insistence on sameness rather than otherness. The two narrative strands that meet in Mackenzie's narrative tell the same story, just as the journey to

Darien only leads to a meeting with an inadequate national self rather than a nationally validating colonial otherness.

The colonial enterprise is explicitly articulated within the framework of national definition: the narrator places himself in the position of 'the historian of Caledonia' (223), while also aspiring to composing the epic of the nation, 'the Scotiad' (12). The double label reiterates Mackenzie's wavering perspective on the events: while as a historian he is required to tell the story of the colonial adventure from an ideal position after its end, as an epic storyteller he will project the tale forward from one event to the next without necessarily envisaging an end. In other words, the nation described is both completed and still in the making at the same time. The flotilla of ships led by the eponymous *Rising Sun* that leaves the port of Leith laden with the trading goods purchased with subscriptions from the entire nation and from all levels of society forms 'a wooden archipelago' (15), with the boats its 'neighbouring villages' (18). Severing itself from the geographical impediment of being attached to England, the expedition embodies the aspiration of a nation to assert its unity and homogeneity by replicating itself first on board the ships, and eventually on the colonised land. And yet, while it may be true, as Mackenzie optimistically suggests, that the expedition contained 'all the lading for a new, human ark; every breed of man and everything they made' (198), its very comprehensiveness harbours the seeds of internal strife: the 'bitter division ... between some of the officers and the clansmen of the Highland regiments' is a legacy of 'the great massacre' of Glencoe only a few years previously (198). Although the physical separation from the mainland signalled by the ships' departure symbolically marks a move towards a national future, the persistence of (and regard for) the past undermines the foundation of a new nation before it has even begun. Deprived of an external object of confrontation, the pattern of self-definition by means of an identifiable statement of difference is turned inward, with the result that '[t]here can be no pretence any more of our being a single colony: Caledonia is divided' (378). The unity of the nation was maintained but briefly in the common prospect of colonising another land and even then, ironically, only by the physical separation enforced by life on different ships. The common project that kept at bay individual rivalries dissolves in the absence of a common present adversary, England and the East India Company being too remote and too intangible to serve as adequate foils. The consequence is a reassertion of personal animosity and the search for distinctions within the would-be colonists. This tendency touches even the narrator. Mackenzie himself admits to being 'the chapman of my own and my people's past' (5): not only does the phrase point to the retrospective nature of his narrative, it also intimates the unresolved relationship (to be found in *The Map of Love* and, more consistently, in the novels discussed in the next chapter) between private and public events, personal and national history. It is only at the end of the novel, when the union with England is inevitable, that Mackenzie can renounce the past and, with it, his allegiance to Scotland: just as he shouts ' "I've lost my country!" ' (516), his friend James Minto adds that 'he had no past and from this day on he would have nothing but a future' (515). That future is as part of Britain and *its* Empire, the new state entity paradoxically created by Scotland's attempt to assert its nationhood, as Mackenzie finally accepts a job connected with 'business … on the Gold Coast' and unconcerned with '[n]ational companies, empires, flags, patriots' (503). In an ironic parallel, he 'sells out' his national loyalty at the very moment when his country literally sells itself to England in exchange for a bailout of the debts incurred as a result of the ill-fated Darien expedition.

Mackenzie thus attains the closest identification with his country in the action of relinquishing it, but in the manner and nature of the loss a different model of supra-national community based not on subjective ideals but on the objective value of precious metal can be discerned. Mackenzie first comes into contact with this unifying force on the arrival in Darien of the pirate ship *Worcester*. The 'essence' that 'binds the crew … together' (328) in spite of their vastly diverging races, nationalities, personal histories and characters, is 'gold', which 'Captain' Green praises as 'a fair master, worth exactly as much to one man as to another. It is our common ground, the value we all agree on' (328). Gold is also distinguished from money, with its national dimension and shifting exchange value, and is at the basis of meaningful action in the modern world (and new state) Scotland is set to join at the end of the novel: modernity offers a more profitable alternative to the literal and ideological bankruptcy of the nation defined by 'honour or pride or loyalties stuffed down your throat before you can say your own name' (516). The same point of view is expressed with rhetorical force by Jewish merchant D'Azevedo, who asks ' "What are [countries] for?" ' before concluding that all they do is 'break our hearts' (516).

The Darien expedition, on the other hand, is founded on, and conducted in the name of, precisely such a pernicious entity as the independent nation. It is presumed to be honourable, is an expression of national pride, and demands of its participants an unquestioning loyalty that proves ultimately impossible. The internal divisions apparent from the moment the ships set off from Scottish shores are exacerbated by the fact that the enterprise is envisaged as having neither a physical enemy nor a confrontation with otherness. In spite of its colonial nature, and regardless of the physical distance travelled and marked by a great unfurling of maps and charts, the Reverend Mackay presents it to Mackenzie as a mythical homecoming and the fulfilment of a Biblical (rather than a historical) omission. The conventional equation of the uncolonised land as 'a paradise' (27) takes on a literal dimension in the complex vision of the religious scholar, as he suggests, firstly, that Gaelic is 'the closest descendant of the Original Tongue' (148) spoken by Adam and Eve; and secondly, that the 'white Indians of Darien' (150) of whom he had read were none other than 'descendants of the first Scots settlers who crossed the ocean centuries ago' (150). The inevitable conclusion is that the colonists 'are not going abroad at all' but rather are about to find their 'home' again (150).

The luxurious vegetation and unknown fauna of Darien seems to confirm the place's paradisal quality, with one of the colonists 'like a latterday Adam' compiling a list of native words 'so that we may know how to describe our new world' (224). It is not, however, an Eden that lets itself be replaced by another model, specifically the one implied in the naming of the settlement New Edinburgh and in the construction of civic, administrative and defensive landmarks. At most, what the colonists achieve is a precarious superimposition, which leaves the underlying pre-existing reality intact. This is the case of the location of the church, one of the earliest buildings to be erected, which coincides with the spot where young Indians traditionally go to have their first experience of sex. In the clash between the two, 'a young Adam and Eve at their carnal devotions' are chased out by Mackay, 'lantern in hand', a new Archangel 'barring the gates of Eden' (267). Ultimately, though, the church is never completed and Mackay himself abandons it to join the white Indians he had so desired to find. The paradise that is Darien has its own defences, from the incessant rains to the stifling heat and the unquenchable vegetation. Indeed the settlers experience an encounter that presages their own future. Venturing inland they find the dilapidated remains of a once beautiful European house whose erector aspired to 'be the author, entirely, of his own paradise' in an enterprise that 'had once been almost as great' as their own (302).

Paradise and national narrative are as mutually exclusive in *The Rising Sun* as they were inherently unsustainable in *English Passengers*. In Kneale's novel the successful historicisation of paradise and even the intimation of a new national identity in Peevay's narrative were achieved at the expense of 'the world' remaining Eden. The very naming of it as Eden deprives the place of its paradisal quality by framing it within a pre-existing system of signification, Christianity, whose starting point is precisely the awareness of the Fall. Galbraith's colonists, on the other hand, refrain from re-articulating their Edenic surroundings within a national history, as the settlement they create aspires to be an exact copy of the capital they left behind. Thus, the narrator muses on how 'in so short a time our New Edinburgh had grown to such a resemblance of the old as to have newsboys running amongst an evening crowd' (269). There is no attempt to incorporate the alien land and its people into a narrative of difference that implicitly asserts the speaker's identity, so that when the colonists experience their first encounter with the Indians in Darien the gaze they turn on them is one of 'fascinated amazement' (238), but it is not accompanied by an articulation of superiority. Indeed, Mackenzie goes so far as to call them 'our compatriots' (238). While lack of the equivalent of Orientalist or ethnographic certainties may be refreshingly contemporary, it is also evidence of the ideological deficiencies of the expedition. The period of national codification of identity for the European nation-states, in fact, coincided with their colonial expansion; inevitably,

the imperial experience ... had a profound imaginative impact on the imagining of national identities within Europe. It generated new ideologies both of national glory and of national destiny ..., new conceptions of service and sacrifice, new breeds of national hero. Assumptions about national character and civilization were given new kinds of definition through contacts – both real and imaginary – with an exotic (and generally politically and militarily subordinated) 'other'. (Cubitt 13)

In the case of Scotland's imperial expansion, however, this process of self-definition by difference in the colonial environment does not occur. Instead, the strength of national feeling that leads to the formation of a colonial trading company for Scotland rests on the assertion of difference from, and animosity towards, England, but it also exhausts itself in the act of founding the Company, making the subsequent colonial enterprise redundant. As a result, the paradise of Darien remains intact both physically and imaginatively, historically and narratively. After the surviving colonists' return to Scotland and on the eve of the Union, however, the myth of the Garden and the Fall are re-encoded to express the situation of the two countries involved in it. In an improvised representation on the back of a cart, Scotland becomes an Eve tempted by the English serpent with the apple of Union, riches and empire and, as the framework chosen for the story predicts, the alluring fruit will be accepted and consumed. What could not be made to contribute to an assertion of national identity in colonial surroundings is successfully co-opted to express Scotland's perspective when the target of that assertion is once again the familiar one of England.

If the a-historical perspective of the Reverend Mackay contributes to the imaginative failure of the national colonial enterprise, the generic uncertainty of Mackenzie's text points to that enterprise's narrative frailty. The tensions between a historical and an epic account of the Darien expedition, a personal and a national history (Mackenzie refers to his work as 'Scotiad' and 'Roriad' [12] in the same sentence) indicate a larger internal contradiction, that between a realistic and a romantic emplotment of the events. The narrative is permeated by an ambiguous intersection of romance and accounting, which begins with the narrator's role in the Company, both chief bookkeeper and unofficial chronicler, and his shifting definitions of himself as 'the historian of these numbers' and 'the Herodotus of our comic tragedy' (3). The former suggests factual accuracy, the latter the complexity and contradictions of a literary endeavour. Bare economics are transformed into the enchanting rhythms of 'the sweet music of so many pounds, so many tons of this or that commodity, so many per cent' (3). Mackenzie's own initial attraction for the prospects of the Company comes from its exotic aura, rather than from pragmatic reflections: he aspires to be 'among men of affairs,' whose talk of '[k]ings, wars, Acts of Parliament, tobacco, grain, Mexico' is 'a poem, an enchantment' (55). The birth of the Company itself is presented as a literary exercise, which 'emerged from its chrysalis of paper and dreams' divulged by ballad sellers who 'stood at every second street-corner selling heroic execrations of the King, the East India Company, the Continental war, the Navigation Acts, the English grain merchants, the English weather' (118). As the last subject of resentment suggests, the legitimate causes of complaint are always in danger of giving way to emotional, irrational resentment.

In the course of the voyage and then through the events in Darien he progressively relinquishes the literal accounting to pursue its narrative counterpart. In so doing he abandons the material power of money in favour of the romantic power of this tale of a failed attempt at national assertion. What remains by the end of the novel is a narrative which seals off this episode of Scottish history from the British reality that follows, thus reproducing the tendency of 'the Scottish imagination' to 'create pasts to mourn the loss of' (Pittock 5). Mackenzie's final act is an ideal retrenchment into his manuscript as a counterpart to his public engagement with the reality of trade in the British Empire: the national aspirations and the physical nation he has lost in the wake of the Union are replaced by their textual private equivalent, the book, which 'has become a shelter, a home of sorts' (493). The move stands at the core of the novels discussed in the next chapter, which grapple with the ethical dimension and respective appeals of public engagement and private integrity at times of significant and openly perceptible historical change.

4
Political Engagement and the Romance of Withdrawal

The Rising Sun left its hero, Roderick Mackenzie, on the verge of a new life outside national considerations, embracing instead the opportunities offered by the imperial expansion of Britain, the new state entity, though not as yet a nation, with whose establishment in 1707 the novel concludes. While the less salubrious aspects of Mackenzie's fledgling career are implied in the mention of the location where it will unfold (the Gold Coast), the final impression is that of the individual's and Scotland's own entry into the modern world, as the narrator listens to scientific discussions on a coach careering at high speed towards the national and imperial centre of London. This ending echoes Sir Walter Scott's emplotment of national history in the Waverley novels, whereby the demise of Highland society and culture with its traditional outlook on personal and economic relations is an instance of the unstoppable march of the bourgeois modernity exemplified by the Lowlands and their allegiance to the Hanoverian dynasty. The Waverley novels thus function as a monument to a lost indigenous tradition, which they enshrine into the realm of romance and therefore outside active political relevance while concomitantly tracing the inevitable triumph of a historical process teleologically oriented towards progress. Indeed, Scotland becomes the destination of nostalgic tourism and its exemplary model: 'the Scotch tour in the wake of the Union and the pacification of the Highlands [the settings for *The Rising Sun* and *Joseph Knight* respectively] is a privatised imperial ceremony which confirms the final reduction of an archaic culture and raises the *genius loci* only as a spirit of elegiac solitude' (Duncan 14). In this respect, Scott's work anticipates the tendencies towards the dwelling on loss and the politically unengaged nostalgia for a national or imperial past which have been identified as consistent features of the works in the preceding chapters, providing further evidence of the generic continuity from the originary form of historical fiction to its contemporary instances. It also participates in the substitution of lived public history with its privately consumed counterpart, heritage, which is a feature of contemporary engagements with the national past. Galbraith's novel projects backward to an earlier period Scott's theme of the move from Scotland's romantic illusions of national independence to the realism of the economic advantages in political union with England, but largely preserves the pattern of historical change identified by the earlier author.

Scotland also acquires an exemplary status as a case study for the trajectory of the historical process, yet paradoxically one that is outlined just at the moment when the pattern is broken. In fact, Galbraith's revisiting of the traditional emplotment of the Scottish past and, as we will see in detail in this chapter, James Robertson's less acquiescent engagement with Scott's work and its influence on the nation's understanding of itself in *Joseph Knight* (2003) coincide with the changed circumstances of national political life following the establishment of devolution and the opening of the new Scottish Parliament (the first since 1707) in July 1999. If the romanticised narration of history owed much to the reality of 'a country which lacks even the façade of conflict in terms of a politics fought out through a parliament' (Craig 120), the resumption of political engagement in a parliamentary arena has proved a stimulus to these authors' attempts to probe and then defy the orthodoxy about the national past. As was the case with the early emergence and definition of the historical novel, the fictional depiction shares its terrain of enquiry with historians, whose renewed interest in the relationship between Scottish national identity and empire is epitomised by T.M. Devine's *Scotland's Empire 1600–1815* (2003). It appears that once again, at the start of the twenty-first century as was the case at the start of the nineteenth, Scotland is taken to be the place where historical events and their narrative articulation find new ground.

In the particular case of Scotland the correspondence between present political events and the narration of the past acquires the features of a veritable restarting of the historical process for a nation that had been kept artificially 'outside the causality of history [...,] a place with a past but a place without a history' (Craig 118) insofar as 'past Scotlands [were] not gathered into the being of modern Scotland' (Craig 21). More generally, however, the novels discussed in this chapter respond, however indirectly, to the pressures of contemporary events, attempting to use narrative modes and narratorial positions to expose and, ambitiously, explain the workings of the historical process. Thus, Philip Hensher's revisiting in *The Mulberry Empire* (2002) of the circumstances, ideologies, and delusions which, from the early 1830s, led to the First Afghan War of 1839–1842 is carried out in the light (or more accurately given the novel's cautionary message, the shadow) of the NATO invasion of Afghanistan following the terrorist strike of 11 September 2001 in New York. Similarly, the background of irreconcilable religious disputes straying into political life in *Havoc in Its Third Year* (2004) and *Ghost Portrait* (2005), both set at the time of the English Civil War, is a lightly veiled reflection of the ideological climate following the Twin Towers attack, which was characterised by a denial of any mediatory middle ground.

In Lukács's definition the historical novel is characterised precisely by this desire to harness past and present to one another ('viewing [historical events] as individual stages in the prehistory of the present', 79) with the aim of extending 'the historical novel into an historical picture of the present... the portrayal of prehistory into the portrayal of self-experienced history' (84). The novels discussed in this chapter signal a return to the early examples of the genre, without however negating or abandoning the formal experimentations that marked the resurgence of the historical novel in the last quarter of the twentieth century. Reprising the terms in which I described the aims of those experiments in previous chapters, Robertson, Hensher, Bennett and Norminton rediscover the seemingly lost innocence of unselfconscious historical representation only after admitting to the impossibility of denying the relevance of self-reflexive representational strategies to the longing for past forms. Indeed, the pliability of historical narrative is exploited to reproduce the double function of the genre, namely, to recreate the contingency of individual moments at specific points in history and yet to configure them in a coherent sequence whose meaning depends on the discovery of historical causality, necessity, and process.

The parallels, divergences and comparisons between events in history can only be drawn with the benefit of hindsight proper of historical narrative, a point not lost on the author of *The Mulberry Empire*. Hensher's self-conscious recognition that, as '[t]he historian', he 'inspects the world from a safe distance' (340) and occupies a privileged position with respect to the events of the past when compared to the only partial knowledge and understanding of the actors in those events, echoes Scott's own, thus demonstrating his awareness of the conventions of the literary tradition in which he is writing. Equally, the points of contact between his novel and Farrell's *The Siege of Krishnapur*, which will become evident in the course of the discussion, suggest that this generic awareness encompasses the experiments with the genre to which the early chapters of this study are dedicated. The most obvious metafictional strategy in the novel is pastiche, with sections and whole chapters written in the manner of Dickens and Tolstoy. Hensher thus chooses to deploy a range of intertextual references to nineteenth-century novelists who sought to represent the perception of the historical process by those individuals who, willingly or otherwise, participated in it. It is also no coincidence that these two authors are cited by Lukács as proof that there is no substantive difference between the realist novel generally and the specific genre of the historical novel. I would argue, firstly, that the novels under consideration in this chapter aspire to the scope of nineteenth-century realism in so far as its narratives encompassed past and present, the individual and society, historical demands and personal choices; secondly, that there is a similarity in the relationship of realism to historical fiction, on the one hand, and experimental and traditional contemporary types of the latter, on the other. In other words, in the nineteenth century the new genre of the historical novel provided an early model of representation of events as part of larger entities (history and the nation) to the realist novel, unto which it was then subsumed. Similarly, in the late twentieth and early twenty-first centuries the (postmodern) experiments of the initial revival of historical fiction, which signalled the search for a viable representational mode for the past in a present that had appeared to reject historicist thinking, are later integrated in the more confident examples of the genre, whose primary concern in substantive rather than formal.

There are, however, considerable differences in the uses to which these self-referential moments are put in *The Mulberry Empire* compared to, for instance, *The French Lieutenant's Woman* or *Possession*.

The redefinition of the historical novel in Britain in the late twenti-eth century relied on metafictional devices to limit the scope of the works' literary, historical and ultimately political intervention (hence, for instance, the emphasis on private over public redemption in the novels in Chapter 2) by placing their representational enter-prises under the aegis of irony and within the escapist compass of romance. This strategy, as I have argued in earlier chapters, acknowl-edged and largely embraced the critique of realist and historical representation articulated by postmodernism, even as it attempted to transcend the dangers of narrative *impasse* the latter posed by identifying romance as the genre that could articulate and overcome the postmodern attitude to history and its rendition in narrative. Conversely, the recuperation of more conventional attitudes towards the intelligibility and representability of the past which can be traced to the novels discussed here points to a waning of the influence of postmodern theory and, less evidently, postmodern narrative prac-tice on the most recent British historical fiction. Thus, Robertson, Hensher, Bennett and Norminton strive to provide a narrative and historical continuity which, by definition, implies a degree of explan-ation for the events and of political commitment by the authors. In relating episodes from history to current events, in fact, these authors inevitably reveal their positions with respect to the present. Although their novels reprise earlier concerns of the contemporary British his-torical novel (most clearly the search for a representational mode that does not preclude the multiplicity of historical experiences at any given moment), they do so from an ideological position which sees engagement as the ideal, even when fraught with personal diffi-culties, and full representation as the achievable aim, whatever the formal compromises needed. The ever-present romance becomes, as a consequence, a narrative mode and an ideologically pregnant genre to be dissected and exposed even while it is being deployed in the novels; retrenchment into a narrow private domain of personal ful-filment and redemption becomes incompatible with the demands of the historical environment and is achieved only at the cost of unsus-tainable ethical compromises; perhaps most significantly, the scepti-cism about the past and the awareness of the difficulties in knowing the truth and the import of events is not elevated to an ontological condition but to the more mundane and contingent partiality and deficiency of point of view.

Arguably, what marks most clearly these novels' difference from the earlier examples of contemporary British historical fiction is the ambition of their subject and their attempt to produce an all-encompassing portrait of a past that intimates the developments in the present. *Joseph Knight*'s subject competes with, and aims to expand, that made famous by Sir Walter Scott, opening up the directions for Scottish history that had been purposefully shut down as a result of the earlier author's commitment to the success of the Hanoverian dynasty. The challenge is all the more significant because the romantic understanding of Scotland's past, with its tartans and heroic defeats and 'heritage' retail outlets that commodify the past for instant present consumption while depriving it of political relevance in the present, is at the basis of the cultural self-definition of the nation in the present. In the process, Robertson demonstrates his awareness not only of the role of literary representation in the shaping of the nation's understanding of itself but also of the impossibility of escaping the power of that representation, as by the end even the revised story of Scotland the novel proposes (a story re-written from within that nation in the present) cannot comprise the experience of those who, like the slave Joseph Knight, have been brought to the country by force. The desire to offer a comprehensive and revised national narrative as a counterpart to the comprehensive and revised form of the historical novel as a genre is therefore made to confront its limits, without however denying the worthiness of the aspiration.

The Mulberry Empire reviews the history of Afghanistan in relation to Britain's own narrative of nationhood as it was progressively articulated through imperial texts, with the unfolding of the plot alternating between the two settings. Not only does the novel suggest that imperial expansion functions as a conduit for national identity for both sides, since it is only the presence of the would-be British conquerors that induces the disparate Afghan genealogical lines to unite behind an idea of sameness to oppose to the otherness of newly arrived Europeans. Hensher also filters the realisation of difference through his use of narrative and representational modes, by contrasting the oral genealogical epics of the Dost of Kabul and his 54 sons, on the one hand, and the ethnological travel writing of the British explorers, coupled with the romance into which their exploits are turned in the mother country, on the other. The latter appear narratively familiar even when they are parodically presented and point to the cultural ground which the British characters, consumers of those narrative forms, share with narrator and readers, respectively purveyor of the same narrative forms and their consumers by proxy. In the course of the novel the reassuring familiarity signals an all too comfortable and unquestioning complicity. Conversely, the artificiality of the epic narrative of Afghanistan in the sections concerning the Amir Dost Mohammed Khan and his 54 sons does not merely heighten the exoticism of this part of the novel; it also foregrounds the strains which the subject poses to a Western genre and narrative form (the historical novel and realism). Like Robertson with respect to his eponymous character, by deploying a codified approach in the tradition of exoticism to the alien territory and its inhabitants Hensher implies that his position as a Western narrator cannot really do justice to the Afghan perspective on the colonial wars of the nineteenth century nor, by extension, can America and Britain really understand the country, society, and civilisation they undertake to change unilaterally in 2001.

The section of the novel labelled 'Anthropological Interlude', which constitutes a conspicuous intrusion into both plot and metafictional devices and is marked by its typographically old-fashioned appearance, serves as a vehicle for this awareness. It features an unnamed traveller, potentially Hensher himself, visiting Afghanistan at the time of the country's occupation by the Soviet Union, and failing to understand his surroundings to such an extent that the title of the section could more aptly refer to the Englishman as the specimen in question than to the supposed subjects of his ethnographic study. The suspension of the plot's thrust engendered by this section is more than an additional layer of self-referentiality. The historical moment in which the 'Interlude' takes place, in fact, provides another step to the novel's goal of tracing a continuous narrative between the past of the setting and the present of the writing, while also complicating the linearity of the historical process. The Soviet presence in Afghanistan is a continuation of the Anglo-Russian conflict at the basis of the First Afghan War that is the primary subject of Hensher's novel. The invasion, and the resistance it engendered by the mujaheddin, is also a primary cause of subsequent events in the history of Afghanistan, not least the political and military success of the Taleban a few years after the withdrawal of Soviet troops. And yet this seemingly clear unfolding of cause and consequence is disrupted by the equally evident circularity of the situation. The Soviet invasion becomes only one instance in a series of attempts at imperial expansion by European powers onto Afghan territory, regularly recurring and just as regularly conforming to a pattern which, starting with the seemingly successful initial imposition of an alien ideology (be it nineteenth-century civilisation, Soviet communism, or Western democracy), is ultimately followed by the defeat and retreat of the invader. In *The Mulberry Empire* the Enlightenment and Victorian models of history as a broadly causal sequence are, at one stroke, prominently deployed and subtly countered by the older use of historical *exempla* as cautionary tales for application to the present, so that the same mistakes can be avoided. The irony of the novel is that the mistakes should be so similar to those of preceding generations and the warning, though clearly pertinent, less heeded.

A notable aspect of this recourse to recognisable versions of the historical process is the retreat from the postmodern rejection of Enlightenment absolutes and the corollary exploration of the discourse of values, private ethics and public morality, and politics. Although the novels in this chapter explore the difficulties of finding a sustainable ethical position for their characters, even weighing the respective merits of the compromises of public engagement and the reassurance of private consistency, they leave characters and readers in no doubt as to the necessity of choosing a course of action. Sustaining the balance between opposites advocated by, for instance, *The Chymical Wedding* and *Possession,* proves not only impossible, but also cowardly. This shift in attitude on the part of Robertson, Hensher, Bennett and Norminton is, I believe, related to the changed political climate in the aftermath of the terrorist attacks on 11 September 2001 – explicitly so in the case of the last three authors, since the consequences of the events of that day colour their stories.

Those events mark the culmination of postmodernism and its demise at once. On the one hand, in fact, the twin towers of the World Trade Center epitomised the global reach of late capitalist postmodernity which provided the socio-economic and cultural conditions for the development of the range of philosophical positions and aesthetic practices that have come to define postmodernism and have made its cultural products recognisable. Their premises were the reproduction of an absent original, self-referential irony, and an oxymoronic uniformity in the multiplicity of voices advocating the local interests of identity politics, which rejected any universal notion of truth as the manifestation of hegemonic oppression. The cultural artefacts thus generated, including literary texts, were expressions of local traditions and yet became instantly marketable at a global level in what amounted to a virtual counterpart of the Victorian passion for museums and exhibitions, albeit one supported by the suggestion, inconceivable in its nineteenth-century predecessor, that these forms of representations, so widely available because so easily reproduced, did not in fact grant access to any reality, either epistemologically or ontologically. The destruction of the Twin Towers seemed to crystallise this postmodern understanding of the world of postmodernity. The unique nature of the event and the reality of the destruction are undeniable, and yet the images that convey it are endlessly reproduced, even today, all over the world; nor did their proliferation aid understanding of the historical chain that preceded the attack. Indeed, in true postmodern fashion the sequence from the crash of the first plane to the collapse of the second tower acquired such an iconic status in its own right as to obscure the reality of what they represented.

At the same time as it confirmed the limits of representation as a vehicle to understand reality, however, 11 September 2001 marks the date when the a-historical tendencies of postmodernity, nourished on the certainties of the end of the Cold War and on the seeming triumph, in that conflict, of the model of society and economics based on liberalism and capitalism, suffer their own (metaphorical) collapse. In the first place, the attacks demonstrated a degree of religiously inspired resentment towards the West's liberalism, secularism and capitalism that belied the claims for an end to ideological juxtapositions in the name of wealth, on the one hand, and micro-politics, on the other, put forward by postmodernism. In the second place, the terrorist action in New York has had as a major theoretical consequence the re-ignition of a polarised, if not Manichean, political debate and the resulting articulation of absolute ideological positions. If the causes of the terrorist attacks on the Twin Towers remain obscure and indeed if even attempting to explain the events of the day may be perceived as an outrage against preserving the horrific uniqueness of the senseless destruction of terrorism, there is no doubt that one can trace the consequences of those events and consider the violent re-irruption of history onto contemporary reality. While *The Mulberry Empire* and *Havoc in Its Third Year* may not necessarily embrace either side of the ideological divide their plots articulate, they certainly acknowledge its existence and use the historical record to probe the origins of early twenty-first century events in the case of Hensher's novel, or to explore the very nature of a climate of clashing ideologies in Bennett's.

1. James Robertson's *Joseph Knight*

The role of narrative and the literary tradition in the articulation of history as process is central to the case of Scotland. The subtitle to Scott's *Waverley* (*'t'is Sixty Years Since*) sanctioned and perpetuated the impression that discontinuity is inherent in Scottish history and that the traumatic events of 1745 are only its latest instance. In this view the romanticised past of the Jacobite rebellion bears no relation to the pragmatic present that confirms Scotland's position within the Union and places its future in a national history that starts at Culloden and unfolds to encompass the empire. The gap of 60 years draws a veil over the personal and national compromises in the period separating the time of *Waverley*'s action from the year of its publication, with the result that 'the Waverley novels represent the historical formation of the modern imperial nation-state in relation to the sentimental formation of the private individual: a homology, a synecdochic equivalence, is asserted between these processes' (Duncan 15).

James Robertson's decision to set *Joseph Knight* precisely during the interval elided in Scott's novel has both political and generic implications. Robertson engages with the earlier writer's role as the initiator of the historical novel at the same time as portraying the insalubrious side to Scotland's continuing participation in the Union. The trajectory of John Wedderburn, one of Robertson's two protagonists, from the battlefield of Culloden to a comfortable country home in Tayside and the restoration of the family's social and economic fortunes, via the ownership of sugar plantations – and of the Gold Coast slaves integral to the business – encompasses the period between 1745 and 1803, the span referred to by the subtitle to Scott's novel. Robertson's graphic depiction of the events at Culloden, with which the novel starts, proves that this correspondence is not coincidental. In a move analogous to the representational gap of 60 years, Scott had also shied away from engaging narratively with the military brutality that marked the threshold of Scotland's second entry into the modernity of Britain: the last battle shown in *Waverley* is the Jacobite victory at Prestonpans, and the novel's protagonist only hears of the Pretender's defeat without witnessing or participating in it. Waverley is therefore implicated neither in the treasonous actions of the rebels nor in the ferocity of the reprisals that followed their rout. He enters the newly confirmed union under the Hanover monarchy untainted by the excesses of either side and ideally placed to be a representative of a new national unity founded on a selective pattern of memory and forgetting, so that '[t]he final image of domestic and political reconciliation is the most fantastic, artful and labyrinthine of all evasions' (Duncan 15).

Joseph Knight, on the other hand, exposes the complicity of the nation and its people in the practices of empire, whose counterpart is the generic influence on national and imperial identity of the novel as Scott first envisaged it: 'After *Waverley* the novel established itself as the pre-eminent literary genre of the Britain of the Imperial era, and the novels of Walter Scott, John Buchan, and other Scottish novelists of the nineteenth and twentieth centuries did much to shape and sustain the Imperial master-narrative' (Mack 12). John Wedderburn's career exactly epitomises the personal and national compromises deriving from the seemingly laudable desire to regain the ancestral home and to preserve a threatened national identity. His undeniable participation in the Jacobite rebellion, the flight from the battlefield, subsequent emigration to Jamaica and the making of a fortune there mean that the author refuses to sanitise the national past just as he shows the sequence of events that causally lead to Wedderburn's present (coinciding with Scott's), exposing the link between national ideals, empire, and individual success. The novel's epigraph, from Ben Okri, exhorts '[n]ations and peoples' to 'tell stories that face their own truths' in order to free their history 'for future flowerings'. The revisionist stance implied here is fulfilled by Robertson's rejection of the romantic emplotment of Scotland's past initiated by Scott and, Okri's words suggest, it reconstitutes a linear narrative that rejoins the past and the present and projects the nation into the future. The epigraph also foreshadows the author's reaction against the elegiac treatment of Scotland's past by asserting itself as a representation of both the horrors of defeat and the moral ambiguities of nationalist action when the latter is inextricable from empire. The self-conscious revising of Scott's influence is apparent: to Wedderburn the work of his contemporary concerns 'nothing that was not safely in the rusted, misty half-dream that was Scotland's past' (5), a blunting of the political realities of the Jacobite rebellion so successful that Wedderburn's daughter can claim that '[a]ll that Jacobite passion belonged to another age, it had nothing to do with her. The Forty-five might have been tragic and stirring but it was also hopeless and useless and ancient' (20). Reflecting that it is 'nearly sixty years' since his participation in the Jacobite rebellion, Sir John envisages with both horror and irony 'somebody ... writing a *novelle* about it' and knows that it will not 'tell the truth' (26). Yet it is precisely the distorted picture of the time painted by the likes of Scott that facilitates Wedderburn's return home to take up his old social position, since that novelist's treatment of them had turned 'their politics ... positively romantic' (68). Sir John, it appears, acquiesces in the romanticised depiction of events in which he participated, separating the public consumption of that depiction from his private knowledge in order to regain the social, and therefore public, position that was his family's before the Jacobite rebellion.

Robertson's response to Scott's perspective in *Waverley*, that the events of the '45 were best remembered as a romantic enterprise irredeemably separated from the modern Hanoverian state, consists of reconstructing the interrupted line of Scottish history. If this attenuates the sense of bifurcation at the point where that history became encompassed into the larger British imperial trajectory, it also deprives the newly de-romanticised and re-historicised past of the national comforts of heroic defeat. *Joseph Knight* shows that the defeated rebels' involvement in the British imperial enterprise can be traced back to their national ideals and that, consequently, the reassertion of the historical process for Scotland is inextricable from a re-evaluation of its role as England's partner in the economic and human exploitation of colonial territories. This reconstructive operation is evident in the novel's structural arrangement. Each of the chapters is headed by a place and a date, giving it a degree of historical and geographical specificity, but their sequence is neither continuous nor chronological. The first two chapters, showing Sir John Wedderburn at his home in Ballindean in 1802 and on the battlefield of Culloden in 1745, set the temporal limits of the narrative and refer to the gap of nearly 60 years during which he went from dispossession to wealth and the social status conferred by the possession of a house with a prospect that includes 'the lawn ... , the little loch, then the parkland dotted with black cattle, sun-haloed sheep and their impossibly white lambs. Thick ranks of sycamore, birch and pine enclosed the house and its immediate grounds' (3). The bucolic idyll of the present, with the intersection of seclusion and ownership implied in the description, could not be more different from the 'sodden moor' (35) where Sir John's story began, a reversal made all the more striking by the knowledge that what had led Sir John's father to join the Jacobite cause was the desire to restore the family's fortunes and reacquire the house and land he had lost through poverty. The chapters that follow, however, undermine the felicitous outcome, once again reminiscent of Scott's *Waverley,* suggested in the initial juxtaposition of Ballindean and Culloden. They show instead the protagonist's morally dubious behaviour in his quest to take up again the position his name commands in Scotland.

The mother country undergoes a process of redefinition by similarity and difference in the course of Wedderburn's profitable exile in Jamaica. Lacking a historical connection with his new land, and unable to access the past in his home country, he relies on a geographical one, building his house in a spot that is 'comfortingly familiar' because 'you could almost believe yourself to be in a Scottish glen' (66) and names the house Glen Isla, transferring what was lost in Scotland onto the Jamaican landscape. There is an essentially contradictory aspect to this reliance on geography as a parameter of the nation in the absence of a viable national narrative. Cairns Craig suggests that '[t]he associations of place ... can bring back into history values denied by the very process of history', allowing to preserve the image of 'a world as yet unmoved by the destructive forces of history' (156). And yet, by his participation in the British Empire, Sir John is contributing to, and profiting from, that same process of history marking the triumph of modernity that drove him from Scotland and which he is now banishing from the confines of his estate symbolically, at the same time as enforcing it in practice. Wedderburn first moulds his Jamaican possessions after the country he left behind, and then proceeds to exploit them systematically, acting at once as a political exile of idealistic convictions and as a representative of imperial success for the country that dispossessed him. Glen Isla, 'picturesque and peaceful' with 'a sense of industry, fertility, domesticity, prosperity' (67) both foreshadows and replicates Ballindean, which it follows in the narrative sequence but precedes in the story. Both estates fulfil the anachronistic Jacobite ideal of 'Scotland's agricultural purity', but they respectively contribute to, and are sustained by, 'the luxuries of imperial Britain' against which the local rural ideal was originally designed as a pure, uncorrupted form of Scottishness (Pittock 36). The historical contradictions inherent in the nostalgic attempt to recreate the lost home while at the same time actively participating in the imperial economy are, in part, obviated by diverting the experience of exile and ownership into myth, turning the 'huge, hot, overgrown garden' of Jamaica into a version of 'the Garden of Eden' (22). Sir John's strategy is analogous to Scott's, whose often admiring stance towards the culture and customs of the Highlands was safely enshrined by the knowledge that they had become redundant in the context of a modern Scotland.

At the basis of the productive activity at Glen Isla are the slaves. Living in a land populated by expatriates and imported slaves, Wedderburn becomes conscious of the centrality of race to their mutual interactions; these reflections then lead to a reassessment of Scotland according to a new parameter, namely, whiteness: 'As his own skin became burnt by the sun ... [h]e thought of home and its whiteness, something to which he had never before given any consideration. Now, surrounded by black people, he saw in his mind the overwhelming whiteness of Scotland' (51). When he envisages his return to Scotland he imagines his position to be determined not only by possession of 'a big house' but also by the acquisition of 'a graceful, lily-white lady' for a wife (73). The insistence on colour as a mark of national self-definition defuses the latter of its political dimension. Firstly, there is neither choice nor gradation in a national allegiance presented as an accident of nature; secondly, the definition denies the possibility of internal divisions (which, the novel makes clear, abounded during the Jacobite rebellion); and finally, it relies on a feature that Scotland shares with England, thus finding a common denominator with the former enemy which is further confirmed by the social context of Jamaica: politically, one of the older colonists tells Wedderburn, '[w]e're an island of tolerance – we're only here to get rich after all' (57). This attitude is comparable to

Roderick Mackenzie's at the end of *The Rising Sun,* when commerce replaces national ideals following the failure and disillusion of Darien. The crisis for Sir John comes when his slave Joseph Knight, whom he has brought back to Scotland with him, appeals to the ideals the Scots rather unquestioningly claim for their own (love of freedom and hate of oppression) and then makes successful use of the Scottish legal institutions to gain his freedom. It is Wedderburn's inability to extend to Knight the same form of ductile national allegiance of which he himself has benefited as a Scottish Jacobite and a British colonist at once that causes the irreconcilable split between the two.

The split, just like the chronologically discontinuous and non-sequential structural arrangement, draws attention to what has been omitted or erased, most notably the eponymous character. He appeared in an amateur painting of a family scene by Sir John's brother Sandy, but was subsequently covered up by dark paint; he features in the delirious diaries kept by that same brother, but these are inaccessible, locked away in a drawer in Sir John's study, where the mutilated painting still hangs. These two physical traces of the slave Joseph Knight mark the simultaneous presence and absence of the past in Wedderburn's life, a traumatic persistence intimated by his equation of Knight and Culloden as 'a knot in time that he could not untie but could not leave alone' (277). In this respect, the fragmented nature of the novel's unfolding reproduces the protagonist's personal narrative and the national narrative of Scotland, whose interrupted sequence Sir John commemorates in 'anniversaries scattered through the calendar ..the martyrdom of Charles I, at the end of January, and the death of his first, dear wife Margaret in March; and late in November he would mourn, yet again, his father. But tomorrow was Culloden' (26). Knight's desertion of his master and the ensuing court action for his freedom are additions to the traumatic sequences, for which there is, however, no formal celebration 'with a sombre heart' (26). The difference is that in the latter case the personal and the political, the economic and idealistic, cannot be incorporated without revealing their incompatibility.

There is a suggestion that Knight is a figure for Scotland's past more broadly and for what is wilfully forgotten in the popularised representations of it. He is alternatively erased or narrativised to fit a pre-existing plot structure, that of Wedderburn's return home,

which, like Scotland's own narrative, is shaped as a romance, yet by
his very existence he disrupts the oblivious comfort of the genre into
which he has been co-opted. Thus, Sir John is 'like the hero in a fairy
tale' and Knight the 'token' of his past (167). The latter's presence
constantly acts 'as a reminder of where he had been and what had
happened there' (167) and intrudes on his gentleman's life in
Scotland, to whose romantic perfection he had aspired even while in
Jamaica. A similar romantic understanding of itself, the novel argues,
contaminates the nation as a whole, protecting it from any responsibility for the actions perpetrated by its representatives in the Empire,
but also preventing it from self-knowledge. The spokesperson for this
position is Maclaurin, Joseph's solicitor in the case against
Wedderburn. In a novel where firmly drawn lines between idealism
and pragmatism, strength of national feeling and expedient compromise are shown to be unsustainable if not the result of wilful
self-delusion, he represents a Scottish identity that preserves its peculiarities, most notably a distinct language, without however turning
those peculiarities, as Scott did, into outmoded antiquarian curiosities that mark the impossibility of a Scottish modernity.

Robertson places Maclaurin in clear juxtaposition to both Sir John
and James Boswell, who makes a brief appearance in *Joseph Knight*.
The latter has embraced a manufactured Englishness to the point of
wincing at his friends' Scottish pronunciation and denigrating his
country's lack of refinement; the former purports to live by a set of
principles that embody Scottish values, but these amount to no more
than the exercise of feudal seigniorial rights which are in any case
sustained by active participation in Britain's imperial enterprise. In
contrast, Maclaurin recognises the undesirable political dimension
of the Jacobite rebellion in spite of the romantic allure of its representation: it is 'tyranny, however gallant it seemed and however bonnie
it looked wi [*sic*] its cockades and plaids' (276–7). Equally, he rejects
the other romantic self-delusion, that Scotland has 'aye been hot for
liberty' and therefore, by some kind of essential national trait ('We're
Scotsmen. It's in oor banes'), its people will 'fecht for the freedom of
the Negroes' (250). His reply to these naïve sentiments is to remind
his interlocutor of the overwhelming Scottish presence in the West
Indies: 'Jamaica reads like an Edinburgh kirkyard! And the plantations are a map o [*sic*] Scotland' (251). This is a statement of national
responsibility: the reference to family and place names expresses the

degree and depth of Scotland's ideological involvement in colonial exploitation.

The suggestion that the map of one country has been superimposed on the colonial territory reprises the earlier connection between nation, on the one hand, and geography and landscape, on the other. Robertson shows that the persuasive force of these elements shapes the nation's search for identifiable markers of itself. In the alien environment of the imperial outposts, the reiteration of the family name recalls the clan structure at the basis of a pre-modern Scotland, that is to say the very social system revived and enforced in the course of the 1745 rebellion, which pitted Highlanders and Lowlanders against each other as much as the Scots against the English. Given the importance of geography for the articulation of a Scottish identity, moreover, the repetition of place names across the ocean is not just an act of colonial imposition but also an attempt to reconstitute and reproduce the nation in exile with a view to preserving it for a triumphant return to Scotland. This is Sir John's trajectory. His move from a Scottish to a Jamaican Glen Isla (whose common name, it is worth remembering, rests on perceived similarities in terrain) and then his return to the landed respectability of Ballindean via the 'substantial and imposing' house he used to imagine for himself (73) is achieved by conflating economic property with social propriety and by investing both with an implicit national moral dimension that both Maclaurin and Knight challenge, one politically, the other personally.

Contrary to Scott's *Waverley*, Robertson's novel does not propose a reconciliation between the private and public domains. *Joseph Knight*'s overarching structure, consisting of four parts named 'Wedderburn', 'Darkness', 'Enlightenment', and 'Knight', signals the failure of attempting to provide an overarching narrative that integrates individual actions and national development. The central, and longest, sections appear to contribute to a generic emplotment of national history founded on progress and as such congruent with Scott's own project in *Waverley*. Its deployment by Robertson, however, is consistently ironic. The trajectory from darkness to enlightenment echoes colonial discourse's justification of imperial expansion, as well as intimating the racist undertones that guided it. The distinction between the two stages and the corollary implication of progress is, furthermore, undermined by the fact that the epigraphs are similar notices for slave ships' departures, rewards for the capture of runaway slaves, or auctions of newly arrived 'cargoes'. There is no change in Wedderburn's attitude towards Knight in the novel, just as his national allegiance remains constant in private; nor does Joseph benefit in any way from a form of enlightenment. On the contrary, by the end of the novel he has reasserted his difference from his adoptive home (the Fife coast) and his individuality even with respect to his Scottish wife. The fact that Wedderburn and Knight frame the attempted master-narrative of the larger sections of the novel confirms that such overarching statement can only be made if individual lives are elided. In this novel, on the other hand, they remain unassimilated to what may be envisaged as a general direction in history, or the fulfilment of the process of history.

Knight, in particular, escapes the boundaries of a narrative of progress just as he broke through the restraints of his condition as a slave: his figure, even in the section that bears his name, remains unknowable in his motivations, desires, actions. To Sir John, this is a feature he shares with all the slaves and the realisation signals the delusions of plantation owners and colonists more generally: he

> had thought he knew his [slaves]. [...] But the truth was, slaves were unknowable. The so-called Coromantees were named after a place neither they nor their masters had even been to. The Africa-born slaves had names and languages that ran like subterranean rivers beneath the surface names and the new language they acquired. They wore their faces like masks. How could they have been anything *but* unknowable? (109–10)

Joseph conceals his African name from everyone around him, including his wife, because '[i]t was the one thing he had left from that other beginning, the one thing that was his and his alone' (352). The suggestion remains that the story the novel tells is unavoidably partial, beginning as it does from the point of enforced submission to the slave traders and planters, so that the narrative cannot reach back to the start of Joseph's life, or perhaps to the core of his identity. This makes the title of the novel intriguing. The name that stares at us on the front cover is the black man's colonial name, imposed by his owners, and Robertson confirms that he is himself implicated in the attempts at limiting and defining the slave by means of the representational codes applied to him. Thus, the novel foregrounds the largely mediated nature of the knowledge we gain of Knight (he is the subject of a painting, a diary, court papers, a letter, personal recollections), while delaying the man's direct representation until the final pages of the novel. Even then, however, there is no access to the African name to which Knight clings as a marker of his original unenslaved identity and which is therefore withheld from the novel.

2. Philip Hensher's *The Mulberry Empire*

Scotland's participation in the imperial enterprise is taken for granted in *The Mulberry Empire*, in the person of its protagonist Alexander Burnes. He is not only a Victorian explorer at the further reaches of the British Empire but also the instigator of that empire's expansion from Punjab into Afghanistan. So unquestioning is Burnes's allegiance to the national enterprise that he even thinks of himself as 'an Englishman' (11). This seeming solecism is in fact a symptom of a more general laxity in the understanding and preservation of historical categories that informs the British society described in the novel and which Hensher, with Dickensian fervour particularly in the rhetorical force of the description of the upper-middle classes, equates with a moral, intellectual, and political laxity verging on bankruptcy. The characters' unwillingness or inability to make morally sound judgements on people and events results in a disastrous naivety with regard to the reality of Empire: not only are its high-minded ideals and practical purposes conflated with indiscriminate ease, both are suffused by a romanticised and textually mediated vision that prevents Burnes and his companions from reacting to events during their stay in Afghanistan. Hensher's own desire to apply that exact discrimination so visibly absent in his characters manifests itself in the ramifications of the plot and the reach (geographical as much as historical) of the novel. The various narrative strands include two expeditions to Afghanistan by Burnes, the first time in secret and the second as part of a large military and bureaucratic movement to take control of Kabul; the Russian machinations aimed at countering British expansion, whose prime mover is first presented with a friend's family in a country retreat in Russia and only subsequently takes up his place in Afghanistan; the deliberations and reactions of the court of the Amir Dost Mohamed Khan in Kabul, including court rituals and etiquette; the unwitting involvement in the events of a homosexual British soldier, Masson, who is caught between the various warring sides; and finally the fate of a society girl in London, which provides the opportunity to dissect the preconceptions and misconceptions of the British upper classes.

To Bella Garraway, the young woman Burnes loves, the Amir Dost Mohammed 'truly sounds like the black villain in a Christmas raree show ... entering, stage left, his face and his intentions for the heroine both as black as pitch' (67). While it is neither surprising nor disturbing that an English girl should rely on her limited cultural boundaries to imagine her friend's adventures in a distant land, the practice of allowing textual evidence pre-eminence over direct experience acquires more sinister connotations when performed by the presumed expert, Burnes himself. Thus, uncertain about the purpose of his presence in the country or its eventual outcome and unable to make sense of Kabul and its inhabitants, Burnes resorts to the discourse of colonial ethnography to domesticate the strangeness of his situation. The Afghans, whose purposes and behaviours the explorer finds unfathomable, become on the page the conventional 'nation of children' who 'cannot conceal their feelings from one another' so that 'a person with any discrimination may at all times pierce their designs' (36). That person, by implication, is an Englishman. The national certainties revived in the course of the writing allow Burnes to quell 'the itch, the uneasy fear' he had felt in the midst of an opaque people and 'to bring the Afghans who surrounded [him], every one under the point of his pen' (36), but the desired or expected perspective is only achieved at the expense of the very investigation of the territory and its inhabitants that was the aim of Burnes's journey. The reality of Afghanistan is made to conform to the preconceived expectations of the would-be colonists, but this fit is forcible rather than natural, and entails a further distancing from its object, even though the latter is within convenient distance for observation, that will have disastrous consequences during the colonial occupation of Afghanistan.

Burnes's discursive negotiations are, of necessity, sophisticated, in so far as they have to elide both the daily experience of living among the inscrutable Afghans and the explorer's own underlying doubts about the outcome of his scouting enterprise. However, less subtle versions of similar operations punctuate the novel: the politicians attempting to replace one just but independently minded ruler with another, crueller but more amenable to furthering British interests, use the discourse of reason and rights to assert that 'this is not an invasion' but rather the restoration of 'the rightful king of the Afghans to his throne', so that the British intervention amounts to no more than 'aid[ing] our neighbours' (366). Even minor characters such as a group of musicians playing at a ball participate in the national rhetoric of empire when they claim with confidence that ' "There's no other nation on earth could have done what we've done, marched in and taken charge, and no other nation could set it to rights like we'll do." ' (418) What these words reveal is the national confidence which is a direct result of imperial expansion and which, in turn, ensures that the expansion is supported in the popular arena. Once again, Burnes is the most forceful proponent of empire but also the most transparent. In reply to Stokes, a sceptical listener who has suggested to him that there is nothing wrong 'with being satisfied with what you have' (55), he embarks on a peroration that unwittingly concedes the less than honourable or disinterested motives of territorial expansion:

> Nothing, sir, unless you have the spirit of a Briton. Our posses-
> sions, sir, are vast new markets. Do you suppose our little island
> can contain our native spirit? Of course it cannot. And should we
> stay at home, relinquish India tomorrow, what would happen?
> Would the natives not slide back into all manner of native barbar-
> ities – the murder of travellers, the suicide of widows? [...] Would
> the precious flame of Christianity survive six months in such a
> poisoned atmosphere? Would India, indeed, be left to its own
> devices? Would not the French perceive an empty space? Would
> not Russia send its vast armies to bring new barbarities to a bar-
> barous land? (55)

What had started as an equation of the imperial enterprise with a natural manifestation of national character and identity soon gives way to more prosaic economic factors, while the emotional rhetoric of civilisation and religion makes way for the pragmatic view of geo-political influence.

The far-reaching implications of the textual dimension of the imperial enterprise are examined not only in these cases of contemporary participation in the discourse of nation and empire but also from a historical perspective. As Charles Masson, Burnes's antagonist in Afghanistan and a man opposed to the goals and means of colonial expansion, compiles a false report of the explorer's actions aimed at discrediting his rival, he relies on the acknowledged historical weight of documentary evidence when direct proof is no longer available, confident that '[o]ne day, these lies would be as true as history' and 'that what he wrote would come to be the truth' (370). This contention is important on two levels. Firstly, it confirms the novel's broader proposition that the experience of empire is ultimately textual, for its participants as for future consumers of it, and foregrounds the suggestion that, in the hands of a skilled narrator such as Masson and Burnes at different times, events are liable to ideological manipulation. Secondly, and arguably more controversially, it questions history's tendency to accept written sources as reliable in the absence of proofs to the contrary: just as the British in Afghanistan are so ensnared by their own falsifications that they forget they are not the truth (with dire consequences for the occupation), so future students of the First Afghan War will be entirely engrossed in the search for and interpretation of extant documents about it that they will forget the real events those texts purport to elucidate. Hensher's warning here may seem little more than a redundant echo of Hayden White's own mistrust of seeming textual transparency. However, the fact that, at the same time, Hensher envisages an oral tradition as a counterpart to the documentary record points to the existence of sources more difficult to trace but for this reason more desirable. One of them is the report of the eye-witness, as is the case with the sole survivor of the defeat of the British army, whose story 'was a single one, and it was all that he could tell' (509). Yet even this testimony cannot encompass the plurality of 'sixteen thousand stories', one for each dead soldier: it would take 'sixteen Scheherazades, telling night after night … and every single story ending in the same way' (509). The historical record, in other words, must of necessity impose boundaries to its subject and rely on typicality of episodes rather than comprehensiveness of narrative.

It is interesting that in order to convey adequately even the British experience in Afghanistan Hensher should call on an Eastern myth and on the related storytelling mode, rather than the dry factual accuracy of the first-person account by a participant, which would be valued by a Western historical tradition. This provides further evidence of the ultimate failure of the rational systems of signification the representatives of imperial power deployed in their attempts to master the country, primary among them written documents. As for the perspective of the victors, 'forever afterwards, when the children of the Dost's empire ... told each other tales of the past to while away a long cold night, they would talk of the great deeds of these years' (519). This story, transmitted from father to son, 'would not be forgotten until Afghanistan itself was destroyed' (519). In other words, oral narrative tradition and the integrity of the nation are inextricable and the ductility of storytelling triumphs over the more rigid structure of narrative in the same way that the unorthodox military and diplomatic tactics of the Afghans prevail over the regimented, regulated army and bureaucratic practices of the British.

The closest equivalent to Afghan orality for the British characters is the romance of adventure. Thus, visiting the docks of London where produce from the furthest corners of the Empire is gathered and looking at the crates and bales being shifted, Burnes entreats Bella to 'think of the journey they have undertaken, through what wastes and deserts, think what hands they have passed through, what fortunes, what hopes rest on these ordinary things' (90). Romance is nevertheless envisaged within a written medium, as Burnes feels 'rather like a novelist must in a crowded room in an inn' ready to prise open 'all the unspeaking secrets contained in it' (89). After leaving Bella to return to Afghanistan and complete his mission – a mission from which he will never return – Burnes writes to her from the ship as to 'a romantic reader', bemoaning the absence of a 'narrative to tempt you onwards [...,] no mutiny ... no typhoon to interest you' (167). The relationship between them, which had been so experiential as to be consummated against all social conventions and which would soon result in the equally real birth of a child, has already been reduced to a textual exchange for vicarious consummation. Nor does romance succeed in sustaining the explorer in his final feat. In fact, far from validating his actions and those of the British colonists generally, in the way that the patrilinear transmission of tales about the Dost does for Afghanistan, romance is revealed to be an inadequate, misleading, ultimately destructive mode of emplotment for the imperial enterprise. When mulberry branches appear in various places at the occupiers' residences in Kabul, the British initially and unsuccessfully strive to explain their presence with reference to romantic gestures, until they have to concede that they have 'some quite specific meaning not apparent to us' (442) and indeed in the novel they precede by only a few days the Dost's final and decisive attack against the British. The episode is reminiscent of the mysterious proliferation of the chapattis, heralding the rebellion of the Sepoys, at the start of J.G. Farrell's *The Siege of Krishnapur*. Not only did they, like the mulberry branches, disrupt the complacency of the colonisers, derived from the belief in their superior understanding and civilisation; they do so, in both cases, because the sheer physical presence of these incongruous objects could not be encompassed within the prevailing discursive structure of the British officials (the adventure romance in Kabul, taxonomic displays in Krishnapur) and their offensiveness to the foundations of colonial identity could not be neutralised.

As was the case for the Scottish colonists in *The Rising Sun,* a romantic paradigm pre-empts the success of the British expedition to Afghanistan. Inder Lal, an Indian impartial observer of the events described in the novel, refers to Shakespeare's *The Tempest* to explain the reasons and meaning of British imperial expansion: although in the process of furthering the frontiers of empire the colonisers may believe that 'you are here to sell us your wonderful English goods, you want to set us free, you want us to grow up, you want to educate us', these are no more than 'fairy stories' (244); the real motive behind aiming for ever vaster territory is in fact, like Prospero, 'to surrender it, to give it up [...] and return nobly' (244). He concludes with what is both an indictment of the romantic framework of empire for its impracticality and a recognition that, at the same time, this is also its only redeeming feature from a human point of view: 'That desire is so strong in you, it makes you build an empire; because if you never had an empire, you would not have one so nobly to surrender' (244). This explanation intimates the tendency towards the celebration of loss and the anticipation of nostalgic retrospection even at the height of, and against, the immediacy of experience, which this study has identified as a constant in the contemporary British historical novel's attitude towards the past it seeks to represent and towards the nation whose foundations it aims to examine. Thus, the displacement of the present reality of empire in favour of a future look back at its achievement (something which, implicitly, can only be done after the end of the experience and at a time of decline from the earlier summit) is conducted in the name of nobility, preserving in spite of all commercial and geopolitical considerations the allegiance to an unviable ideal. The reliance on a romantic understanding of the imperial enterprise, initially signalled by adventure but ultimately revealed to be nostalgic in nature, becomes in the novel a conscious and wilful act of self-undermining that defines the nation both at home and abroad.

In Britain, at the close of the novel, the reaction and re-emplotment of the disastrous defeat in Afghanistan is encapsulated in the popular performance at Astley's circus of a private scene, the reunion of General Sale, commander of colonial troops in Punjab, with his wife Florentia, who had been stranded in Kabul. The strategic and political humiliation at the hands of the Afghans is elided to be replaced by a moment of private triumph invested with national overtones: ' "So Britons shall never come to harm ... while hearth and home ... and LOVE is warm" ' (522). The success of the scene rests on the fact that it presents 'heroism made small and put on stage' (522), in other words a celebration of private virtues that implies a withdrawal from the public arena. And yet, however heart-warming to a British audience thousands of miles away from the events, this portrait of the two characters is no less misleading than the version of the siege in the celebratory painting of General Sinclair in *The Siege of Krishnapur*. The weight of the preceding pages of the novel has shown that, far from being loving, relations between the General and his wife, an ambitious and bossy woman, were decidedly frosty. The impression that the circus performance is a convenient reduction of the truth to an acceptable myth is clearly heightened for the reader, who has experienced Sale and Florentia in action.

Among the applauding spectators at Astley's circus are Mr Stokes and Bella. The former, as we saw earlier, dared to challenge Burnes's imperial certainties at the height of the nation's enthusiasm for the Afghan enterprise; the latter had herself 'been in the war, the real one' (522) when she found that she was pregnant and had to retire from society to her family's country estate. A different version of the intersection of romance and reality can be traced in the novel, centring on Bella's experiences at home as opposed to Burnes's abroad.

The unsuitable, old, damp house at the bottom of a misty vale in the Gloucestershire countryside, with countless rooms only four of which are in use, as in a kind of living ruin, becomes a source of personal and national identity alternative to both the brilliant world of London society and the adventurous one of Kabul. Against the instability of the former's changing fashions and the latter's shifting fortunes, the house offers continuity, as '[i]t slept on, without annoyance or disturbance, much as it had done for three centuries' (255). It is marked by a conscious retrenchment into an ever decreasing space, as the public and reception rooms are shut up one by one, but is also characterised by the intensity with which Bella lives her new situation, without any attempts to apply to it a framework of behaviour or understanding: 'There was so much … that Bella did not think about; there was so much that did not enter her thoughts, so much that lay unconsidered in a life that was now past, that might have been that of a distant acquaintance. [...] Her happiness was of an oblivious, uncontemplative nature' (262). Stokes, who, like the hero of a conventional romance, chances upon the house while riding in the countryside without knowing to whom it belongs, equally struggles to put into words the experience he has in Bella's company. He realises that '[s]omething – some story, true – had been vouchsafed to him' and, at the same time, that 'there was no betrayal like the telling of it' (265). It remains experience not revisited with the benefit of retrospection and not reshaped to the parameters of narrative. While Stokes thinks of the unexpected visit as having 'a distinct whiff of the fairy tale about it', with himself as the 'hero' (266), the analogy is neither pursued nor contested.

As a result, the episode remains to the side of the main thrust of the plot, and outside the relentless unfolding of history the novel depicts. Its historical significance is uncertain and its only perceivable effect is on Stokes's changed outlook on his public role as consummate satirist of society's foibles, which lessens in comparison with his private reflections on ethics. It is therefore interesting that the same two characters should find themselves together at the close of the novel, the moment when the nation collectively participates in the withdrawal from history and the embracing of an ideologically motivated version of domesticity. It is Bella's son, Henry, who implicitly challenges the construction of domesticity on the stage, juxtaposing it with his experience of it in reality, even as a child, as 'his little face shone with the memory of his quiet acres, of birds flying over the still ponds of his own land' (523). Uttered as it is by a child, the sentence suggests a retrenchment even before public engagement has been experienced. In the by now predictable equation of the ancestral house with the nation, the ending also points to what is ultimately a pre-modern national model of inherited land ownership, which shuns further acquisition but, in so doing, prevents the kind of social mobility fostered by the opportunities afforded in imperial outposts from which Burnes and Masson benefited.

3. Ronan Bennett's *Havoc in Its Third Year* and Gregory Norminton's *Ghost Portrait*

The Mulberry Empire juxtaposes its own model of historical writing, based on comprehensiveness and retrospection, to that of historical romancers, for whom the past is little more than an exotic background to formulaic action. A representative of this literary strand, Stapleton, makes a brief appearance in the novel. Among his successes are 'a romance of old Byzantium [...,] a romance of life among the Vikings' (152–3) and even more remote settings such as Medieval China and Abyssinia, none of which are the product of first-hand research, as Stapleton admits: ' "Oh, I made it all up" [...] "Invented. The whole caboodle, anthropofagy, sacred tigers, ritual dances with cowcumbers, all of it" ' (153). The common feature in these works is the absence of any sense of historical process, with the result that plots are devised purely for the sake of adventurous or exotic events: the Vikings in Stapleton's second novel were 'meant...to invade Britain' but 'in the end, they were so interesting that –' (152). Stapleton's example introduces a degree of generic self-referentiality, to accompany its narrative counterpart, in Hensher's novel. From the earliest examples of historical fiction (and the novel's setting in the 1830s is not significantly distant from the publication of Scott's works), in fact, a distinction developed between 'the recovered past – in historical novels based on a careful study of books, documents, archives, and visits to sites that had figured prominently in actual events – and the "felt" past – in a historical novel that imagined the emotional responses of fictional characters who lived at some moment prior to the novelist's lifetime' (Orel 1). The latter became known as 'costume novels' and were characterised by 'the element of play and of good-natured fun [...]: fun in the plotting for its own sake rather than as a subsidiary aspect of dialogue or character development' (Orel 3).

Hensher's insertion of a foil to his own emphasis on the concatenation of events according to relations of cause and consequence serves as a commentary on historical fiction generally: it acknowledges that, in spite of its name, the genre had, from its origins, contained an element of a-historical escapism. In Ronan Bennett's *Havoc in Its Third Year*, on the other hand, the plot itself centres on the irreconcilable conflict between the a-historical understanding of the world fostered by religious belief and the very real workings of causality and consequentiality in events that define history as process. The historical setting (the 1630s) places the characters at the cusp of momentous events of national significance, the Civil War and its religiously scandalous outcome of the deposition and execution of an anointed king, while the fact that the action takes place in an isolated town in the North, removed from the centre of political power and national decision-making, emphasises that the reach of history is inescapable and its effects inevitable. John Brigge, the novel's protagonist, embodies this conflict and is ultimately defeated in all he holds dear because of his inability to reconcile his double allegiance, to Catholicism and to the government of the town.

Brigge is himself a governor of the town and its coroner, for whom 'the law is the law, duty is duty' (1). He is dedicated to the implementation of policies, from the prevention of crime to the relief of the poor, that respond to the necessities of the people at the time and as a result he finds himself attempting to understand and influence the course of events: he is, in other words, eminently involved in shaping the future by active human intervention, which amounts to a definition of history-making. When, for instance, a few years before the action of the novel begins, he had participated with the other governors in the deposition of the tyrannical Lord Savile and had voted for his replacement by a council of godly men (including himself), Brigge had unknowingly anticipated the actions of Parliament towards Charles I which would occur on a much larger historical and national stage. And yet, the novel suggests that even at this moment when his historical involvement was greatest and most effective, the seeds of the defeat of the project and of Brigge himself are apparent, since the effect of the demand that the town's government be conducted according to the principles of the Bible is to bring to the fore the religious differences between the governors. These, in turn, are more complex than the doctrinal distinction between Catholicism and Reform; rather, they consist of a fundamental divergence in the understanding of God as merciful or as vengeful. The extremism of the reformer Favour is matched by the belligerent pronouncement of the priest Father Edward: both men succumb to the demands of history, which will require only one to triumph while the other pays with his life, and in so doing they betray their stated religious purpose.

Brigge is the only one who succeeds in preserving his ethical integrity, but he can do so only at the expense of any attempt to intervene in historically significant ways and ultimately only at the cost of losing his possessions, his family, and his life. His religious outlook, which is never relinquished but at most subdued during the time of his active participation in government, affects every aspect of his existence: 'Brigge lived with signs and saints; they were everywhere in his life. To his mind nothing in the world was without signification: dreams were portents, phantoms real, and only a fool believed in such a thing as chance' (1). As a man who 'desperately wanted to know the future [...]. What was God's plan for him?' (2), he conceives of the world and everything in it as part of a predetermined, if still obscure, outcome, already in place in the timelessness of God's omniscient framework, even though men are compelled to live in the historical uncertainty of human time. The significance of human action diminishes when set against the comprehensiveness of eternity, with the result that the historical specificity of his circumstances is subsumed to a system of signification that transcends history. He even reads the disruption he witnesses in the town in terms of universality, claiming that ' "[w]hen I was a child there were also men who prophesied calamity and preached harshness and rigour. Every age, it seems, is the most dangerous there has even been" ' (96). His interlocutor replies by emphasising that ' "[t]his age is particular. Darkness threatens to overwhelm us as it never has before" ' (96). The irony is that Brigge is right, but his position is out of tune with the prevalent understanding of themselves as actors in history on the part of the other characters in the novel. The crisis for Brigge (the point of rupture in what had been an outward allegiance to political participation and a private belief in the pre-eminence of obedience to religious life) comes when demands are made on him that conflate the two and, at the same time, make an ethically and politically sustainable choice impossible.

On his way to the town to fulfil his function as a coroner, Brigge encounters a group of squatters illegally camped at the edges of his land. His duty as an official representative and upholder of the law of the town requires him to enforce their removal, while the compassionate attitude he owes his religion stays his hand, and he resolves to ignore the impasse and do nothing. What is interesting, however, in the squatters' plea for their right is that they shift the argument beyond the legal confines of the local government and the moral boundaries of religion, referring to themselves as 'Englishmen' who 'must live somewhere' (6). As the stories of the group of vagrants are pieced together, it emerges that they have indeed travelled all over the country, from the Fens to the South West and now the North, forced to move from place to place by the lack of labour and means of supporting themselves. They are victims of history but also the only group who appropriate for themselves a national identity: thus, where Brigge perceives his existence within the compass of God's will and his adversaries mould their actions to the contingent and local context of the events of the town, the vagrants introduce a third term of reference in the debate, nationality. Although neither Brigge nor the politicians take up the implicit question of a communal identity, with the duties and responsibilities that entails, the knowledge that the events in this remote town are part of a larger national conflagration, which comes from the readers' and author's historical perspective, implicitly invites a reflection on the broader national significance of the novel's plot.

The second challenge comes in the person of Katherine Shay, an Irishwoman accused of infanticide whom Brigge, as a coroner, is called to examine. Although Brigge meets her in his official capacity, which involves among other duties the investigation of clues and the pursuit of logical explanations and therefore ought to place him firmly within the historical dimension, her first hearing takes on religious overtones that disrupt the separation of worldly and devotional behaviours by which the magistrate defines his existence. To his question ' "Is your name Katherine Shay" ' she replies with an echo of Jesus's words to Pilate at his hearing for an unjust charge: ' "If you say it is, then it is" ' (14) and then goes on to claim to claim ' "I owe nothing to any court of any pretended power or magistrate put over

me [...]. I owe obedience to no one on this earth"' (15). The Biblical
resonance of her words places the everyday situation in which Brigge
finds himself (one to which he is used and whose duties he can carry
out competently) unto the plane of timelessness, requiring a reaction
which the coroner is incapable of providing because the two systems
of signification that guide the separate areas of his life have been
scandalously conflated. The probing of Brigge's certainties is relentless. At her second appearance in front of the magistrate, Shay urges
him to take on the role of St. Germanus, freer of prisoners in unjust
circumstances, and open the very real barred gates of the town's
prison. In other words, she is inciting political action on the part of
Brigge by articulating it within the competing framework of religion
and appealing to the very aspect (the depth of his religious conviction as a Catholic at odds with the prevalent reformist climate in the
town) that had motivated his reluctance to become more deeply
involved in public life.

Brigge had previously responded to calls for his loyalty not only in
'outward conformity' but in the absoluteness of 'your heart' (35) by
retreating further into the private seclusion of his land. Unsurprisingly,
the seclusion is envisaged as a real and ideal paradise: he wishes to
'build a wall to keep his family safe' and contain the privacy of '[m]an,
woman, child, home' (117). He imagines their existence there with
reference to the iconography of the Edenic Garden and the Madonna
and Child, superimposed on the reality of his land:

> a child, healthy and whole, plump and laughing, its eyes curious
> and frank, its mouth fringed with milk. Elizabeth recovered in
> her spirits, restored to the woman she had been before. A crop
> carpeting the long slopes stretching out from the house as far as
> the little beck that marked the boundary of his land, endless ears
> of corn fat enough to please a pharaoh. Sheep with lambs and
> long wool and no sign of the rot or the turn. (58)

The wish, however, is only briefly sustained for a few 'warm spring
days' that 'were like a term in paradise' (162) and is ultimately
destroyed by the fact that Brigge's is already a post-lapsarian world of
poor land where, in contrast with the plentiful natural riches of paradise, '[l]ittle grew' (2), where few rewards are gained despite much
toil, and where Elizabeth gives birth after much pain and danger to

a child who will not suck. The story Brigge finds himself enacting instead is a conflation of Jesus's entrance in Jerusalem on the eve of his Passion and death and the flight into Egypt to escape Herod's persecution, when after the death of his wife he moves from village to village around the town, from which he has been banished, with his son and the wet nurse on a donkey and a motley following of former prisoners, and they are greeted on arrival by waving of branches and cries of welcome. What the two episodes from the Gospels have in common is that actions inspired by God have to confront the political reality of the historical context in which they take place.

The echoes of the same conflict reverberate into Brigge's life to the end, when he dies reconciled with his principles and reaches 'paradise' (227) in its religious sense of the soul's place after death, where his wife and child await him. This final personal fulfilment, however, is ineffectual in any political sense, since his journey through the country does not lead to a resolution to the town's divided state. Nor does the travelling offer a more successful counterpart to the wandering of the vagrants in the name of their right as Englishmen: Brigge's trajectory in the novel fails to provide a viable model of existence that reconciles opposing forces, as once again the religious framework (accompanied by the distinctively Biblical tone of Bennett's prose) within which they are envisaged grants these moments a significance that transcends history, and yet at the same time it deprives them of relevance for the particular historical moment in which they take place. On the eve of the Civil War, historical action is all-consuming and the historical understanding of the competing factions all-encompassing. The consciousness of the specificity of the historical moment belongs to Brigge's clerk and reform sympathiser Adam, who reminds his master that ' "[w]e live in bitter times and the world is divided in two: those who live inside the godly nation, and those outside. Inside is righteousness and strength. Outside is barbarism and terror. You chose to live outside" ' (229). Brigge's reply to the effect that he ' "chose rather not to live inside" ' (229) is disingenuous, since in the divided town ' "There is nothing in between" ' (229). *Havoc in Its Third Year* thus identifies the ineluctable thrust of the historical process, which sweeps all attempts at resistance in the name of personal belief or ethical integrity in its wake. The final proof of its force comes when the town is razed to the ground by its unnamed enemies: throughout, Brigge had denied their existence and, in what appeared to be a correct surmise, had taken them to have been spectres raised by the governors who sought more extensive powers for themselves. Yet by the end these apparent phantoms take on physical shape and perform real actions.

The starting point for Gregory Norminton's *Ghost Portrait* is an apparently successful instance of retrenchment into the private domain of the kind Brigge envisaged but could not fulfil and which is represented, unsurprisingly, by ownership of a house and garden. The former is 'a refuge ... where a man may believe the world to be good' (18), while the latter takes on the semblance of 'Paradise' (69) in its traditional iconography of the '[h]ortus conclusus' or enclosed garden, which '[i]n times of crisis, of discord ... means order, peace, abundance' (68). And yet the completeness of this initial situation is progressively undermined as the novel retraces backwards the events of Nathaniel Deller's life, revealing the ethical compromises to which he subjected himself in order to gain the desired withdrawal from public life and their consequences into the present.

At the start of the novel, in 1680, Deller is an old man and a painter forced into retirement by his blindness, whose wife died in giving birth to their daughter. Although he attained success in his career as a court painter after the restoration of Charles II to the throne, the mannerist nature of the work required of him by his patrons and clients has left him, now that it is too late to amend his style, deeply dissatisfied. The novel constructs a complex argument around painting which combines representational form and national identity: Deller's wish as a young apprentice training in Holland amongst artists dedicated to minute realism was to import it into England and create a new kind of painting. This was his 'earthly purpose', to 'invent that English art, sprung from our native soil, imbued with the genius of the country' (80). He finds the ideal subject in 1650 in the Diggers that had colonised the empty land around Cobham after they had been deprived of their livelihoods by a programme of enclosures, a political counterpart, with very public effects, to the retreat into privacy represented by the walled garden of the house. To Deller the Diggers' unembellished state provides the perfect test for his philosophy of an unembellished art: representation, at this point in the novel, consists of a coincidence of subject and method. And yet, by virtue of the fact that he is the observer and they are the specimen under scrutiny as potential subjects of art as much as because of any difference in class, Deller never belongs with the dispossessed settlers. The situation suggests ironic parallels between Deller's present metaphorical understanding of paradise as a private garden and the Diggers' attempt to reproduce paradise literally in the unwelcoming surroundings of St. George's Hill, a 'harsh and ancient garden: fallen Eden, whose fruits were sharp and bitter' (126). Their actions are an attempt to re-encode the myth of the garden within a political context, as they demand *'our heaven here ... and heaven hereafter too'* (129), while Deller's intervention in the national definition is solely through the medium of art: the immortalising of the present in the faces of the settlers implicitly counters the possibility of their significant development as historical actors.

Deller's ostensible and frequently stated wish to represent the world as it presents itself to his eyes (a statement of radical realism) is undercut by his inability to see that the form he seeks to pursue entails a political closeness to the project of his prospective subjects which he simply does not possess. When the army charges the settlers in Cobham to clear the site, the difference in class, status, and in what they have to lose between the painter and his subjects is brought to his consciousness and he flees without confronting the soldiers or helping the others, admitting that 'now he recognised all that was at stake. Radical groups had exhausted their license. If it became known that he had lived among Diggers, the consequences for his art and his family might be serious' (167). It is at this point that Deller realises that the ideals and aims he proclaimed to share with the settlers were only a cover for the pursuit of his artistic goals in what he deemed to be the best circumstances: in his first full experience of a historical event and of the relationship between power and the historical process, his conscious decision is to withdraw from the action in the name of art, even if that art had been imagined (while still untested) as having a national and therefore political dimension.

Although it gains him social position and the house and grounds that confirm it, this dereliction of political and human solidarity affects Deller's entire life and taints his art, which had been the very reason for joining the Diggers in the first place as well as the reason for abandoning their fight. Not only does he never return to the project of devising an English style of representational realism, he also fails in what is for him the most important painting, a portrait from memory of his late wife, who has been dead for over 20 years. The sitter is represented as 'an English Madonna seated in the oak tree's shade' framed by nature, including 'the gathered splendour of an ancient oak, a few leaves precisely rendered in the foliage and the knotted trunk furrowed in brown ink. Vague premonitions of a garden' (37). But the garden, 'a landscape of civility and order' (37), has purely symbolic and conventional generic existence and is no longer a viable paradise on earth, while the woman's face remains unpainted as Deller, attempting to recapture the reality of his beloved wife by means of art, in fact 'found only artifice' (37). He is also reminded of the past by the unexpected arrival of Thomas Digby, who was with him on St. George's Hill, on the same day as the King's return from France and on the eve of his wife's death. The novel's structure unveils the layers of Deller's disillusion in reverse, so that what at the start of the novel, in the section dated 1680, had seemed artistic disappointment and private grief at the loss of his wife, becomes in the second section set in 1660 also a political disappointment and grief at the loss of his companions and their ideals, and finally in the narrative of the events of 1650 Deller's own betrayal of the Diggers is revealed.

Digby openly places in front of Deller the same objection to his choice of a life of private fulfilment over public intervention that was raised against Brigge, namely that ' "[t]he test of spiritual value is in community. Your seclusion here is ungodly" ', to which the painter replies, ' "Vice has ever been the fruit of power. Virtue, redemption, love – these exist only in private" ' (62). What is interesting in this exchange is that Digby's appeal to active participation in history is made in the name of religion and morality, so that like Katherine Shay he conflates political intervention and religious consistency, while the response shifts the ground of the argument to an equation of participation in historical events with political struggles for power and only then introduces moral (or immoral) elements in the debate. If the association of virtue, redemption, and love with a withdrawal to private life is familiar, Deller's statement is nevertheless coloured by the fact that it appears in the narrative sequence after the consequences of his actions in the present have already been shown. We therefore know that he has lost his wife, is professionally and personally disillusioned, and regrets his past actions: redemption seems impossible and virtue is applied to a very limited compass, particularly in Deller's treatment of his daughter Cynthia.

Digby too, however, shows a degree of moral ambivalence that arises precisely from the consistency of his beliefs. Following the failure of the Diggers' project, he proposes to '[s]et sail for the colonies. *America.* Think of it, friend. Virgin territory – a land without history, without boundaries' (57–8). It is impossible not to read this statement with the benefit of retrospection and in the light of the novels discussed in the previous chapter: the assumption that the lands of the New World are empty of inhabitants, that they have no past of their own (since history is, in colonial discourse, a Western prerogative), that they are gendered female and waiting for their conqueror, even if a benevolent one, all form the background to the imperial expansion accompanied by ideological mastery of discourse which fosters national self-definition. It is no coincidence that Digby outlines his plans for emigration just after dramatically declaring that 'England is lost' (57). The expansionary aim is articulated within a double framework, national (historical) and religious (mythical). The colonisation of the new territory becomes a way of finding a new location to reassert the ideals that were to form a community of equal men in England but were first betrayed by the Commonwealth and then destroyed by the intervention of the army on government orders. At the same time, the move from Cobham to America is a geographical counterpart to the displacement of Eden ever further into the past, which underscores the impossibility of its historical recreation in the present. Ideologically, then, Digby's project is doomed to fail again.

While the reverse chronological sequence of the novel's structure emphasises the chain of cause and consequence from the past into the present, and indeed the hold of the former over the latter, the fact that neither Deller nor Digby have been able to live fruitfully in the present and the noted absence of a future for either man suggests that the model of historical causality on which the novel and the characters rely for an explanation of events may in fact be inadequate. The possibility of a future is, nevertheless, asserted at the very end of the novel, in the promised union of Deller's daughter Cynthia with his former pupil William Stroud. Their vows are exchanged in the grounds of the house 'which were forbidden to [Stroud] in his youth' (172) while he was apprenticed to Deller and mark a physical repossession of the garden in contrast to the failed attempt at its ideal representation in the portrait of Belinda Deller and the limited scope of its metaphorical investment as a sanctuary and a retreat from the world. Indeed, this final episode situates the younger generation firmly in the world as active participants: Cynthia welcomes William's renunciation of artistic aspirations, for which he admits 'no true calling' (190) in favour of pursuing his father's job as a miller. She suggests that the practical, even mundane role he will take up is comparable to the higher goals he nurtured as a young man, since ' "[n]othing can exist without bread. You are a maker, William" ' (191). The garden *has* been regained, but it is a contingent, actual paradise of everyday life, rather than a mythically desirable and unattainable site of (past) delight.

Conclusion: Fictions of the Garden

In an essay written only a few years before *The French Lieutenant's Woman*, John Fowles singles out withdrawal from the public arena as the defining trait of the English (as opposed to the British) character. Like the novels with which the previous chapter ended, Fowles shows a degree of sympathy with the desire for retrenchment into the private domain, but again like them he disputes its ultimate goal, reflecting that while 'withdrawal is a kind of movement' or, in other words, an act significant in a historical context, it is 'not necessarily a kind of morality' (1964: 85). The statement in many ways sums up the concern with the relationship between the individual and the historical process that pervades the 13 novels discussed in this study. They outline not only the predicament of characters caught up in situations over which they can exercise limited control and torn between active if uncertain intervention in history and the passive rewards of private fulfilment, but also the comparable quandary of the historical novelist (and, vicariously, his or her proxy in the novels, the quester after the past), who must navigate between truthfulness of representation, with its corollary partiality of vision, and historical comprehensiveness, which can only be achieved by resorting to invention.

The previous four chapters have recorded a movement from one strategy to the other, thus signalling the genre's progressively more established confidence in its representational possibilities. Thus, once the epistemological and ontological questions consonant with the preoccupations of postmodernism in fiction, which had been raised by historical fiction in the late twentieth century, had also been answered by the same novels' formal innovation and self-conscious attention to their representational practice, later examples of the genre could turn their attention to particular aspects of the national past (most notably empire) and undertake a comprehensive and ideologically astute probing of its historical significance and its reverberations into the present. Interestingly, though, one can trace a reverse relationship between the contemporary historical novel's assertiveness of its generic viability and the increasingly pessimistic framework for the comprehensive representation of the past the genre can lay claim to. The formal negotiations of *The French Lieutenant's Woman, The Siege of Krishnapur* or *Heat and Dust,* in fact, concerned the individual's ability to find redemption within his or her historical situation: Charles Smithson's final parting from Sarah signals a newly discovered ethical integrity, while the Collector's insight into the real forces of history largely atones for his earlier unquestioning adherence to colonial discourse, and Jhabvala's narrator's decision to remain in India frees her from the apparent historical determinism of her actions throughout the novel. On the other hand, in the most recent examples of historical fiction I examined, personal redemption in a private context is either unattainable or achieved at an unsustainable ethical cost, with the result that there appears to be a disconnection between the nation in its historical existence and the individual's ability to act as representative of the community of which he or she is imaginatively part.

The shift in outcome marks the progressive gaining of prominence in the novels of the uncertain fate and diminished congruence of the nation over the place of the individual in that nation and in history. It is therefore especially appropriate that Fowles's mention of withdrawal into the private sphere should appear in a discussion of national identity, and particularly of the difference between Englishness and Britishness. Fowles associates 'Red-White-and-Blue Britain' with 'the Hanoverian dynasty and the Victorian and Edwardian ages...of Empire' (82): its national identity coalesces around the perceived 'historical duty to be a powerful military nation' on a global scale (79). Given that 'Britain' does not, for Fowles, refer to any specific element of the nation but is merely a 'slogan word' (79) to meet the demands of a particular historical moment, it fails to achieve a continuity of national identification. It is worth pointing out that the periodisation the essay associates with the concept of Britain coincides with the time of the historical novel's first emergence as a recognisable genre (as in Scott's allegiance to Hanoverian Britain over Jacobite Scotland), the period of greatest expansion of its methods and principles to encompass the novel *tout court* (the Victorian era of realist fiction), and the historical moments to which contemporary examples of the genre return most frequently for the settings of their stories (the late eighteenth, nineteenth, and early twentieth centuries). In this respect, the engagement with questions of national identity in the novels examined in this study and their attempt to put forward and probe different models of national identity can be related to the need to invest the *fait accompli* of the political entity of Britain with a national dimension. Conversely, in view of the contemporary historical novel's task, to which I referred in the Introduction, to cast a retrospective glance over the seemingly continuous narrative of the nation and pinpoint the moments when the seams are at their weakest, it would seem that the deterioration of a sense of the nation in the aftermath of the loss of the Empire can be traced to the fact that the nation (Britain) needed the presence of empire to sustain its definition of itself. In the late twentieth century, when all the former colonies had achieved independence, the incongruity between the grandiloquent and expansionary associations of the term 'Britain' and the reality of a country reduced from the near-global reach of its political control to the relative paucity of its physical island borders had become inescapable.

It is in this climate of national retrenchment to the literary myth of the garden of England – a case of romanticising loss and turning it into the foundation of identity which recurs in the plots of the novels discussed in the preceding chapters – that Fowles's essay must be placed. Its title, 'On Being English but Not British', performs an ideological sleight of hand which turns the necessary contraction of the national outlook into an affirmation of positive difference from the past, even though in the process Fowles has to acknowledge that he is trying to give shape to something that is 'far more an emotional than an intellectual concept' (87). This concept is 'Green England', whose sense of identity relies on such traditionally established, yet curiously ineffable, traits as fairness and justice and whose representative is Robin Hood, a political outlaw fighting for liberty for the people (83). In spite of its instinctive attractiveness, this articulation of national identity contains the contradictions inherent in the disparate models of the nation proposed by the novels in the earlier chapters, from the governmentally sanctioned wildness of Ware Common to the enclosed gardens of *Possession* and *Ever After* to the imposition of an Edenic model on colonial territories, to the garden of a private home or the lands of a country house. Robin Hood's alliance with 'the people' was historically only temporary and motivated by the loss of his lands, expropriated by King John; his lineage and values are those of an older feudal order that denies the historical relevance of the community of the nation and seeks to perpetuate the narrower relations of personal kinship and vassalage, while his loyalty to an absentee king is declared in the name of tradition and against the changes (even the modernity) introduced by the presumed usurper John.

An interesting echo of Fowles's mention of Robin Hood as the representative of the nation can be found in *The Siege of Krishnapur*. At the height of the siege, Fleury receives as a birthday present 'a coat of Lincoln green together with a cap of the same material, garnished with a turquoise peacock's feather' (Farrell 192) which had been fashioned by cutting off the green baize from the billiard tables. Harry Dunstaple immediately observes that 'he looks as if he has just come from Sherwood Forest' (192) and, in spite of the ludicrousness of the outfit in the context of the Indian heat and the dangers of the siege (the bright green makes him stand out as a target for the sepoy muskets), Fleury is 'secretly pleased to be compared with Robin Hood' (192). The suit becomes a mark of personal and national identity, as Fleury aims to imitate the heroism associated with the original wearer of the clothes and to distinguish himself from the bedraggled survivors of the siege as much as from their Indian adversaries. He certainly succeeds in surviving the ordeal relatively unscathed; he gains the woman he desires in the person of Louisa Dunstaple, and by the end of the novel he has acquired all the least attractive characteristics of the typical Englishman of his time. In what is a reversal of the trajectory undergone by the Collector, in fact, Fleury goes from his Krishnapur days of being the voice of Romantic equality amongst cultures to owning a vast collection of artefacts that stand for the superiority of Western ideas and confidently talking about progress, while at the same time 'hector[ing]' his children 'with his views' (312) and betraying Louise with 'a young lady of passionate disposition' (313). Interestingly, the myth of Robin

Hood is perpetuated most effectively in the colonial context, whereas its relevance subsides when it is applied to its original location of England, as once he has returned from India Fleury gives up any heroic endeavours or ideologically transgressive positions. As I noted on several occasions with respect to the novels' projection of national attributes to physical locations or metaphorical repositories, this incongruity indicates the difficulties of sustaining a representation of the nation in the present which does not also contain the seeds of its failure, most notably the overwhelming sense of loss of wholeness and development inherent in the shift from a (diachronic) narrative articulation of the nation to its (synchronic) location in a fixed image, however resonant the latter's associations may be. Geoffrey Cubitt (1998) has noted the shift from the 'grand and essentially linear narratives of nationalist historiography' of the nineteenth century, which 'supply the most obvious framework within which the elements of a national past may be assembled' (10) to '[t]he twentieth century ... impulses to process the national past in other ways', whose emphasis is less on linearity and more on physical synchronicity (10). Among the contemporary strategies Cubitt identifies as providing a framework for national articulation are 'to organize commemorative rituals around its heroes and salient events, to conserve its material remains, to reconstruct its way of life for public consumption' (10). The result is 'a conception of the national past that is at once more cumulative and more fragmented – a past shaped less as progression than as selectively remembered accretion, less as story than as memory and heritage' (10).

The 13 novels that form the subject of this study conform to Cubitt's description in their efforts to replace a narrative strategy widely perceived as inadequate (linear historical narrative and its corollary claim to realism) with alternative modes of representation, such as romance, which defy the periodicity and sequentiality inherent in nationalist historiography. The novels' self-conscious abandonment of realism at the level of form results, substantively, in a changed framework for the provision of models of national identification. In so doing, however, they also acknowledge the unstable nature of a national model that contravenes one of the fundamental attributes of the nation as imagined community, namely its trajectory in time from the shared past to the experienced present and into a commonly envisaged future. It is no coincidence that arguably the only fully successful articulation of a narrative trajectory that encompasses a possible future as well as recording the past is Peevay's in *English Passengers*: his model is founded on the appropriation and redeployment of the very narrative and representational strategies of imperial discourse that had begun to fail the colonists. At the opposite end of the national-representational spectrum are the gardens of *The Chymical Wedding*, *Possession*, and *Ever After*: their physical boundaries are transcended in the name of the metaphorical resonance of their implications for a story of Fall and redemption with the eventual regaining of paradise, but it is a paradise which has been largely deprived of communal value and whose experience is confined to the individual. The preservation of Agnew Hall or Seal Court gestures towards the location of the nation in a particular place, but even this has to confront the competing embodiment of the nation in its cultural remnants, the documents from the past, whose potential for disaggregation and monetary value, however, militates against an enduring role as repositories of the national imagination.

The recurrence of the trope of the garden, in its widest associations, as a vehicle for imagining the nation is significant in so far as it points to an attempt to locate a minimal common ground for a shared experience of natural existence to counter the artificiality and ideological exclusions of more complex (man-made) national referents. Hobsbawm (1994) refers to the 'paradox' of 'modern nations', which 'claim to be the opposite of novel, namely rooted in the remotest antiquity, and the opposite of constructed, namely human communities so "natural" as to require no definition other than self-assertion' (76). There is no furthest point of origin than the Edenic garden, a place situated before the onset of history, while the perception of a natural community requiring no external element to define itself becomes especially attractive following the demise of the obvious terms of comparison to validate British identity, namely, the colonial territories. In English, there are particular benefits to the appropriation of the natural landscape for nationally imaginative purposes: ' "country" is both a nation and a part of a "land"; "the country" can be the whole society or its rural area' (Williams 1); the language, in other words, sustains the illusion of naturalness to which references to the garden appeal. The country is also, in the literary tradition of the pastoral as well as in the social contemporary phenomenon of leaving an urban life for a rural one, identified as the site 'of a natural way of life: of peace, innocence, and simple virtue' (Williams 1), on which can be bestowed a moral dimension. Interestingly, this is a myth shared by the Left as well as the Right: 'There is a powerful myth of prelapsarian agricultural simplicity that has survived, even been encouraged by, 300 years of industrialisation; the emergence of an urban proletariat has led to memories of community and class solidarity which are summoned up to confront contemporary conflicts and defeat' (Hewison 47). What is more, the appearance of immutability generated by the idea (and the ideal) of a life subjected only to the rhythms of nature and oblivious of the demands of artificial routines fosters the desirable myth of the country as a place beyond the reach of history and where, therefore, the individual pressed into historically significant actions can escape. So can the nation, in order to forget or even deny its defeat in the process of history which resulted in decolonisation. Ironically, the word 'colony' also etymologically derives from the Latin for countryside: the site of retrenchment contains the possibility of expansion.

Yet even the greenness that is the only attribute Fowles bestows on England is part of a complex ideological construct that combines nostalgia with escapism and projects a far from comprehensive image of the nation. Not only is the image of the countryside promoted as a national symbol largely removed from the reality of actual locations and lived-in landscapes (hence the appeal of the mythical site of the Edenic Garden). It is also an instance of imagining the nation 'through the deployment of a notion of "typicality"' whereby 'selected specimens or images of the local or particular are woven into the symbolic fabric of the national' (Cubitt 7): for instance, 'the landscape of the southern downlands becomes the typical scenery of rural England' (7) or even of England *tout court*.

Privileged but decontextualized, these selected fragments of a socially and regionally differentiated culture service the illusion of national homogeneity, and encourage the transfer to the imagined community of the nation of at least some of the affective capital that attaches to other, more localised, experiences. The cost of this, of course, is the implicit marginalisation, in national terms, of lifestyles, landscapes, cultures and traditions that do not attain this emblematic status. (Cubitt 7)

Even within the confines of the nation, it appears, the tendency is towards retrenchment from part of its reality – the part, notably its urban landscape, which is more evidently subject to change and historical intervention. What is interesting about the ideological operation Cubitt describes is the fact that it succeeds in making the limited frame of reference not only desirable but also actively sought. However unconscious, this is the result of a largely unquestioned and paradoxical historical sense that associates the countryside in all its forms of greenness with the wholeness of the nation within its physical boundaries, before its fall into modernity, imperial expansion and eventual loss of status.

The idea of a natural, whole nation, however far into the past it is projected, is of course no more than a consoling myth. Raymond Williams (1973) notes that the idealisation of the countryside entails the erasure of the very real conditions of economic pressure and class exploitation. Far from being immune from the reach of capitalism (and with it, of historical change), the countryside is in fact the place where the first experiments with capital, the application of technological innovations and the effects of social mobility occur. The very gardens and country estates which, in so many of the novels discussed in this study, come to stand for the nation withdrawn from history and its ills were the culmination of changes in traditional rural life ruthlessly imposed in the name of progress, modernity, efficiency of production, which produced the capital to be spent on erecting the future metonyms of the nation. Nevertheless, the persistence and success of the erasure of history from the country house and its garden are apparent in their significance as representatives of the nation to the present day, in spite of or perhaps because of its reactionary (if misleading) association with 'feudal and immediately post-feudal values: of an order based on settled and reciprocal social and economic relations of an avowedly total kind' (Williams 35). Nor can the influence of the continuous tradition of literary representations of the country estate from Renaissance poetry to the early novel in the eighteenth century to the tales of decline in the interwar years be discounted, particularly in view of the contemporary reliance on textual mediation for access to the past. The 'cult of the country house' (Hewison 53) also responds to the general sense, which I have traced in the novels under consideration, of an irrecoverable loss of the past, which is then recast as the unattainable object of a never-extinguished desire. It is '[a] building that can only be glimpsed' from far away and as such 'becomes the erotic object of desire of a lover locked out. Yet he seems unaware of his exclusion. By a mystical process of identification the country house becomes the nation, and love of one's country makes obligatory a love of the country house. We have been re-admitted to paradise lost' (Hewison 53), physically so on payment of an entrance fee to the heritage site. Even in the ultimate attempt to flee from modern constraints into a past codified as outside history and available for emotional communion, it seems, we are reminded of the inescapable modern condition of dependence on money. In so far as the country house itself was an expression of monetary confidence and the display of wealth, this is an unintended aspect of historical accuracy in the experience of the products of the heritage industry.

In the course of the discussion the focus has shifted from the identification of the nation with the countryside in general, to the selection of particularly evocative parts of the country, to the clearly defined and privately owned estate and garden. Although the progressive contraction of the space imagined for the nation suggests a narrowing of ambition in the representational enterprise, the semantic and referential richness of the trope of the garden does nevertheless confer some ductility on contemporary historical fiction's use of it to explore questions of national identity. As Shelley Saguaro points out, combining physical and metaphorical dimensions the image of the garden '[o]n the one hand... can signify a pre-lapsarian and harmonic bliss; on the other, the inevitability of the Fall' (x). The private, preferably secluded garden is 'a testament to a place which serves as a pleasure-filled retreat from the urban world's harrying strictures of business, commerce and politics' (x), while the tilled gardens in a class- or race-conscious context 'can serve to show the duress of toil, slave-labour and the disenfranchisement of the poor, where nothing of pastoral pleasure is realised but only inescapable hardship and meagre subsistence' (x).

The 13 novels that form the subject of this study variously exploit the wealth of associations of the garden trope which Saguaro details. In *The French Lieutenant's Woman,* Ware Common becomes the site for freedom and transgression, with the dangers for the position of the individual in society this carries; these dangers are even more acute, coloured as they are by the question of race, in a colonial context, as Olivia's fate in *Heat and Dust* shows. Conversely, the ordered English garden in the grounds of the residency of Krishnapur acquire symbolic value for the British colonists because of their associations with the social model of existence of the imperial metropolis. *The Chymical Wedding, Possession* and *Ever After* combine the presence of a physical garden, a site of desire for a nostalgic national unity centred on the social and economic arrangements of the country house or the Oxbridge college, with a metaphorical use of Eden to articulate their narrative longings and negotiations and re-encode the postmodern condition as a loss of paradise. Where in these novels the superimposition of metaphorical value and Biblical resonance onto a physical space is largely benign, *The Map of Love, English Passengers,* and *The Rising Sun* probe the pernicious effects of this operation in a colonial context. The myth of the Edenic garden thus becomes a function of colonial discourse, which at one stroke removes the imperial territories from history and deprives their inhabitants of any possibility of historically meaningful action within that discourse. The publicly validated use of the garden trope in these novels is countered by the investment in the garden as a retreat from history in *Joseph Knight, The Mulberry Empire, Havoc in Its Third Year* and *Ghost Portrait,* at the same time as, in the case of the first two novels, relating it to both the national imagination and colonial exploitation. If there is one common aspect emerging from this consistent reliance on the trope of the garden to variously articulate narrative and national desires, it is precisely the variety of the trope's associations and the precariousness of any embodiment, symbolic or otherwise, of the nation within the confines of the garden. What the search for a viable location for the national imagining reveals is in fact its multifariousness and instability, perhaps an appropriate statement for a changing modern nation, Britain in the twenty-first century, to counter the seeming nostalgia inherent in the image of the garden itself.

Bibliography

Primary texts

Bennett, Ronan, *Havoc in Its Third Year* (London: Bloomsbury, 2004).
Byatt, A.S., *Possession: A Romance* (London: Vintage, 1991 [1990]).
Clarke, Lindsay, *The Chymical Wedding: A Romance* (London: Picador, 1990 [1989]).
Farrell, J.G., *The Siege of Krishnapur* (London: Phoenix, 2001 [1973]).
Fowles, John, *The French Lieutenant's Woman* (London: Vintage, 1996 [1969]).
Galbraith, Douglas, *The Rising Sun* (London: Picador, 2001 [2000]).
Hensher, Philip, *The Mulberry Empire; or, The Two Virtuous Journeys of the Amir Dost Mohammed Khan* (London: Flamingo, 2003 [2002]).
Jhabvala, Ruth Prawer, *Heat and Dust* (London: Penguin, 1994 [1975]).
Kneale, Matthew, *English Passengers* (London: Penguin, 2001 [2000]).
Normington, Gregory, *Ghost Portrait* (London: Sceptre, 2005).
Robertson, James, *Joseph Knight* (London: Fourth Estate, 2003).
Scott, Sir Walter, *Waverley; or, 'tis Sixty Years Since* (London: Penguin, 1980 [1813]).
Soueif, Ahdaf, *The Map of Love* (London: Bloomsbury, 2000 [1999]).
Swift, Graham, *Ever After* (London: Picador, 1993 [1992]).

Secondary texts

Anderson, Benedict, *Imagined Communities* (London: Verso, 2006).
Baucom, Ian, *Out of Place: Englishness, Empire, and the Location of Identity* (Princeton: Princeton University Press, 1999).
Bennett, Tony, *Pasts Beyond Memory: Evolution, Museums, Colonialism* (London: Routledge, 2004).
Bergonzi, Bernard, *The Situation of the Novel*, 2nd edition (London: Macmillan, 1979).
Bhabha, Homi K., *The Location of Culture* (London: Routledge, 1994).
Binns, Ronald, *J.G. Farrell* (London: Methuen, 1986).
Booker, M. Keith, 'What We Have Instead of God: Sexuality, Textuality and Infinity in *The French Lieutenant's Woman*', *NOVEL: A Forum on Fiction* 24.2 (Winter 1991), 178–98.
——, *Colonial Power, Colonial Texts: India in the Modern British Novel* (Ann Arbor: The University of Michigan Press, 1997).
Botting, Fred, *Gothic* (London: Routledge, 1996).
Brannigan, John, *Orwell to the Present 1945–2000* (Basingstoke: Palgrave 2003).

Brennan, Timothy, 'The National Longing for Form' in Homi K. Bhabha (ed.), *Nation and Narration* (London: Routledge, 1990).

Brooks, Peter, *Reading for the Plot: Desire and Intention in Narrative* (Cambridge: Harvard University Press, 1988).

Buxton, Jackie, '"What's Love Got to Do with It?" Postmodernism and *Possession'*, *English Studies in Canada* 22.2 (1996), 199–219.

Byatt, A.S., *On Histories and Stories: Selected Essays* (London: Chatto & Windus, 2000).

Colón, Susan E., 'The Possession of Paradise: A.S. Byatt's Reinscription of Milton', *Christianity and Literature* 53.1 (2003), 77–97.

Connor, Steven, *The English Novel in History 1950–1995* (London: Routledge, 1996).

Conradi, Peter, *John Fowles* (London: Methuen, 1982).

Costantini, Mariaconcetta, 'Crossing Boundaries: The Revision of Gothic Paradigms in *Heat and Dust*' in Andrew Smith and William Hughes (eds), *Empire and the Gothic: The Politics of Genre* (Basingstoke: Macmillan, 2004).

Cowart, David, *History and the Contemporary Novel* (Carbondale and Edwardsville: Southern Illinois University Press, 1989).

Craig, Cairns, *The Modern Scottish Novel: Narrative and the National Imagination* (Edinburgh: Edinburgh University Press, 1999).

Crane, Ralph J., 'Introduction' in Ralph J. Crane (ed.), *J.G. Farrell: The Critical Grip* (Dublin: Four Courts, 1999).

Cronin, Richard, *Imagining India* (Basingstoke: Macmillan, 1989).

Cubitt, Geoffrey, 'Introduction' in Geoffrey Cubitt (ed.), *Imagining Nations* (Manchester: Manchester University Press, 1998).

Currie, Mark, *Postmodern Narrative Theory* (Basingstoke: Palgrave, 1998).

Darraj, Susan Muaddi, 'Narrating English and Egypt: The Hybrid Fiction of Ahdaf Soueif', *Studies in the Humanities* 30.1/2 (2003), 91–107.

Dennis, Ian, *Nationalism and Desire in Historical Fiction* (Basingstoke: Macmillan, 1997).

De Vitiis, A.A. and William J. Palmer, '*A Pair of Blue Eyes* Flash at *The French Lieutenant's Woman'*, *Contemporary Literature* 15.1 (Winter 1974), 90–101.

Eco, Umberto, *A Postscript to The Name of the Rose*, trans. William Weaver (London: Secker & Warburg, 1998).

Elam, Diane, *Romancing the Postmodern* (London: Routledge, 1988).

Ermarth, Elizabeth Deeds, *Sequel to History: Postmodernism and the Crisis of Representational Time* (Princeton: Princeton University Press, 1992).

Ferns, Chris, '"First as Tragedy, then as Farce": J.G. Farrell's Retelling of History', *Dalhousie Review* 208.20 (1994), 275–85.

——, 'Walter Scott, J.G. Farrell, and the Dialogics of Historical Fiction' in Ralph J. Crane (ed.), *J.G. Farrell: The Critical Grip* (Dublin: Four Courts, 1999).

Finney, Brian, *English Fiction since 1984: Narrating a Nation* (Basingstoke: Palgrave 2006).

Flegel, Monica, 'Enchanted Readings and Fairy-Tale Endings in A.S. Byatt's *Possession'*, *English Studies in Canada* 24.4 (1998), 413–30.

Fleishman, Avrom, *The English Historical Novel: Walter Scott to Virginia Woolf* (Baltimore: The Johns Hopkins Press, 1971).

Fowles, John, 'On Being English but Not British' in Jan Relf (ed.), *Wormholes: Essays and Occasional Writings* (New York: Vintage, 1999).

Frye, Northrop, *Anatomy of Criticism: Four Essays* (Princeton: Princeton University Press, 1957).

Gasiorek, Andrzej, *Post-war British Fiction: Realism and After* (London: Arnold, 1995).

Gaston, Patricia S., *Prefacing the Waverley Novels: A Reading of Sir Walter Scott's Prefaces to the Waverley Novels* (New York: Peter Lang, 1991).

Gauthier, Tim S., *Narrative Desire and Historical Reparations: A.S. Byatt, Ian McEwan, Salman Rushdie* (New York: Routledge, 2005).

George, Rosemary Marangoly, *The Politics of Home: Post-Colonial Relocations and Twentieth-Century Fiction* (Cambridge: Cambridge University Press, 1996).

Green, Martin, *The Adventurous Male: Chapters in the History of the White Male Mind* (University Park: Pennsylvania State University Press, 1993).

Greenhalgh, Paul, *Ephemeral Vistas: The Expositions Universelles, Great Exhibitions and Fairs, 1851–1939* (Manchester: Manchester University Press, 1988).

Griffiths, Gareth, 'Being there, Being There: Kosinski and Malouf' in Ian Adam and Helen Tiffin (eds), *Past the Last Post: Theorising Post-Colonialism and Post-modernism* (New York: Harvester Wheatsheaf, 1994).

Gutleben, Christian, *Nostalgic Postmodernism: The Victorian Tradition and the Contemporary British Novel* (Amsterdam: Rodopi, 2001).

Hartveit, Lars, 'The Imprint of Recorded Events in the Narrative Form of J.G. Farrell's *The Siege of Krishnapur*', *English Studies* 5 (1993), 451–69.

Hassan, Wail S., 'Agency and Translational Literature: Ahdaf Soueif's *The Map of Love*', *PMLA* 121.3 (2006), 753–68.

Hennelly, Mark M. Jr., ' "Repeating Patterns" and Textual Pleasures: Reading (in) A.S. Byatt's *Possession: A Romance*', *Contemporary Literature* 44.3 (2003), 442–71.

Herman, Arthur, *The Scottish Enlightenment: The Scots' Invention of the Modern World* (London: Fourth Estate, 2002).

Hewison, Robert, *The Heritage Industry: Britain in a Climate of Decline* (London: Methuen, 1987).

Higdon, David Leon, *Shadows of the Past in Contemporary British Fiction* (London: Macmillan, 1984).

Hobsbawm, Eric, 'The Nation as Invented Tradition' in John Hutchinson and Anthony D. Smith (eds), *Nationalism* (Oxford: Oxford University Press, 1994).

Holmes, Frederick M., *The Historical Imagination: Postmodernism and the Treatment of the Past in Contemporary British Fiction* (Victoria: University of Victoria Press, 1997).

Huggan, Graham, 'Decolonising the Map: Post-Colonialism, Post-Structuralism, and the Cartographic Connection' in Ian Adam and Helen

Tiffin (eds), *Past the Last Post: Theorising Post-Colonialism and Post-Modernism* (New York: Harvester Wheatsheaf, 1994).

Hutcheon, Linda, *A Poetics of Postmodernism: History, Theory, Fiction* (London: Routledge, 1988).

Jackson, Tony E., 'The Desires of History, Old and New', *CLIO: A Review of Literature, History, and the Philosophy of History* 28.2 (Winter 1999), 169–87.

Jameson, Fredric, *Postmodernism, or, the Cultural Logic of Late Capitalism* (Durham: Duke University Press, 1991).

Janik, Del Ivan, 'No End of History: Evidence from the Contemporary English Novel', *Twentieth-Century Literature* 41.2 (Summer 1995), 160–89.

Kabbani, Rana, *Europe's Myths of the Orient* (London: Pandora Press, 1986).

Kaplan, Cora, *Victoriana: Histories, Fictions, Criticism* (Edinburgh: Edinburgh University Press, 2007).

Keen, Suzanne, *Romances of the Archive in Contemporary British Fiction* (Toronto: University of Toronto Press, 2001).

Kermode, Frank, *The Sense of an Ending: Studies in the Theory of Fiction,* new edition with a new epilogue (Oxford: Oxford University Press, 2000 [1966]).

Lea, Daniel, 'Parodic Strategy and the Mutiny Romance in *The Siege of Krishnapur*' in Ralph J. Crane (ed.), *J.G. Farrell: The Critical Grip* (Dublin: Four Courts, 1999).

Lerner, Lawrence, *The Uses of Nostalgia: Studies in Pastoral Poetry* (London: Chatto & Windus, 1972).

Lukács, Georg, *The Historical Novel,* trans. Hannah and Stanley Mitchell (London: Merlin Press, 1989 [1937]).

Mack, Douglas S., *Scottish Fiction and the British Empire* (Edinburgh: Edinburgh University Press, 2006).

MacQueen, John, *The Rise of the Historical Novel: The Enlightenment and Scottish Literature* (Edinburgh: Scottish Academic Press, 1989).

Martyniuk, Irene, '"This is Not Science. This is Storytelling": The Place of the Individual and the Community in A.S. Byatt's *Possession* and Tom Stoppard's *Arcadia*', *CLIO: A Review of Literature, History and the Philosophy of History* 33.3 (2004), 265–86.

Massie, Allan, *The Novel Today: A Critical Guide to the British Novel 1970–1989* (London: Longman, 1990).

McEwan, Neil, *The Survival of the Novel: British Fiction in the Late Twentieth Century* (London: Macmillan, 1981).

McLeod, John, 'Exhibiting Empire in J.G. Farrell's *The Siege of Krishnapur*', *Journal of Commonwealth Literature* 29.2 (1986), 117–32.

Mink, Louis O., *Historical Understanding,* ed. Brian Fay, Eugene O. Golob and Richard T. Vann (Ithaca: Cornell University Press, 1987).

Newman, Judie, *The Ballistic Bard: Postcolonial Fictions* (London: Arnold, 1995).

Pearce, Susan M., *On Collecting: An Investigation into Collecting in the European Tradition* (London: Routledge, 1995).

Pratt, Mary Louise, 'Transculturation and Autoethnography: Peru 1625/1980' in Francis Barker, Peter Hulme and Margaret Iversen (eds), *Colonial*

Discourse/ Postcolonial Theory (Manchester: Manchester University Press, 1994).

Punter, David, *The Literature of Terror volume 1: The Gothic Tradition* (London: Longman, 1996).

Richards, Thomas, *The Imperial Archive: Knowledge and the Fantasy of Empire* (London: Verso, 1993).

Rignall, J.M., 'Walter Scott, J.G. Farrell, and Fictions of Empire', *Essays in Criticism* 41 (1991), 11–27.

Rigney, Ann, *The Rhetoric of Historical Representation: Three Narrative Histories of the French Revolution* (Cambridge: Cambridge University Press, 1990).

——, *Imperfect Histories: The Elusive Past and the Legacy of Romantic Historicism* (Ithaca: Cornell University Press, 2001).

Sadoff, Dianne E. and John Kucich (eds), *Victorian Afterlives: Postmodern Culture Rewrites the Nineteenth Century* (Minneapolis: University of Minnesota Press, 2000).

Sage, Victor, 'The Ghastly and the Ghostly: The Gothic Farce of Farrell's "Empire Trilogy"' in Andrew Smith and William Hughes (eds), *Empire and the Gothic: The Politics of Genre* (Basingstoke: Macmillan, 2004).

Saguaro, Shelley, *Garden Plots: The Politics and Poetics of Gardens* (Aldershot: Ashgate, 2006).

Said, Edward, *Orientalism* (London: Penguin, 1987 [1978]).

Sanders, Andrew, *The Victorian Historical Novel 1840–1880* (New York: St Martin's Press, 1979).

Scanlan, Margaret, *Traces of Another Time: History and Politics in Postwar British Fiction* (Princeton: Princeton University Press, 1990).

Schmitt, Cannon, *Alien Nation: Nineteenth-Century Gothic Fiction and English Nationality* (Philadelphia: University of Pennsylvania Press, 1997).

Shaw, Harry E., *The Forms of Historical Fiction: Sir Walter Scott and His Successors* (Ithaca: Cornell University Press, 1983).

Shiller, Dana, 'The Redemptive Past in the Neo-Victorian Novel', *Studies in the Novel* 29.4 (1997), 538–60.

Slemon, Stephen, 'Modernism's Last Post' in Ian Adam and Helen Tiffin (eds), *Past the Last Post: Theorising Post-Colonialism and Post-Modernism* (New York: Harvester Wheatsheaf, 1994).

Stevenson, Randall, *The Last of England? The Oxford Literary History*, vol. 12 (Oxford: Oxford University Press, 2004).

Strobl, Gerwin, *The Challenge of Cross-Cultural Interpretation in the Anglo-Indian Novel: The Raj Revisited* (Lewiston: Edwin Mellen, 1995).

Su, John J., 'Fantasies of (Re)collection: Collecting and Imagination in A.S. Byatt's *Possession: A Romance*', *Contemporary Literature* 45.4 (2004), 684–712.

——, *Ethics and Nostalgia in the Contemporary Novel* (Cambridge: Cambridge University Press, 2005).

Sucher, Laurie, *The Fiction of Ruth Prawer Jhabvala: The Politics of Passion* (Basingstoke: Macmillan, 1989).

Suleri, Sara, *The Rhetoric of English India* (Chicago: The University of Chicago Press, 1992).

Thorpe, Michael, 'Making History: Fiction, History and the Indian "Mutiny"', *World Literature Written in English* 26.1 (1986), 179–87.

Waugh, Patricia (ed.), *Postmodernism: A Reader* (London: Edward Arnold, 1992).

Wells, Lynn, *Allegories of Telling: Self-Referential Narrative in Contemporary British Fiction* (Amsterdam: Rodopi, 2003).

Wenstein, Mark A. (ed.), *The Prefaces to the Waverley Novels* (Lincoln: University of Nebraska Press, 1978).

White, Hayden, *Metahistory: The Historical Imagination in Nineteenth-Century Europe* (Baltimore: The Johns Hopkins University Press, 1973).

——, *The Content of the Form: Narrative Discourse and Historical Representation* (Baltimore: The Johns Hopkins University Press, 1987).

Williams, Raymond, *The Country and the City* (London: Chatto & Windus, 1973).

Young, Robert J.C., *Colonial Desire: Hybridity in Theory, Culture and Race* (London: Routledge, 1995).

Index

The Siege of Krishnapur 24, 28–9,
44–54, 56
collection 49–50
colonialism 48–9
and *The French Lieutenant's
Woman* 45
historical positioning 32–3
identity and location 49
materials used 36
and *The Mulberry Empire* 135
Mutiny romance 45–6
narrative forms 35–6
nostalgia 46
objects and possessions 49–50
and *A Passage to India* 45
Robin Hood 172–3
taxonomy 47–8
undermining of generic
convention 47
theory, as representation of the
nation 61
timeframes, alternating
63–4
Tolstoy, Leo 135
trade, as romance 130–1
tradition, resurrection of
Victorian 62
translation 112–13
truthfulness 7–8, 40

uncolonised land, as
paradise 128–9
understanding 23, 108–9, 159
unity 64–5, 67

Victorian crisis, and modernity 69
Victorian fiction, reference to 24
Victorian novel, preoccupations 89
Victorian period 2, 12, 22, 33, 51, 63
Victorian realism 37, 65
Victorian tradition, resurrection of 62
Victorians, scientific
obsessions 40–1
violence, textual expression 106–7

Waugh, Patricia 17, 61–2
Waverley novels 132–3
*Waverley, or 'tis sixty years
since* 5–6, 14–15, 141–2
Wells, Lynn 39
Wenstein, Mark A. 14
White, Hayden 6–7, 18–19, 153
wholeness 64–5
Williams, Raymond 175–6
withdrawal from public life 169
women, solidarity 113
World War II, effect on novel 29

Young, Robert J.C. 105